Edge of the Glen

2002

EDGE OF THE GLEN

A Novel

by Clifford Geddes

To
Mary Collins
With the author's compliments
and
very best wishes,
Mike (Lambs)
i.e. "Clifford Geddes"

Writers Club Press
San Jose New York Lincoln Shanghai

Edge of the Glen
A Novel

Writers Club Press
an imprint of iUniverse, Inc.

For information address:
iUniverse, Inc.
5220 S. 16th St., Suite 200
Lincoln, NE 68512
www.iuniverse.com

ISBN: 0-595-23621-9

Printed in the United States of America

Contents

CHAPTER 1

I Hear About Myself

I abandoned the humdrum of my life one day early in autumn. I remember it well because I'd come down from the north and could hardly believe how warm was the morning and blue the sky. Pocketing my cap, I'd flung my mackintosh over my shoulder in a gesture of chagrin. London was indeed a far cry from Lancashire.

I was not then due to meet my friend until half past noon and had ample time to spare, yet I had had more than enough of London's hectic streets so that when I came at last in sight of St. Paul's the prospect there of cool and quiet proved irresistible. I found a corner of relative solitude and fell shortly to ruminating upon my remembered past.

My problem, I should say, was that I was unable to connect the last eight years of my life with what had gone before, albeit a piecemeal picture had gradually begun to emerge owing to visits from friends, an aunt of mine in Winchester, and an inevitably episodic collection of letters. Nevertheless, precisely what had happened to me before the battle for the Falklands was a matter to be discovered through the narration of others and not through any recollection of my own. The amnesia brought about by the conflict of '82 had been total, and therefore I had had to find some means of starting again.

Just the same, I had clearly been fortunate in my choice of companions, all of whom had exhibited a remarkable degree of loyalty—a fact nowhere more in evidence than in the case of my oldest acquaintance, Montagu Fiennes. We had been at the same private school in Valetta and had together gone up to Oxford as thick as thieves, Monty to take up anthropology and I to become a student of theology. It had been to witness my graduation there, *maxima cum laude*, that my parents had made their ill-fated flight from the island of Malta. Insidiously, and without their knowledge, the plane they had chartered had been cruelly sabotaged, offering no chance whatever of survival. At the same time two Sicilians—loyal descendants of the old Black Hand—had completely destroyed the Delman-family residence on the outskirts of Attard. My father, it seemed, had acquired for himself something of a reputation in textiles but in the process had made contacts of a doubtful nature and not easily abandoned: his attempts to rid himself of unwanted embarrassment had, in addition, merely compounded his initial imprudence; he himself had already been blackmailed—and his chauffeur mysteriously disappeared—when the decision had been made to attend the graduation ceremony.

During the agonising days that had followed Monty had proved himself to be a continual source of support. While I had reacted to the tragedy by blaspheming the Almighty and, worse still, doubting God's existence, Monty—himself an ardent atheist—had made every attempt imaginable to return me to my moorings. Such indeed was the selfless nature of my friend. In the event, however, I proved too obdurate to be so persuaded, and he was finally obliged to take me on board the Good Ship Reason—a fully paid-up passenger on a course-without-compass. I had become as convinced then that God was nothing more than a figment of man's weary mind and pitiful loss of nerve as I had earlier been that without God's existence life could have no meaning and bear no purpose. As I sat within the safe haven of St. Paul's I shuddered to contemplate my erstwhile derision.

However, such is life's curious design that within only a few years I was to return to my original tack and for the better part of twelve months appear set for the austere and often silent rule of a Carthusian monk. Indeed, my brother Miles had already made considerable progress along that same path. His own reaction to tragedy, then, had not been to make war upon God and His Creation but to draw closer to his Maker and so discern more fully the intentions of the Divine. After the trauma of the Falklands and the loss of my memory, Miles had secured sanctuary for me at a far-flung abbey to the north of the Tweed. There, labouring peacefully on an adjacent farm and making vigorous sorties into the Lammermuir Hills, I had gradually regained my composure and discovered anew the delights of prayer. So much did I then despise the rationale of conflict—not to mention my own part in settling it—that I would have nothing to do with my former life: for six months all correspondence to me lay unopened and all attempts at contact were thus contemptuously rebuffed; I wanted only to do good honest work, eat simple fare, and to enjoy such temper of mind as comes from a life lived in the open and in proximity to the elements.

In the end it had been the prior himself who had brought me to my senses: I was, paradoxically, living in a world adjoining reality yet not conterminous with it—and the good man wasted no sentiment in telling me so. Whatever I chose to do, be it to return to regular civilian life or to seek the path to ordination, I had first to confront my earlier experiences. Reading the rapidly thinning stream of letters ought, he said, to be my first task. Bit by bit, then, did the puzzle of my life begin to emerge. Nonetheless, in one capacity or another, I stayed in that place for two whole years.

The reader, I fear, must make allowances for my tardiness: remember, I was like a man who sets forth upon a distant planet—when he is told there are inhabitants who claim already to be his friends, he will be apt to rejoin them with incredulity if not suspicion. Faces had to be learnt anew and the bonds of familiarity built afresh; so, for the next two years I travelled sometimes absurd distances in search of myself. By the end of that time I had indeed a clearer picture of my true identity and a network of acquaintances I was welcome to call friends. All the same, the reality of who I might once have been still seemed disconnected from the person I'd become. I was in need of a source of income too and, even more than that, an occupation.

It was at this juncture that Montagu Fiennes again proved to be invaluable, for he gave me the exclusive use of a part of his house—the ground floor, no less, of a stately building in one of the better parts of Axminster. There I must own to having spent three miserable years as an assistant in an up-and-coming estate agency. I fancy I did the job efficiently, and certainly secured a modest salary; but, it was a tedious and irregular affair and to my way of thinking highlighted some of our nation's diametric excesses. On the one hand, there were the enormous manors and palatial homes looking like the follies of some bygone era, and, on the other, the box-like and soulless dwellings of the modern industrial estate. As the interest rates in the City began to reach infamous proportions, ordinary hard-working folk seemed obliged to endure ongoing confinement, or, in certain severe cases, were forced to sell up their homes lock, stock and barrel. Purchasing of holiday-lets and the increase in long-distance commuting conspired alike to oust the local from the community he loved: sometimes whole families were required to seek accommodation in a more northerly county. As for myself, I knew I wanted to spend more time out in the open and less in having to pick up a receiver and stare at a screen. Suffice it to say that by the end of that period I had got myself into a funk, good and proper.

Then Monty again came to my assistance. It seemed that among his many hideaways—my friend was a man of considerable resourcefulness and many assets—was an agreeable apartment in the Lancashire town of Morecambe. When he heard of a vacancy with the R. S. P. B.—at a sanctuary close to Leighton Moss—he suggested at once that I apply for it and take with it the use of his flat. "You wouldn't get paid much," he admonished, "but I can certainly put in a good word for you, and it would get you out of that infernal motor car and—more to the point—out of that damned office."

As it happened I jumped at the chance. Not only was it an offer that would free me from the rut into which I'd sunk, but it would also allow me to indulge a hobby which by then had become a passion. Ever since I'd heard the call of the curlew in the north—its intriguing, liquid trill high over the moorland hills—and had seen a harrier and a buzzard jostle in flight, I had been both captivated and inspired. My savings during the previous three years, taken with my pension from the army, meant that for a while at least I could wander at will. The prospect alike of being able to use my hands and to dabble in the practice of ornithology seemed altogether too good to dismiss. Besides, I had discovered something else about myself: I adored the sea.

At this point further ruminations upon life—either past or present—became impossible due to the abrupt interruption of a verger. Having been roped in to give some sort of an address the fellow was declaiming to a party of sixth-formers on the grandeur of the design and the beneficence of the Almighty. I got up and began to pick my way through the crowds till once again I was stepping out alone along Ludgate Hill. Next, I turned into New Bridge Street and struck out there for the Embankment, proceeding finally toward my destination, the City Livery Club.

One legacy of mine unaffected by the intrusion of the mafiosi had been my freemanship of the City. Waiting until I was twenty-one, during what was then my penultimate year at Oxford, my brother Miles and I had gone up to London, become members of one of the great historic trade-guilds—in our case the Company of Mercers—and had become admitted to our hereditary freedom. Our family could trace its antecedents back to the fourteenth century, though if ever the line were to continue it would not be due to any endeavour on the part of Miles: he'd chosen a rule debarring progeny in favour of the lifelong canon of celibacy.

After the initial thrill of being dubbed a freeman had diminished, I confess I myself had had little interest in the matter: I'd never had any intention of following in my father's footsteps and yet couldn't see any other way of serving the Company. In due course I'd received an invitation to join the livery, but, frankly, couldn't view it with sufficient seriousness actually to proceed. However, when the City Livery Club decided to open its doors to freemen generally, and not simply to liverymen, I determined to take advantage of the option. Besides, Monty had already done so and it would make a convenient rendezvous at the centre of the capital. As I came to the corner of John Carpenter Street I smiled wryly: the thought of Montagu Fiennes being a "worshipful member"—in his case of the Drapers Company—bore with it a certain incongruity.

A little later I was looking across the Thames—through one of the club's windows and in the direction of the National Theatre—when I heard a familiar voice.

"Major Delman, so there you are! Good to see you, old chap, good to see you."

My friend, it should be said, had the infuriating habit of according me my military status whenever we were in company.

"Less of your old," I rejoined. "I feel my years well enough—the more so when I watch those lads there running along The Queens Walk."

I pointed to a line of brightly-clad joggers, just then circumventing a bemused fiddler on the opposite side of the river.

"Cheer up, Fred, you look in pretty good shape to me. I'd say your work at the sanctuary is doing you the power of good. Now, be a good fellow there and let's have some lunch. My morning at the Foreign Office has given me a mighty fine appetite."

We dined well and supped a very passable bottle of Medoc with the distinctive accent of the Sauvignon grape. Monty was keen I should sample a glass of what he called "The Chairman's Late Bottled Port," and so we repaired to the Library.

Monty had said I looked well and that my present occupation suited me. Up to a point, of course, he was right; and, as I have indicated, there was that about Leighton Moss which pleased me. All the same it was only ever a temporary appointment and the nature of the work itself was bound to be peripheral. Suddenly I was envious—envious of Monty and of his work at Westminster, envious of his adventuring in centres of change, envious of his reputation as *un homme formidable.*

During the Falklands Campaign, Montagu Fiennes had served with me as a captain, but when the fighting was over he'd got into the world of counterespionage and had, after several ugly scraps in undeniably tight corners, gained for himself a considerable following. It seemed that wherever there was internal conflict or growing international tension that somehow or other Monty was in the thick of it; occasionally he would play the part of the agent provocateur—inciting riots or strategically planting units of rebellion in corrupt quarters of the globe. Most of the time, though, he worked through diplomatic channels, astounding his peers by an adroit ability to disappear at the opportune moment or else cut through red tape where others before had either been denied access or summarily disposed of. He had, too, an uncanny ability to infiltrate the minds and hearts of such disparate creatures as oil tycoons, city magnates, army chiefs, and foreign royalty. His speciality, it appeared, lay in befriending politicians. He had operated in the Punjab, been shot at in Nicaragua, been imprisoned in East Germany and had escaped from Albania. Also, he had been consulted by the Kremlin. In all of these activities he had been admirably served not simply by his postgraduate work at Oxford in anthropological studies, but also, and variously, by an enviable network of family contacts, by a marked flair for languages, and by the resolute and indomitable spirit of the 2nd Battalion Parachute Regiment. So successful had he become that he had been put in charge of a special department dealing with top-secret information and with such far-ranging powers that even I baulked to hear of them: he referred to his department, somewhat enigmatically, as MQ1, boasting that he had commandeered some of the best men and women that virtue and high principle could buy.

Now, as I stared disconsolately into my drink, Monty seemed to sense my despondency, for he suddenly spoke up.

"What's bothering you, Fred? There's nothing much wrong with the port, so I must hazard that you're keeping something back."

"Oh, don't mind me," I replied. "In truth, I've plenty to be grateful for. I've got my strength, my limbs intact, a pleasant enough occupation, sufficient money to keep me, and a wealth of friends who are the best of company."

"But—for I think there is a but—you are wondering what it's all been for: your life, that is. What was the point of winning the struggle down in the South Atlantic—I mean for you, yourself—the point of all those years of training, of military endeavour? And now you look at yourself and still you seem to be adrift, floating upon some becalmed patch of sea, not sure if you want to be rescued or not, but sometimes hoping that a vessel will chance by just to break the monotony. And here's a funny thing, too. It doesn't matter if she intends you help or harm: either will do, just as long as you get a fillip to action or challenge to venture. I know you, Fred; better than you think. You may look at me at times with an element of curiosity, wondering how I fit into your life and whether or not you are becoming too indebted to me. I understand, I assure you. But there is no need on that account. It will always be I who owe you. And if you look at me with admiration, remember the path of action may be yours again—as once it was—and, as for myself, I should not be where I am today had not a certain Major Delman come to my aid. As I've insisted before, were it not for the job you did that week in May of '82 the tide of history might well have been reversed. Our chaps could have come off a good deal worse than they did and it is questionable at least whether we would have delivered Port Stanley."

Monty was warming once more to the task of narration. I had heard it all before, of course; for, many times and with infinite patience had my friend laboured to inspire me with a sense of identity. He lowered his glass and began again.

"You see, Fred, even today nobody knows what brought that helicopter down—sabotage, mechanical fault—an albatross, as some would have it—but on board there were eighteen of the best trained Sass then available. I reckon it was that which scuppered the original operation for Fanning Head. Anyhow, the loss of those brave stalwarts—all the more tragic in view of their success on Pebble Island—inevitably meant a rearrangement of manpower. That was where you came in. You had, you see, already demonstrated considerable surveillance-skills in Northern Ireland—where for a while you were with the Guards—and had displayed an unhealthy interest in defusing bombs. Now, shortly after the crash, word arrived that an attempt was being made to halt the advance of the Paras in the direction of Goose Green. Yet the taking of that settlement was of strategic importance to the whole operation. It was vital that it should proceed as planned. Unfortunately, the three men of the S.A.S. who would have gone forward under normal circumstances had all been transferred to a different task. That's when you were singled out; and, typically, like a fox at a hen, you seized the opportunity. I myself meantime, in receipt of treatment for trench foot, was thought not fit enough to engage in combat. On the other hand, the powers-that-be didn't want to send you in all on your own. So, yours truly—not for the first time in his life—found himself by your side."

"Honestly, Monty," I cried, "it's like something from a dream!"

"A nightmare, more like. Well, our first task was to negotiate the southeast flank of the Sussex Mountains separating Darwin from San Carlos. We had a fair old time, I can tell you, trying to skirt those hills undetected and more than once were forced to take out an

Argentinean snooper. Considering you weren't exactly in our regiment you seemed mighty keen on having a banjo at the enemy! It was quite disconcerting, for it was as much as I could do to keep up with you. In due course, however—after much wriggling and worming through bracken and wet bent—we alighted upon a spot from where we were able to observe Camilla Creek and the Darwin Isthmus. You at once pinpointed a prominent house—painted white and standing out on the flat landscape—and with it a variety of farm-outbuildings. This was, you reckoned, a likely venue at which the battalion might reassemble and from there await the command for a forward attack. But, before doing anything else we got back our breath and had something to eat. For the most part the going had been either very quick or very slow, and both of us were feeling the effects of what had been rather a long haul—in addition to which we'd eaten nothing at all since our departure at first light. I recall it well because you yourself declined any tinned meat in favour of a large ration of chocolate! You said as well you were ready and the rest for a damned good smoke! However, after what seemed only a handful of minutes, we set off again."

At this point Monty paused and proceeded to pour a black coffee for us both. His comment about my eating habits—my disinclination for real food when there was a job to be done—certainly accorded with my experience since leaving the monastery. He began again.

"Well, Fred, if we'd had a hard time of it till then the way forward seemed more arduous yet. You insisted we keep our heads down for the bulk of the way, so our progress as we hurtled towards the farm was unnervingly slow. I remember thinking that we must be terribly exposed. You yourself, moreover, were anxious to approach from behind rather than in front, and this involved us in a long detour around the side of the farm. Still, you hoped that our retreat would be quicker, noting that the dusk was already upon us. With what remaining light there was you infiltrated the premises and began the search. Sure enough, within the rotten timbers were concealed enough booby-traps to blow the place apart ten times over. As a matter of fact you said you'd been damned lucky to have spotted one of the kind used, for it was of a type you'd not previously encountered. In the meantime I myself did a recce outside and examined a couple of the ruining sheds standing there. Before long it became sufficiently dark for us to venture a return and to lope back to higher ground. It was then disaster struck."

"Yes," I broke in. "This must be where the three fraudulent paratroopers came onto the scene. I recall it from one of your earlier accounts."

"That's right. It's a deuce of a pity all the same you can't contact it properly, for you were devilish brave."

"Perhaps it's just as well then," I grinned back.

"Anyway, there they were and even by our standards they were big! What with that and the wings on their maroon berets we were quite taken in. Fortunately—and just before they saw us—we heard one of them broach something in Spanish, and it was that that put us on our guard. You immediately stepped forward and greeted them in their native tongue. When they replied in kind your first reaction was to make a bluff of the thing and to act as if we ourselves were similarly disguised. Alas! just when all seemed well one of them addressed me and—idiot that I was—I replied in too refined an accent. The game was up and they were on us in an instant. You yourself were knocked unconscious by the butt of a rifle while I was pinned down by the other two combatants. A bayonet was already raised above my head when, *mirabile dictu*! you re-emerged. You struck my opponent hard in the back, making him collapse at once. Before I could join in myself, however, I was summarily kicked in the head and thereafter lost consciousness—though I remember as I did so reaching wide across the fallen Argentinian. Then it was just you yourself against them.

"When I awoke, several seconds later, I heard a cry of anguish and with it the heavy breathing of someone labouring towards me. That was it I thought; if I'd been lucky till then my number now—as they say—was well and truly up. Yet it was not to be. For none other than a certain Major Delman raised himself up at last and asked me how I was. To hear those words in English was already to feel invigorated. However, though our enemies had been successfully dispatched—or so it seemed—it was plain the price you yourself had paid had been considerable. Your face was all bloodied, you had a tooth half out and a number of gashes both to your upper arm and right hand. In fact the first thing I did was to put a dislocated thumb back into place.

"Next we turned to the fellow over whom I had fallen. He was slowly coming round. We had no time for civilities and could not afford to be gentle. We interrogated him in Spanish, and at the sight of blood issuing from his mouth he began to babble something about his home and how he'd never had any interest in securing the Malvinas. I thumped him again and he started to mutter something about having put a reserve in one of the outhouses. He pointed to a small shed. Then he blacked out. I was about to finish the poor devil when you checked his pulse. He'd already gone."

As Monty described this incident I couldn't help but wonder that it was I and not he who had felled such contenders. As I looked at my friend's tall athletic build, his rugged face, his lantern jaw, I marvelled at how such a one could have been downed at all. He himself believed it was his height which had proved to be his undoing, for he supposed that the taller a man be the easier it was to upset his balance. Now, as I admired his neatly cropped hair and thick, jet moustache, he seemed to me to be every bit the military man—the epitome of all that's finest in the ranks of our combatants.

"I was all for getting out, there and then," he went on, "and for helping you back to our boys as soon as I could. For, like I said, you were in quite a mess. You yourself though would have none of it and commanded me instead to help you to the small outbuilding signalled by the Argentinian. You found the explosive, defused it, and we returned to the main house. I did what I could for your wounds but in the event you still lost another tooth. Then, as we closed the door behind us, a chunk of loose masonry broke off and it caught you on the back of the head. You looked a little stunned for an instant, but did not at that stage lose consciousness. In fact we continued to make our way back towards the Sussex foothills. It was not until an hour later, at about a quarter past midnight, that you finally passed out. Fortunately it was only a few minutes before I chanced to come across a scout from my own company. Together we were able to get you to the nearest wireless, and within a couple of hours a Sea King helicopter had you up and away. You woke later that morning having no idea who you were nor able to make head nor tail of all this Falkland's business! Only the chaplain seemed able to reassure you."

"I should be grateful to you—and so I am, Monty—for saving my life. I'll always, I fear, be considerably in your debt; unless the tables be turned, that is, and I be afforded the opportunity of repaying the compliment."

"But, my dear friend," he replied, "you are sorely distracted or you would have heard me say that it was you who saved me! I merely got you the assistance you temporarily required. Anyhow, a scupper the size intended for our paratroopers at Camilla Creek would have had devastating consequences, and not simply in terms of consolidating the enemy forces down in Darwin. Any advance of our chaps in the direction of Port Stanley would have remained vulnerable thenceforward to forays from the rear. It is likely our final push would never have passed off so well—had it indeed passed off at all. Rest easy, Fred. All those for whom liberty, courage and truthfulness still matter are indebted to you. I ask merely to be counted in their number."

I suggested to my friend he take another coffee but could have appeared little altered in my prevailing mood, for he began again.

"Know what I really believe you need, Fred? It's what the Americans call a piece of the action, and I could give it to you right now if only you would let me."

"You may well be right, Monty. Maybe I'm a fool not to seize the moment. But as you may have guessed, I don't know if I'm fit for the job. I might just make an ass of myself, then let you down at the critical juncture. What I would need would be a slow introduction—an easy way in—so I've time to test the waters and find my feet, yet still to withdraw if I start to make a mess of things. But my hunch is that in the sort of game you people play there's no room for the amateur or fair-weather participant. You need good honest commitment and a rigorous professionalism."

"Yes, I don't deny that. On the other hand I know your credentials to be good even if you don't. What I have in mind in any case involves a trip to the Scottish Highlands. Long ago that was a favourite haunt of yours. Another thing, you are more than welcome to come along just for the ride. Not only that, but you'd enjoy the company of Rupert Malahide. He's one of the old school—about your own age, as tough as a gnarl, and as fine a gentleman as you could hope to find. He's also, poor fellow, as bald as a coot. Unlike Samson, though, the source of his strength lies in his will and not in his hair. Also, his own Delilah let him down when he was scarcely twenty and he's reputed never to have looked at a woman since!"

"It all sounds very fine," said I—and indeed I meant it, for I could see Monty was pressing me most generously. I was tempted to push him to comment further. Instead I added, "Delilah or no, there is one Freya Boyesen who awaits my company in Brighton today, while the week ahead I'm afraid is already booked. I shall be staying in Winchester where my aunt has persuaded Freya and her niece Rachel to join us—so you must permit me to turn down your offer."

Even as I spoke, however, I noticed my friend appeared distracted, as if troubled by some thought that hitherto had been kept at bay but which now surfaced, unwanted and unbidden.

"The game as it stands, I can tell you, concerns drugs—cocaine and several kilos of it. Malahide first picked up the scent out in Iran, pursued it to Athens only to lose it somewhere between there and Venice. He picked it up again, by chance, from a pedlar operating outside of St. Marc's. This pedlar, I might add, has been an informant of ours for many years. The good fortune was he'd gotten into the same show in which Malahide was engaged. However, the name of the main player had changed. No longer was it Ramadan—a disillusioned mercenary out to make a proverbial fast buck; by now the protagonist had become a malefactor known as Ishbaal. Say, Fred, you're a man who knows his Bible—tell me what can you offer on this fellow Ishbaal?"

I replied the only thing to come to mind was the name itself, for it was later changed to that of Ishbosheth. It seemed the scribe in question was anxious to point up the man's evil intent, in particular, his disloyalty to the covenant.

"Well, Ishbosheth, then?" interjected Monty.

I paused for a moment, then commented, "Bosheth, if I remember correctly, was the Hebrew term for a thing of shame…"

"Exactly," butted in my friend. "And it still is. For this fellow makes a mockery of all that is decent, genuine, or worthy of respect. He's intent only on harm. It used to be thought he was a Muslim fanatic, one of those infernal and warring sectarians. Now it seems he's turned his wrath against Allah and wants only to wreak havoc wherever he can. On civilians, on children, on simple sisters of religious orders you name it, and this man's either doing it or has done it already."

For a while Monty fell silent. It was clear that the joy of our meeting had temporarily evaporated.

"And?" I queried.

"What's bothering me is that this mischief-maker is too much of a devil simply to be making money or putting the spanner into the lives of ordinary folk—even if it be through pushing drugs and master-minding a network of villains and street-wise junkies. I don't deny that that's about as nasty and vicious a game as your average rascal would wish to play. But then this man is no ordinary or normal mortal. He thinks big and he acts big. His stage is the theatre of politics or the arena of war. He stands for nothing. He's an atheist all right, but he's fanatical with it. Equally, he's out of sympathy with your ordinary doubter or your English sceptic. It's sometimes said of him that his goal is the seizing of pleasure—the snatching of ill-gotten happiness wherever it may be found. But that's to make of the man something too intelligible, too readily appreciated, tolerated even. No, the man's game is deeper, much deeper. Malahide's convinced of it, and I believe him to be right. While you're taking tea with Freya today I shall be meeting up with one of Malahide's aides. So by tonight I should know more."

Then Monty leaned towards me, allowing his hand to rest on my arm. He looked into my eyes with a steely glint, then whispered hoarsely.

"Perhaps, after all, it's for the best. If our suspicions be only a quarter correct, then this is not the one to come in on. Drugs may only be the cover while my jaunt to the west coast may turn out to be perilous enough. It's been nice talking to you, Fred. Look after yourself now. My regards to Freya. There'll be another time, old friend, don't worry. Never fear, never fear."

So saying Monty got to his feet and strolled to the cloakroom. Time was pressing and when I left the club I took advantage of a nearby cab. As I looked out through the taxi-window onto the Thames I felt a sudden pang of conscience. There was my friend about to engage in some dastardly venture, in which heaven only knew what odds were stacked against him, and here was I making for Victoria and a rendezvous with a woman! And that intriguing companion of his—what was the fellow called?—Rupert Malahide. Now there was a name to conjure with.

CHAPTER 2

First Dealings With An Old Etonian

As I settled into a first class compartment to look out onto the dwindling city I was by turn confused, irritated and apprehensive: first, confused by my friend's partial confidences; then, irritated that the elements of danger and uncertainty had in his eyes put me out of the show; and, finally, apprehensive about my intended meeting with Freya Boyesen. I knew of course the first two of these reactions were borne of nothing more than my own pride. That Monty had confided in me as much as he had was enough to indicate the high regard in which I was held, while his caveat at the close had been entirely in keeping with my own hesitation. Still, I couldn't help but feel nettled by the business and there and then felt a resolve to prove myself of worth at the earliest opportunity.

And so to my anxiety over having tea in Brighton with a beautiful lady. I may as well confess at once I have no skill whatever when it comes to dealing with what is oft termed "the fairer sex." Fairer they may be, but women as a whole have nearly always eluded my attempts at companionship, while more than once I have felt supremely foolish in my endeavour to engage them. The fact of the matter is, you see, I am a pretty straightforward sort of chap whose main line of work has always been with other men—be that in connection with the interests of the church or within the ranks of the army. Somehow I have always felt at a disadvantage in the presence of women, imagining my bluff overtures or awkward stammerings to elicit either mere amusement or—worse still—downright pity. My mother on the other hand—the most wonderful woman I have ever known—was gradually attaining substance again in my beleaguered consciousness: when I thought of what had happened to her and to father I found my fists clenched and my jaw rigid. Then there was Freya.

Freya Boyesen was a psychotherapist from Scandinavia. She had been studying a new technique in dealing with emotional disturbance, a method that added to the more traditional form of psychoanalysis—the use of massage allied to physical exercise. However, Freya had lost patience with the slowness of the approach and in the Spring of 1982 had come to London to explore a more dynamic mode—one fostered in the first instance by a medical practitioner operating in America. She was at that time but twenty years of age and boasted the blonde hair and comely figure so suggestive to men of feminine loveliness. Furthermore, the features of her face were the finest and prettiest that I—in seeking help to access my memory—had ever encountered. Any person under her charge, however, who expected either to have a quiet time of it or to be the recipient of intriguing explanations, would have been sorely disappointed. As for myself I found it difficult to take it all seriously. The whole thing seemed to depend upon one's acting as much like a child as was humanly possible. This involved such bizarre behaviours as throwing tantrums, kicking and screaming upon a mattress, gesticulating wildly into the air, and even at one point hitting a punch bag with her grandfather's walking stick. The idea, I gathered, was to contact one's childhood by abandoning adult inhibitions and to gain thereby a measure of catharsis. There was a lot more to it than that, but acting out and a rather crude sort of abreaction nonetheless played an integral part.

In the teeth of such unusual treatment I suggest your ordinary Britisher's response would be an instinctive one of "fight or flight." Bearing in mind our nation's reputation for reserve I suppose an average Englishman would retire into embarrassment and subsequently fail to keep any future appointment. In my own case, however, I must hazard that the disciplining of my sergeant major had got the better of me, as my own response comprised an energetic if compliant desire to obey along with the motivation instilled in me to achieve. I now blush if ever I contemplate it. After a few sessions, nonetheless, I was more than ever convinced that this Swede was the most ravishing beauty I'd ever set eyes on, while the young "bio-energetic analyst" for her part was looking more and more bewildered and at times concealed her fear through drinking coffee or writing notes.

However, when I look back to that episode and to the correspondence it generated, two qualities stand out imbuing her fairness with a rigour and genuineness I have been forced to admire and to cherish. For Freya Boyesen had the courage to concede she had erred with regard to the therapy undertaken and demonstrated thereby the openness of mind of the authentic healer: she was less troubled by conformity to method than the return of a distressed soul to peace of mind and the journey it must make towards inner wholeness. All the same her letters too had lain unopened as I sought sanctuary in the process of denial and the neglect of others. Indeed it grieves me now to think how obdurate I had become. When at last I followed the prior's advice, Freya's half-dozen letters were the first that I elected to answer. It turned out that she had come to reject the earlier "energetic" model in favour of one she described as "relational"—which was to say a style of therapy that was slower, more gentle; one where the accent was on natural development rather than on any artificially induced behaviour. Might she, her letter intimated, see me again? Would I agree to a fresh course of treatment? I had to say no.

The fact of the matter was I valued Freya more as a person than as a therapist—although I admired her in that light too. But it was as a companion, perhaps even a friend and lover, that I courted her now. Besides, I happened to know—from a few pages I'd once read in a paperback—something about the process within the therapeutic alliance called "transference," and how that and "counter-transference" could alter the relationship between client and analyst: indeed, the former was sometimes cultivated as a necessary prerequisite for a successful outcome. On the whole I felt I'd rather trust to our own instincts and innate sensibilities. I wanted to know Freya as an equal, to be someone who could give as well as receive; I did not wish merely to be one more person awaiting recovery.

Freya consented to this. During the long months of my experiment with the monastic discipline she'd kept faith and, like Monty, did not try to superimpose her own judgements or personal beliefs. Twice after I had returned to the secular domain we met and exchanged news and confidences. Then, out of the blue one day, she telephoned me at Axminster to say she was going to California in order to pursue some research into the work of a therapist by the name of Moreno. I could detect the emotion in her voice, and it was as much as I could do to wish her good luck and to beg her not to tarry there for too many days.

Now Freya was back. And what was more, she would shortly be meeting me. And what was more than that, in a day or two's time, she and her niece would be staying with me in my aunt's ivy-coloured cottage on the outskirts of Winchester. The thought of it both delighted and terrified me.

You may judge from my agitation that when the train pulled up at East Croyden and a man got into my compartment I was heartily glad of the distraction he provided. He was a tallish fellow done out in a pin-striped suit, so that I wondered at his going down to the coast and not up to the city. That said, he was surprisingly tanned and looked lean and fit enough to be an army-recruit officer. I was just debating with myself whether or not to say something when he produced from his pocket a pipe, a companion set, and a tin of tobacco. This last he slammed down on the table-leaf at the edge of the window.

"Punchbowl!" I cried, seeing the name on the tin. "Why, that's the very brand my father used to smoke!"

"And your own preference?" he asked roundly.

"How do you know I smoke?" I queried.

"Partly because your memory has included a fact which might otherwise have been forgotten, and partly because—unless I am mistaken—that bulge in your coat pocket testifies to the habit."

"Elementary!" I laughed back. "Though nowadays it's not often I do, and when I am so inclined it's to the pack on whose flap is etched a rather familiar vulture."

"I know it of old," he rejoined. "Personally I prefer something with more of a bite and a keener scent."

The mention of smoking—coupled to the nervous state I was already in—at last made me pull from my pocket a little used Barling inherited from my father. Before two more minutes had elapsed both of us were watching hanks of smoke curl and eddy upwards, a look on our faces as contented no doubt as that worn by two satiated infants. It wasn't a practice I indulged in often, but when (as now) I succumbed it afforded a rare sense of relief and an agreeable degree of calm.

Looking at my fellow-passenger I found I rather took to him. Although he might have been a few years older than I he had not a trace of grey hair on his head, while he had about him an oddly restless air, for he kept thrumming forefinger and middle-index on the top of his tobacco-box. After a while I commented on the small black case he'd put on the seat beside him. I wondered aloud if he might be a musician, as well as the master of other accomplishments.

"So now," he made reply, "it's your turn to act the detective. Not, I might add, without a measure of success. I play the flute, as it happens, and have done so for quite a while. It seems my playing, moreover, meets with approval. A friend of mine on the backbenches—who claims by the way to be a friend of the P.M.—put in a word for me recently suggesting I might like to perform at the party conference. So, that's where I'm bound—for the Grand Hotel in order to entertain Tory politicians! I suppose there are worse ways of spending a few days respite."

"From what?" I asked, noting the import of his coda.

"Shall we just say I lead a more active life than this suit suggests? Ah, we've passed Three Bridges. How marvellously the landscape here unfolds—those stretches so green and pleasant, as the poet says."

"Indeed, indeed," I averred, not at all failing to spy his elusive answer—though entirely sharing his sense of delight as well. By his tone of voice, and somewhat too by his confident air and that special quality denoted by the word poise, I became persuaded that he might once have stood on the creases on the fields of Eton. He had that love of country, moreover, which is the boast of every true Englishman and which I too possessed in no small degree. As the train sped past Wivelsfield, and the first views of the Sussex Downs opened out before us, I was at once transported back to journeys I'd made earlier—from my place of work at Axminster to the company's headquarters at Waterloo. However bored or dispirited I'd felt then about the property business, the sight of the Wiltshire Downs and the Wyle Valley had never ceased to inspire me. Something within me responded to those folds of hill and meandering rivers, and, deep down, I knew that whatever our forbears had struggled for had not been an illusion, and, if I too had been drawn in some small measure to emulate their example, I could not despise the sacrifice. Now, as we passed all too quickly through Burgess Hill towards the town of Hassocks, the sight of those rounded slopes and eye-catching copses convinced me once more—whatever the perplexities of the moment—that my life could not with reason be thought to be in vain.

In due course we emerged from a tunnel and were put in prospect of a newly built road traversing the countryside. I could see by the expression on my companion's face that he did not approve.

"Will they leave us nothing?" he complained.

I started to quote from *The Ballad Of The White Horse*, and the Old Etonian nodded in approval.

When I had finished he put in, "They would make away with all King Arthur's ancient meades and the lovely world of Avalon. But we are here, my friend, and I have not a moment to lose. It's been a pleasure meeting you."

With that my anonymous musician stepped down to the platform and instantly was lost amidst the departing throng.

I looked at my watch. It was shortly before three o'clock. That meant I had a little over half an hour to go. And that would be if Freya were on time—for I fully expected to be kept waiting when I myself arrived (on the very dot) at Harrington's tearooms. Women were not, at least in my own experience, renowned for their punctuality.

I decided to make the best of it and slipped into a bookshop down Queen's Road. There I picked up three hard-backed volumes for the price of a Scotch: a charmingly illustrated item on wild flowers by Marjorie Blamey—it would do for my niece's birthday; a collection of sermons by a certain nineteenth-century preacher, much associated with Brighton—and, by name, F. W. Robertson; and a novel by a former Governor General of Canada which was, I declared—lying through my teeth—for a teenage nephew of mine. With these books carefully wrapped up I set off for the Lanes and there had just enough time to purchase a rather neat-looking pocket-telescope before rushing up some stairs to the appointed venue.

Freya, to my amazement, was already there.

"Round one to you!" I said, scarcely disguising my asperity.

"Take it easy, Fred," she replied, holding out her hand. "This is not a boxing match, you know."

I recovered my composure and sat down.

"My apologies. It's just—it's so very nice to see you again."

The next few minutes passed with each of us making the kind of pleasantries to which friends are apt to resort when they have been parted for any length of time; until, that is, the waters have been tested and a more natural and meaningful exchange may begin. However, the latter was short-lived.

"Fred," Freya said suddenly, "I'm afraid I must try your patience."

"What is it?" I queried, now conscious of feeling warm and comfortable in the old-world charm of the place with its linen napkins and smartly attired waitresses. "Nothing serious, I hope."

"Not really, just a slight change of plan. I'll see you in Winchester as arranged on the Monday or Tuesday of next week. The problem is this evening. I'm afraid you must dine alone: worse, in thirty minutes I'm supposed to see a colleague of mine outside her flat by the Seven Dials. Can you forgive me?"

What could I say? I was scarcely back in the company of this adorable young woman and already she was making for her cardigan and shopping-basket. On the other hand (I cajoled myself) wasn't this precisely what a gentleman should expect? Were not women as will o' the wisp? They could not be tied down. *La donna e mobile.* At least Freya was not leaving me to see another man…

I kissed her on the cheek, told her it was quite all right and that I should see her again shortly. At this she started to flush slightly, her gorgeous eyes melting deliciously, until with a solemn smile she bade me farewell.

I sat for a while staring into an empty cup trying to recapture the deep blue of Miss Boyesen's gaze.

Still, I could see that this was doing me no good, so I got to my feet, paid the girl at the counter, and with a greater spring in my step than usual set off in the direction of Brighton promenade. It remained a beautiful day—the person of my dreams had been near to me and would be so again shortly.

In my haste to be quit of the department store, however, I nearly knocked down a decrepit, blind gentleman teetering towards the corner and tapping in front of him a white telescopic stick. I apologised copiously and pushed into his hand a ten-pound note. He was, he said, making his way to the York Villas. I suggested he might like to take a taxi, for there were several standing vacant at a nearby rank. I took my leave of him, in any case, and at once put the incident out of my mind.

A few minutes later I'd reached the lower promenade and began striding out in the direction of Hove, observing as I did so both the fading Regency splendour of former times and the ultramarine windswept sea. For the second time that day I became aware of a party of runners, this time loping regularly along the opposite way: and there was indeed that about the air which inclined one naturally to turn one's walk into a jog and one's jog into a run: I should, moreover, have enjoyed putting this party through its paces for I'd once enjoyed a certain stamina and could claim even now a respectable speed. In fact there was in me just then a fresh upsurge of all the old feelings—of strength in combat, vigour for the hunt, a determination to achieve.

As I was making my way back, and under the collapsed west pier—and noticing again the signs of decay and how the corrosive force of the elements had combined with those of indifference and diluted wealth—I came within sight of what is arguably the most recognisable hotel the length and breadth of Britain. There can be few who are not familiar—be it from their own experience or from images borrowed from the media—with the imposing and dignified façade of the Grand Hotel. Especially, alas, after the attempt made there on the life of our prime minister.

Now I am myself, I suppose, by temperament a pretty conservative sort of chap, yet I like to think I'm alive both to the occasional need for reform and the necessity for social change. Now and then, moreover, I've been tempted to wonder whether enough is being done to protect the most vulnerable in our society. But to attempt to deprive the nation of its elected leader is, to my way of thinking, to try to let in the forces of violence and anarchy and thereby replace a properly elected government with some ill-conceived junta or the terrorist dictatorship of a Pol Pot. Nothing but mayhem would ensue. It was an endeavour to be resisted by all possible means. If security-measures as a consequence sometime seem too elaborate or authorities heavy handed, so be it. For sad though it be in a free and open society such as ours, tough means are sometimes required to halt the criminal in his tracks, the assassin in his devilish pursuit.

I was just turning over such thoughts in my mind when I recalled seeing a placard at the railway station informing travellers of a temporary withdrawal of left-luggage facilities. Presumably, I reflected—though I'd hardly been aware of it at the time—because the party in power was on the point of holding its annual conference. A pity, perhaps, to inconvenience seaside commuters—yet it was surely wise to take every precaution.

At that moment there occurred one of those incidents to make even the most agnostic of fellows a proselyte to providence or the handiwork of fate. For, just as I was gazing up at the front of the hotel—and contemplating the need to safeguard our country's top leaders—I saw from the window above the top balcony, at the farthest left-hand corner, a flash of light. Then another. And again, another. It must, I considered, be the sun reflecting back on some surface or other mirroring its glare. But what was the surface?

A sudden impulse made me pull out of my coat pocket the newly acquired telescope, and—whilst feeling every kind of fool—train it at once on the source of that reflection. I could hardly believe what I saw. By some stroke of serendipity I was looking straight into the muzzle of a pointed gun! What sort of firearm it was or who was holding it, I could not of course tell. Yet the possibility that this was some would-be assassin, who even now was getting his anticipated target in sight, could not be ignored.

Without a moment's delay—nearly getting myself killed in the process—I dashed across the road and hurled myself through the revolving doors of the hotel.

Concierge, constables, a stammering receptionist—I ignored them all. I leapt up the stairs two at a time. I had wanted to prove myself of worth—this was my opportunity.

Half way up, I stopped. What on earth did I think I was doing? What was I hoping to achieve? Supposing I found the right door, most probably it would be locked. Was I going to break it down? And suppose I came across the armed gunman? What was I going to say? What could I do? More to the point, what could I prove? As the absurdity of my actions bore in upon me I hastily began to retrace my steps. I should need to go about this altogether differently: introduce myself, explain what I thought I'd seen—already I was no longer so sure!—and request that somebody else investigate with all due haste.

Then as I approached the corner of the lounge I thought I heard a voice that sounded familiar. I could not at first place it, nor could I be sure of what was being said. But I believed I could make out the following words:

"Quick—all right, two hundred then—out, now—lose yourself!"

Not that those words formed themselves properly at the time. Only later, looking back on the event, did the staccato message sink in and only later again did it acquire any meaning. Right then I spun round the corner to discover a pale-looking youth in denims—a small black case clutched to his bosom—look up at me in alarm and dive for the entrance. Just before he turned though he threw his incriminating package in my direction. Like an idiot, I caught it!

"Stop that boy!" I heard myself yell.

The response that evoked, however, caught me by surprise. In a voice, rich and sombre, my former fellow-passenger commanded two policemen present to "Arrest that man!" And he was pointing, emphatically, at *me!*

Now though I've every respect for the British bobby I'm bound to say I've never been unduly impressed by his powers of imagination. Try as I might to explain myself, I could make no headway whatever, whilst the more I struggled the more I seemed to damn myself. Already the receptionist had opened the case, the weapon of misadventure there for all the world to see.

And what, you might ask, of the Old Etonian? I am obliged to say that he looked calmly on, protesting that he'd never in his life set eyes upon me, that he was an advertising consultant from London, and then—just for good measure—he added that he'd not be coming back to the Grand Hotel ever again. Full marks to him—he played his part brilliantly. All at once that dignified face and manly bearing, which earlier had excited my admiration, now only filled me with contempt and outrage. The more I stuttered to explain my presence, the more coolly he regarded me and the more softly, it seemed, did he speak.

And all the while that I stood there, flurried and flabbergasted, the real villain was making his escape! Or was he? For, who *was* the real villain? Could it really have been the boy? And then there was that voice I'd heard so full of urgency and alarm. Had it not indeed been that of the Etonian? If so, was he not horribly implicated in the whole affair?

But there was now no time to pursue these questions, for I saw I was soon to be carted off to the nearest police station. The receptionist had already telephoned for two more constables.

There was only one thing left to do. I should have to apply myself in earnest to escape from the law. If I were the only one prepared to believe my story, then it would be up to me to follow it through—whatever the outcome.

I made a start by entirely altering my state of mind. I became composed and well-mannered. I apologised for my unruliness, and, to make the change seem authentic, I even owned up to being the guilty person. That, especially, put them at their ease—so much so in fact that the one on the left relaxed his grip. Officers of the law or no, I should have to make a break for it.

In what seemed less than a second the bobby to my right found he was nursing a severely kicked shin; his assistant, meantime, was careering across the reception area into the arms of the Etonian. It was fortunate for me that I've a sturdy frame and a solid build. My army training, of course, had placed me in good stead and on returning to normal civilian life I'd taken regular exercise. Even so I surprised myself at the speed and agility with which I affected my exit, as I made hurriedly for the nearest street corner without a plan in my head bar a bolt to the station.

Two pieces of luck, however, assisted me in the harum-scarum egress I now essayed. The first was the sighting of an underground concourse—which dipped beneath the road at the very corner I was making for and opposite which stood a large cinema. When I reached the latter I pulled from my pocket a large silk handkerchief with the letters F. D. embroidered in its quarter. Aiming awkwardly I threw it towards the palings at the top of the steps where I half-expected to see it blown away by a gust of wind. But, as I have said, fortune was with me. The handkerchief became attached to the side of the railings, and, by the time the two constables had seized it and noticed the pair of initials, I was securely hidden in a semi-derelict building-site between the cinema and a nearby church. I was just wondering what to do next when a second break came my way.

On the other side of the road there was a public house. Now who should be emerging from its doors but the very blind person I'd almost knocked down but thirty minutes beforehand. Straightaway I saw my chance. While the police were temporarily diverted in the subway I crossed over the road, seized the poor fellow by the arm, and this time properly began to introduce myself. Instead of feeding him the correct story, though, I spun him a cock-and-bull yarn about running away from my estranged wife and needing a quick disguise to lose her forever. I'd judged his mood correctly since this tale—together with the notes I pressed into his hand—quite won him over. What I was after was his telescopic stick and his threadbare greatcoat. These he gladly handed over before plunging through the doors whence two minutes earlier he'd so fortuitously emerged. As he did so I called out to the man, telling him I should send on his belongings via the York Villas—for I had not yet forgotten his address—at the earliest possible convenience.

My next move was to cross the road and so return to the building site. The two constables were still engaged in what looked like a game of trivial pursuits and thereby left me enough time to hide behind a large skip affording me an ideal occasion for contriving a disguise. Amongst the rubble lying there was the usual bonanza of discarded items which such receptacles invariably seem to contain. What I myself needed was a piece of string and some brown paper. In the event I found both of them beside an abandoned spectacle-case. This last, it turned out, contained a very old pair of wire frames with one lens intact, the other entirely missing. By the time I'd wrapped up my jacket and mackintosh, donned the greatcoat, scuffed my shoes in the stony dust and put on the spectacles I quite looked the part—so, when minutes later a pair of flustered policemen ran past me at full pelt they got for their pains a patently vernacular oath delivered by a hunched-up blind man carrying an extended white cane in one hand and a shabby brown parcel in the other. They did not even bother to look back!

Incidentally it was a good thing one of my lenses was missing, for the single round of glass remaining was so thick that it was impossible to discern anything by it. It may have been this fact which prompted me to affect the queer habit of squinting and—from time to time—looking up to the sky. In addition to which every few hundred yards I would place my parcel on the ground, make as if to straighten up my back, but then almost immediately fall forward as though in a paroxysm of pain and a fit of coughing. You see I'd decided from the beginning I couldn't afford to mimic my thirsty helpmate but would be better advised to contrive my own strange, eccentric part. By behaving as if I were half in pain, three-quarters without sight, and completely without sense I believed I might go where I would yet remain undetected—and precisely by attracting to my figure as much attention as was possible. That way too I could enjoy a certain leeway in the matter of observation, for I was able to look about me in my curious fashion, watching out for any familiar person making in my direction. The only ones I saw comprised the handful of joggers I'd earlier observed running along the promenade. One in particular I recognised due to his youthful good looks and his bright shock of ginger-red hair. There was something about the lad, too, which caused me to wonder—but I couldn't quite place it.

It wasn't very long after this that I succeeded in reaching the station, but once there a fresh difficulty presented itself in the dearth of a ticket. In my understandable haste I'd left this and a wallet in my jacket pocket so both were now securely contained within the brown paper package I carried. On the other hand, even if I'd had enough change accessible to purchase a fresh ticket, the long queues of persons waiting to do likewise meant I should surely have missed my train. It was now rush hour with the next departure for Victoria imminent.

Then I spotted a tramp. How often in the past had I bemoaned their presence in our nation's railway-terminals. The invasion of one's privacy, the smell of alcohol, the inevitable call upon one's funds. Now I thanked God for the fact, for in a moment an idea had occurred to me. I went over to the poor unfortunate and sitting down beside him at once began to curse the railway official collecting the tickets. I made a point of speaking in a rich Irish brogue and threw in every foul word my mind could invent. The gist of what I'd to say was that I had been most viciously insulted, I had been refused admission to the platform, and—worst of all—it seemed that folk like us were to get back to the peat bogs whence originally we hailed. This last tack—as I'd fancied at the outset—worked a veritable treat. Without further ado my companion-of-the-road went over to the hapless official and thereupon proceeded to engage him in a most frightful harangue. Whilst the hectoring acquired both colour and volume I myself was able to dart behind the collector, nod surreptitiously at my disreputable redeemer, and thence make a dive for the nearest carriage.

As the train pulled out of the station I might have been heard resorting to the same spicy vocabulary as that of the ruffian behind. Only it consisted now of a heartfelt indictment of a third-class W.C.

CHAPTER 3

A Change of Trains

The contrast between my journey in a first class compartment from Victoria station and the accommodation afforded on my return could hardly have been more marked. Earlier I had been lulled into a consideration of how admirable was our countryside—a meditation that had left me in a state of euphoria and a mood of anticipation. Now I felt only a kind of dread—a cold fear if you will—both of being caught by the police and of being discovered in apparel more suited to a bedlam. Dread, though, was not the only sensation to accompany me, for I soon began physically to shake in the wake of my adventures. It was as if the effort required to loose me from such an absurd situation had finally caught up with me, and, in consequence, I felt shocked and stunned. I shivered when I thought of the pickle I was in, and then and there was all for handing myself in. It was the contemplation of another contrast that prevented me.

The upshot of my reflections turned on how mighty had been the alteration wrought in my travelling companion. Why had he not assisted me at the hotel? Why had he lied? And was it not his own voice I'd heard as I'd rushed to reception? It came back to me then how in travelling to Brighton the Etonian had dodged my question: he would not name that from which he sought respite. And then there was that mysterious case he'd carried. Presumably it had harboured the gun and the only tune no doubt would be as infamous as a dervish in hell. As for myself it seemed I might as well have been a puppet—with the Etonian pulling the strings. I think it was this consideration that finally brought me to my senses. Somehow I had to remain free from captivity for as long as it would take me to warn the authorities. The planned assassination had to be stopped—although I could hardly expect to be taken seriously in my present guise with, in all probability, a warrant out for my arrest. If only I could contact Monty then perhaps the situation might yet be redeemed.

It was then I remembered Monty's invitation to accompany him to the north of Scotland. I couldn't help but reflect that had I done so at once I should never have got myself into such a terrible mess. Surely how right I had been, though, to judge myself "not fit for play." Had I not handled my own affairs abysmally? Still, I remained hopeful that my friend could turn even a person's ineptitude to some advantage. My immediate problem then—always supposing I was not discovered in my present confinement—was how I might get to St. Pancras station for seven fifteen, the time the northbound train was due to depart. I knew this schedule because Monty had kicked up a fuss about travelling in some style and had booked his passage on an Intercity Land-Cruise. Though he was forever lamenting British Rail, he insisted that when the effort was made the service was nigh unbeatable. This meant that Monty journeyed in the elegance and comfort of the Pullman whenever he could. The fact that he might not be returning with the other passengers, and so half the cruise be lost, abashed him not one whit—the point being to arrive at one's destination refreshed and, where possible, with one's spirits raised. But how was I to reach St. Pancras by a quarter past seven?

A disreputable blind man weaving his antic way through an impatient throng may not expect sympathy from a jostling taxi-queue. However, an upright gentleman in a mackintosh with his shoes cleaned and with a parcel held out for all the world like a gift might well anticipate a more favourable hearing: especially if he can carry forth both a military bearing and an earnest if lost sight at one and the same time. Thus it was I came to affront a restless and suspicious line of travellers with the cry, "Anyone making for St. Pancras?"

As I fielded my poser I stared innocuously at a poor specimen in navy blue wielding a beer can almost to my face. Fortunately there came then immediately to my aid someone whom I opined to be a middle-aged stockbroker. Abandoning every pretence to British reserve, this fellow marched to the front of the queue, opened the door of a cab, and almost pushed me inside. He called to the driver my destination and then sat down beside me. I noticed he was carrying a duffle-bag, and this struck me as a trifle odd for one I took to be a City gent dealing in stocks and shares.

In order to get a better view of my importunate helper I stated a preference for having my back to the engine. However, the move did me no good at all as I got nothing more than a first rate view of *The Financial Times*. Eventually, though, there came a moment at some traffic lights at which my *vis-a-vis* lowered his paper to address the driver. To my surprise he spoke something in a foreign language, a tongue alien to me but which I fancied belonged either to the Middle or Near East. More curious yet, the cabby responded with the same accent! The consequence of this was that when the vehicle set off again, and my fellow passenger was once more lost to view on the far side of his journal, I turned round behind to squinny at the cabman. The stockbroker himself (I had noticed) was of rather a swarthy complexion, with broad features and a much lined forehead: his hair was jet black and was set fast in a mass of curls. Now to my alarm I discovered the driver of the taxi was of almost identical appearance: only he had sideburns flecked with grey and, as far as I could judge, his face evidenced fewer wrinkles. It was patent that the two men were twins!

As carefully as I could I glanced at my watch. It was now almost ten past seven. I couldn't see how I could possibly catch the train, my only hope being that the time of departure would be delayed. As passengers would have needed to reserve their places it was just possible one or two tardy comers might set back the schedule for as long as it would take a fellow to step from his taxi and come to his platform. For, by now, we had arrived at St. Pancras where I was as efficiently bundled out as I had enthusiastically been bundled in. My conspiratorial aids left me to my stick and to my vacant looks.

There was now too little time to be detained either by a form of charade or a case of myopia. I pocketed my shortened stick and went haring off towards platform-seven where I knew The West Highlander must either be stationed or about to depart. Luck was with me, for it had not yet gone.

My problem at this stage was how I might get onto the train without due documentation or requisite ticket. I decided to use a ploy I'd often entertained in fancy but never had the nerve actually to perform. I bounded towards the end of the platform holding up my left hand and in it a wallet that displayed several bank notes along its edges. As I did so I yelled out at the top of my voice, "Natasha, Natasha! You've forgotten your tickets and all your visas!...Natasha...just a minute, dear...I'm coming."

As a matter of fact this created very little stir, and I soon reached the sleeper-section of the train indicated by the letters P to X. Unfortunately, a square-looking chap was there standing armed with a clipboard and apparently ready to arrest my progress. I made as if to be lost and backtracked a couple of hundred yards down the platform. Then I dived into a carriage situated between the staff car and the kitchen. As I did so I collided into a passenger, prompting the poor fellow to go staggering down the aisle. When the latter had regained his stance he called out in astonishment, "Good God, it's you, Fred! What on earth's up? Have you changed your mind or Freya her's?"

It was Monty, and a more welcome countenance could not be imagined.

"Look, old friend," I explained in haste, "I'm on the run from the police, possibly from an assassin. Can you hide me somewhere? I'm done for if you don't."

"Lord, looks as if you've quit the quiet life after all! Anyhow you can calm down now, this train is considerably under booked despite the usual nonsense about advanced reservations to avoid disappointment. Besides, I carry a certain amount of clout on a trip like this. Sir George Rawlinson is, as I think you know, a personal friend of mine. And he engineered the initial enterprise on which this is based. So, worry not. In addition to which it's a marvel what a little lucre can do in a tight corner! Rest easy, Fred, it seems we're off—and I for one intend to enjoy myself!"

So saying, and incorrigible optimist that he is, Montague Fiennes of MQ1 picked up the menu card, announced that we shall have darne of salmon and summer pudding, and that we must discard the Bordeaux in favour of the Sancerre. The other passengers assembled while he made for the manager; but he turned round and roared out jovially, "Aye, an' dinna forget the Haggis and Neeps!" I smiled, being a touch bemused, peered out into the fall of the night and wondered how on earth I'd made it thus far.

The train had, I remember, a number of stops to make on a journey scheduled via Stirling, picking up itinerants from St. Albans, Leicester and Derby. Mostly these comprised middle-aged couples—some of whom were to celebrate an anniversary—but which also included an occasional pair of young folk destined for heather and starlight and a handful or so of single people who seemed rather to stand out as if lost or of the kind who tend to bore one with a vast and abstruse knowledge of the locomotive. There was a priest, too, and an ancient gentleman in tweeds for whom this seemed a somewhat curious diversion.

The evening passed by pleasantly enough. The seating was comfortable, the lighting discreet, and the service friendly but not obtrusive. We dined well, smoked a cheroot, and after ten o'clock repaired to our sleepers. It was then that I filled in my friend regarding my doings in Brighton. I confess I was dismayed by his reaction. It was not at all sympathetic.

"To start with," he began, "I'm not even sure it's Brighton where the Tories are having their conference. I'd rather thought it was Blackpool's turn to play host to the P.M. Next, I'm bound to say your little escapade will by now have been forgotten. You've made it here, all right, but I doubt if it's all been down to your skill in covert operations. Numbers are pretty thin on the ground these days while the lads of the Yard have better things to think about than a guy with a gun claiming to know an Etonian—even if he's supposed to be a flautist hired by the Cabinet! I fancy, old friend, you could have come over as a bit of a clown. You know nowadays there are those who will actually plead that they be considered as villains, rapists, despicable murderers. I suppose it's their way of calling attention to themselves, strange enough though that may seem to the likes of you or me. Anyhow, you'll find them by the dozen every time a serious crime's reported in the media. There's not a yard in the land but that it doesn't boast a handful of such cranks or criminals *manques*. No Fred, I think your antics will have fooled no-one. Nonetheless, you've raised the alarm. Security, which to begin with would have been tight in such a noted watering hole, will by now have been tripled. Fear not, of that you may be sure."

Never, I believe, have I felt so deflated! Here was I at the end of a chase, reckless in itself and littered with suspicious circumstances, and Monty was treating me as if I were guilty of Quixotism or mere self-delusion. I stammered out a half-hearted protest and reminded him of the turncoat behaviour of the Etonian and of the peculiar duo I'd encountered in the taxi.

"Yes, you may have something there, though as it stands it's all purely circumstantial, a series of details quirky enough in themselves but hardly enough to constitute a case. Myself, I seem to be the victim of such coincidence every other day. But I'm glad you're safe and I can see that it's put some colour back in your cheeks."

I was all for remonstrating against Monty's equanimity when I saw a troubled look come into his eyes and noticed how his brow had become tightly furrowed. Then I remembered he himself was up against something unquestionably big, that he'd seen fit to warn me away from it and had been going to meet a colleague of Malahide's to deracinate the truth—in the teeth of which my own amateurish pranking must have seemed, to him, the height of tomfoolery. For the time being I decided to forget about the entire episode and see if I couldn't be of use to my anxious companion. As I stood looking at him in the dimness of that compartment I was able to see behind any momentary impatience or show of irritability the loneliness of a man on whose shoulders are placed burdens of which the ordinary fellow in the street can know little or nothing.

I fell silent then and began to study the expression of my former captain. He had pulled from a small wooden box a half-corona and now proceeded to light the thing, sending up thick rounds of smoke swirling into the air. But the usual look of relish did not adorn his face. Momentarily did he gaze through the window into the rush of darkness beyond; then he turned to me and fixing me with that indomitable stare—a look which invariably presaged a statement of some import—he proclaimed the events of his day since the moment we'd parted.

First of all, then, he had gone up to the House of Commons where he'd been due to meet up with a certain M.P. There he had had confirmed to him earlier suspicions about a prominent backbencher. He discovered that this man was actually in the employ of a chap Malahide had been tailing on his journey through France. The politician, said Monty, was a plausible and much admired dealer in foreign art but also part of a network now spearheaded by the infamous Ishbaal. The latter had gained control of the entire gang and had transformed it from a plainly disreputable organization, intent solely on gaining wealth, to an important wing of his own fanatical and evil empire.

"I was," continued Monty, "thoroughly disturbed by the matter, and as you might imagine got one of my boys to pump X's secretary for everything he could get. He's a politician who's going to need careful watching. In the meantime, however, I'd had to hop across smartly to a venue in Little Venice where I was to meet Malahide's second-in-command. He was the one I mentioned to you this morning. What he had to convey was the worst news possible. Drug running—bad though it be—is as naught compared to the evil that this maniac's plotting. Anyhow, at length I left behind our contact—on board a boat called *The Eligibility* that we'd hired for the day—and I was in the process of hailing a taxi when there was this almighty explosion."

"Good God!" I interrupted. "Whatever was it?"

"It was *The Eligibility*, her splintered remnants scattered far and wide, so many scraps for the city scavengers. She was blown to smithereens. Our man—a first class graduate from the L.S.E.—would have been killed instantly. And, if I hadn't been catching this train, so should I."

I was appalled at what Monty had narrated and had no idea what to say to him.

"We must hope," I blurted out, "that he has passed on the baton to the next runner and with sufficient time for MQ1 to be the winner of the race."

"That's true, Fred. And you're right to say it. But if you'd had to break the news to his wife, down some wretched, crackling telephone wire you might be forgiven for wishing to throw in the towel on the whole sorry sordid affair. Good riddance to espionage, let the world go its own sweet crazy course—and let yours truly find some peace at last. Then, when I heard there was a little girl of five—bereft of her father—I knew I was deluding myself. I cannot stop, Fred. I'm a driven man. As long as the likes of your Ishbosheth are tramping the globe, I cannot rest easy."

"And the message?" I quizzed, for I was determined to keep up my friend's resolve, though how he had the nerve for it all I shall never know.

"Well, like a lot of his type he's a master of disguise. Which probably accounts for the way he's slipped our net on several occasions. However, the gallant Welshman I met this afternoon informed me that the last time Ishbaal escaped our clutches he'd apparently worn a shoe on his left foot built up three inches higher than the one on his right. Is it possible, therefore, that he suffers from some physical disability? We can't be sure, for he may have been acting. Yet I'm inclined to think he does harbour such a handicap, for he seemed very natural on the occasion mentioned and because at the time of his temporary arrest he was making his way out of a well-known concert hall in Paris."

"The performance?" I asked.

"*Carmina Burrana*. In Russian, would you believe? Part of the new *entente cordiale* with the improved Soviets."

Monty shrugged. His optimism evidently did not extend to the Great Bear. There were, he once commented, too many hard-liners standing in the wings. He resumed his account.

"For the rest he is a man between five feet ten and six feet two, rather brown in the face—as if he has travelled long distances in the sun—slight in build but as strong as an ox and as taut as a hawser stretched-to-its-limits. In truth do I pity the poor unfortunate who would choose combat with that one. Apart from being preternaturally fit he is something of an expert it seems in martial arts. What drives him, Lord only knows. He is a man of exceptional abilities, extraordinary endurance, and a most astute mind. Yet his sole *raison d' être* seems to be the execution of perfidy on the largest possible scale. He is hell bent on wickedness and calamity and if he can effect them in gargantuan proportions, so much the better. Never forget, Fred, this man is evil incarnate. And I don't believe in the devil any more than I do in God. A thing of shame—yes, he is that all right."

"And his present purposes?" I queried, being somewhat vexed by me friend's elusiveness.

"Forgive me, Fred, but I'm tired. You know it's a heavy load with which to encumber a person one doesn't like, let alone with which to shackle a friend."

This of course made me more avid than ever. I seemed to be standing on the very edge of a precipice looking down into an abyss—yet not knowing what the murky deeps below contained. Only my companion knew that and he was keeping it from me. Yet I forbore and held in check my growing impatience. It was late, after all, and I could see that the fatigue of the day demanded its natural remedy.

I myself, moreover, had been on no mere picnic. I had found my way to safety, discovered my best friend and ally, heard more of Ishbaal and—who knew but in the morning to come—might be entrusted to learn at last what lay at the heart of Monty's misery. And this fellow, Ishbaal—clearly he was no panjandrum. If Monty was to be believed we were dealing more with a monster than any normal man. And my friend never lied and was rarely if ever wrong.

CHAPTER 4

We Travel To Oban

Truth to tell I was relieved I'd not had to double up in the same berth as my companion. By the time I'd left him his cabin was full of cigar smoke and seemed entirely without air. When I saw him at breakfast the next day Monty looked as though he were in rather a rough temper, as though he had not slept well and as though the conversation of the night before had eclipsed all the good the *vin blanc* had wrought. In this there was small matter for wonder.

By contrast, I myself was feeling as merry as a sandpiper and as ravenous as a wolf. I'd taken advantage of the stop at Stirling during the relative quiet of dawn and had gone out for a run along its city streets. Then I'd returned to my berth where—leaning against the washbasin—I'd done a hundred or so press-ups with very little fuss. I had, in any case, slept soundly and was feeling more alive now at six fifteen in the morning than I had done for many a long month. I suppose I must have been seized by the sheer adventure of it, even if it did promise to be a most sinister and deadly affair and even if the rules were liable to be broken at any moment.

The consequence of all this was that I myself ate a hearty breakfast, supplementing the usual combination of eggs, bacon, sausage and tomato, with black pudding and sauté potatoes. Monty, on the other hand, looked on regretfully and nibbled at a piece of overdone toast. However, two cups of dark coffee revived my friend, and a Fribourg and Treyer Virginia No 6 restored his mind to its earlier and customary sharpness. At Taynuilt he declared he had some phone calls to make and made off in the direction of the staff car—leaving me in ignorance to contemplate his next possible move.

I should inform the reader at this juncture that the bright sunny weather of Sussex had quickly deteriorated—as soon in fact as the train had departed the Capital. We'd left behind the Indian Summer and in exchange were treated to as thick a mist as to render sightseeing impossible. Some paper towels we'd been given—with which to wipe away condensation from the windows—seemed at the time as superfluous as they did incongruous. The passengers themselves, strange to say, did not seem at all disgruntled by this absent prospect. Most of them had turned their attention to other matters, becoming busy with maps and guides or else becoming deeply absorbed in their own conversation.

At Taynuilt, however, there was a slight break in the mist, sufficient I decided to try to take in the locale of the station. Alas! I need hardly have bothered. I stuck my head through the open window only to be rewarded with a dismal view of the diminishing line. I fancied that in this respect my fellow travellers on the other side of the aisle might be faring better than I.

I was just wondering then whether I ought not to go to the door in the corridor when I got the fright of my life. No sooner had I turned my head round to view the eastern end of the track than I found myself looking straight into the face of the very same stockbroker who, but hours beforehand, had assisted me in my journey to St. Pancras. I recognised him at once: the same dark countenance, the same shock of hair, the same set of quizzical furrows. You may well imagine I lost little time in withdrawing my head into the anonymity of the carriage. The truth, however, was that I acted more calmly than that; for first I turned my head to the right and only after pausing for some seconds did I actually step back. You see I did not wish to arouse suspicion, whilst something inside of me—instinct I suppose—told me that I had not been wrong about the events of the previous day and that I should need to deal with whatever transpired next with a cool head and a steady hand.

It was with a mixture of excitement and anticipation that I sat back then to await the return of my friend. After all, surely this was a coincidence Monty could not ignore. The minutes passed by with an unbearable slowness. I am not a patient person at the best of times, but this delay in communicating news to the only person I could was nigh intolerable. I was about to go pacing up to the other end of the train when I thought the better of it. Better lie low, better keep my face hid behind a paper. Well, I had no newspaper but I did have a copy of the Sermons of F. W. Robertson of Brighton. Very quickly, then, did I become a myopic student of nineteenth-century theology.

It is now time to say something about the four persons occupying the seats across the intervening aisle, for their conversation was soon to take a turn relevant to my tale. They were all associated, it seemed, with a certain public school situated in Dorset. The one sitting at the window, his back towards Oban, was the chaplain there: he was a stoutish man distinguished by a sanguine complexion and thinning grey hair. To his left, wearing an expression of perpetual concentration, there lounged a tall youth whom I discovered later to be the head boy. Opposite him was an earnest looking chap in his late twenties, done out in a soft tweed suit and sounding as if he might well be a teacher of physics. Beside him there sat a civil servant of some sort who enjoyed a prominent position on the Board of Governors. What they were all doing on a West Highland Land Cruise was hard to say, but at that stage in the journey I surmised it to be an interest of one of them in rail-travel and the need for all four to become better acquainted at the start of their year.

They were talking about the Holy Land. The teacher had chanced to comment on the change of weather and how some splendid hill scenery was being hid from view. That had prompted the civil servant to remind the chaplain of a pilgrimage to Jerusalem during the previous year. It seemed that they had undertaken a period of hill-trekking in the country around Hebron and that the blazing and magnificent vistas of that place were on no account to be missed. How glorious the climate! How striking the terrain!—this was the gist of their discourse. Then the priest turned his attention to the problem of conflict within the city of Jerusalem, "that celebrated *omphalos* (he said) of the Semitic world."

"What a place!" he pronounced enthusiastically, but then added, "Yet more for the heart and imagination than the intellect, so ultimately it satisfies not. It is too much given over to religious and historical wrangling; hence it serves as a source for factional unrest of every description. It is, I fear, ever in peril of losing its proper meaning. Instead of its being a genuine sanctuary enhancing the spiritual life of our race it has become an arena for hot political contest and is only a little disguised by the trappings of religion."

"Oh you are too gloomy, Father," replied the civil servant. "To stand upon Mount Scopus and to gaze out across the Kidron Valley, to feel the rapture of dusk as one strolls besides the Mount of Olives, to kneel in the Garden of Gethsemane and to conceive of that solitary and anguished figure, or to fancy one hears the Lord's declaration to his persecutors—in the words of St. John, *Ego eimi*, 'I am he'—to remember that is surely to be inspired, to be encouraged for evermore."

"Yes, yes. I agree with you, but only so far. You see, for Christians some of those sites are indeed aids to devotion, and as such they may be welcomed as constituting a healthy distraction from Lourdes, or Fatima, or from Garrabandal—even, one might add, from Rome itself. But how so for the Jew? Consider how sad, how pathetic, that all that remains of his beloved temple is a single wall at which he weeps and wails, issues his endless discontent. The cry goes up from the heart that his fallible dream is broken. Alas! Alas!"

Although it was all too easy to hear this colloquy, in the normal way of things I should have kept any opinion of my own strictly to myself. What made me depart from the norm was the particular sermon I happened to be reading—for it was entitled, 'The Illusiveness of Life.' In it the Victorian preacher had seized on the fact that the promises of Revelation are never fulfilled in the manner anticipated, but are only ever realised in some deeper sense: the material letter of the promise might act to motivate man, but fulfilment would always be according to the spirit. I couldn't resist the temptation to bring these *pensées* to bear upon the sentiments so recently expressed. Indeed I went further, for I actually quoted from the sermon itself:

> And such is life's disappointment. Its promise is, you shall have a Canaan; it turns out to be a baseless airy dream—toil and warfare—nothing that we can call our own; not the land of rest, by any means.

"Exactly so, exactly so," the chaplain murmured, looking vexed, as if perhaps I was stealing his thunder.

Still there was no sign of the stockbroker and still I had not been rejoined by my friend. I was debating with myself whether I should seek inclusion in the party from the school when the present conversation took an altogether different turn. I sat back and decided simply to listen, this time with my face in the text of a homily headed, 'The Law of Christian Conscience.'

It was the physics teacher who spoke first.

"What you've been saying, Father, makes me reflect on Iran and Iraq, and I begin to wonder whether the whole of the Near East is nothing but a hotbed of unrest and damnable sedition. Is there a clear, sane head to be discovered anywhere under the Eastern sun? What perturbs me most is how the fanatical element seems to be able to manipulate our own government, for even now I cannot accept the response she made to the plight—not to mention barbarous execution—of Farzad Bazoft."

The name was instantly familiar. I remembered well the accounts of the Iranian journalist who had disguised himself as an Indian doctor and had set forth in an ambulance to the missile plant at Al-Iskandaria, south of Baghdad. His arrest and subsequent hanging had been the cause of much contentious debate if not also of public outcry. I myself had not quite been persuaded by the government's line and in my own mind had looked back ruefully on the Don Pacifico business and Palmerston's famous speech, *Civis Romanus Sum.* I was thinking the same again when the chaplain responded, and, rather uncannily, to the point.

"My dear fellow, we sympathise with your wish to take vigorous, positive action but the days of gunboat diplomacy are over. We recalled our ambassador, after all, and we withdrew support for a Midland's trade mission about to take off for Baghdad."

"I recall," replied the teacher, "that the D.T.I. made a saving of £4,000. Not much for a man's life—shall we say thirty pieces of silver?"

"No, no, I cannot go along with that," interjected the civil servant. "Father Rand is surely correct. There was nothing else to be done. Besides, the fellow was caught red-handed with soil samples and his address book had the number of that chap Nimrodi in it. Remember?—The one who supplied arms in the Iran-contra dealings. I know the Metropolitan police denied any connection and the Foreign Secretary ruled out espionage, but then they were bound to do that."

"All the same," continued the teacher, "it made our Minister of State at the Foreign Office look pretty gullible, not to mention robbing him of any credibility which hitherto he might have enjoyed. Don't forget, he'd already warned of grave consequences for Anglo-Iraqi relations should the execution be carried out. The flimsy measures announced could hardly be said to put the wind up Saddam Hussein, let alone the fear of Allah."

As I listened I began to warm to this lecturer in physics and I felt I'd chanced upon a man after my own heart. The image of the wooden box dumped summarily at our embassy had stuck uncomfortably in the imagination. It had seemed then, and still did, like the casting down of an iron gauntlet.

Next it was the turn of the acescent youth, whose words were delivered in a clear, clipped fashion and with a sureness one might have opined to belong less to wisdom, more to precocity.

"I fear, sir, if you continue to pursue such a line of argument you will be dubbed an educator who is surprisingly jejune. You seem to forget the safety of the British nurse imprisoned for fifteen years, the businessman serving a life sentence in the President's jail, and the ten thousand Britons working in Iraq. Moreover, having already broken ties with Iran, with Syria, and with Libya, the British government could hardly be expected to sever its connection with Iraq as well. I'm sure I don't need to remind you that it is an oil-rich country. To close London's £250 million credit line to Baghdad would have been the height of folly. You may belittle, if you must, the interests of Western imperialism in the Gulf, but commercial expediency must remain the political imperative."

"Perhaps naivety is going a trifle far," commented the chaplain, apparently enjoying the discomfort of the teacher yet not wishing to convey any partiality. "Or, if not, then the same charge must be levelled at the Liberal Democrats and the Socialists. They, too, demanded the expulsion of the Iraqi ambassador, and there were some in their ranks who called for a review of British trade credits and the cancellation of missions in their entirety."

"And arms trafficking?" queried the teacher. "A ban on that might not have gone amiss?"

"Oh, I don't know, the reports are often exaggerated. You can't believe everything you read."

"You mean like the seizure of forty detonators designed for use in the triggering of nuclear explosions? I suppose Iraq wouldn't know what to do with them."

"These things, they take place the world over and always have done ever since Eve took a bite at the apple. When it comes down to it there's very little we can do about them. Be assured though, we share your horror at such a brutal regime. Thank God we can trust in Christ and look forward to a resurrection."

"Amen to that, Father," concurred the teacher. "Yet I sometimes wonder whether that doctrine ought not to make us more daring and that sublime person not inspire us to exceed expediency. Amnesty has reported that children in Iraq are routinely tortured, even executed: what is worse, in front of their parents. Then there is the matter of the attack with chemical gas on the Kurds at Halabja, and before that the bulldozing of Al-Dujail following the failed attempt on Saddam's life. Are you aware their doctors have been ordered to bleed people to death? There's no end to the brutality of Hussain's regime: he is a madman who will stop at nothing. Artistic expression is virtually forbidden, while journalists of course are everywhere oppressed. And what do Western governments do? First they support Saddam in his war against Iran, then they speak of expanding commercial ties! Bazoft may have been foolish, but was he not also a brave man? Would to God the bureaucrats and politicians showed as much fortitude as he. The world will be lost to those devils for no other reason than silence."

And silence it was then that fell on that party in its solemn deliberation.

As I say, increasingly I found myself liking this young man. I was impressed by his forthright speech, his account of simple, heartfelt feeling, and the common civilised decency he espoused in the teeth of such patent injustice. Then again, I rather admired the cut of his jib and the way he eschewed the approval of his peers. I might easily have backed the fellow up, as I could have added to his overall indictment the recent legal exemption for Iraqi men to dispose of their womenfolk summarily and without proof: if the charge conceived was adultery, then suspicion alone was enough. Indeed, I should certainly have done so were it not that upon lowering my book I found myself looking at the worried and now disapproving mien of my friend and had I not felt also the pressure of his foot placed firmly upon my own.

By now the train had descended to the village of Connel, where through shifting spectres of mist we could make out a bridge spanning the narrows at Loch Etive. A turbulence of water sped under the old line fallen into disuse from Oban to Fort William. What with the fine structure of the edifice, the churning current below and the vapours from the adjoining firth, the whole scene made a most evocative and splendid sight.

From then on Monty was clearly anxious I steer clear of all matters raised by our companions-of-the-way. On each occasion I was about to speak he would point out to me some noted landmark, or comment perhaps on the beauty of the mixed woodland, or admire the enthusiasm of nearby walkers marching along the Glen Cruittern Road.

It was not long, though, before the train camc juddcring to a halt and cheers went up from tiring passengers that we had arrived at last. Our guide for the journey proceeded to advise us that the mist was doubtless confined to the mainland and to certain parts of Mull. We were not, therefore, to be discouraged. There was every chance, he insisted, that the sun would break through and that the trip planned to the island of Iona would remain the highlight of the entire excursion.

Most of the travellers in our carriage appeared to be uplifted by his testimony of faith and looked ready to accept the spirit of his gospel, feathers and all. Not so Montagu Fiennes. As he strode down the edge of the platform he pronounced his own verdict on the weather-prospects for the day: "Not enough breeze," he proclaimed, "and the fog's too thick. I'm off for a drink. Come along, Fred."

So saying, Monty practically manhandled me away from the others and made post-haste for the nearest hotel. While I accompanied him, however, I started to feel a strong breeze blowing off the sea and saw in the sky above the pale disc of the sun straining to emerge. Any protestation, however, would have been thoughtless, and churlish besides: without Monty's generous assistance I should as likely as not by now have been detected, and I knew myself that it made every bit of sense to avoid company and to stay out of sight. Moreover it was just possible I was about to be roped into something more adventurous than a voyage to an abbey—less picturesque perhaps, but more piquant to my taste: I was straining at the leash of my friend and did but await his command.

But when the order came it was not to my liking.

"Look, I haven't got time to talk now—except to say that the pace is quickening down at Westminster and I need to be on hand as much as possible. What I'm going to do is to book a room at the Regent Hotel. What I'd like you to do is to stay out of trouble but to join me for tea later at 4 o'clock. By then I should know if this thing is as big as it looks and whether or not you yourself ought to come in on it. For it is indeed a dangerous game."

"Then perhaps, Monty, I am your man, especially if you're prepared to stand by your commentary in London."

"About yourself, you mean?"

"Quite so."

"Doubt it not. You're in, Fred. I'll expect to see you at 4 o'clock sharp. Remember, though, stay out of trouble."

The injunction did not seem difficult. The tardy sun was recalcitrant and I doubted that I could be recognised by anyone at all. As Monty went off towards the Regent Hotel I made my way towards Argyll Square but without knowing where to go next or what to do thereafter. Still, at least I'd the knowledge that by the time we quit

Oban I'd be fully advised of the task to which hitherto I'd been so curiously directed. All in all I felt remarkably bold. Indeed, I strolled out more as if I were heading for the crease on a cricket run than walking into the hands of one hell-bent on wickedness whose sole aim was the expedition of crime. Then came the first yorker to shake my confidence.

I was walking through what passed for a moderate drizzle when I noticed I was staring at several passers-by and that they, disconcertingly, were staring back. It dawned on me then that the effect of poor visibility—in foreshortening a person's gaze—made one turn one's attention inevitably to those people and buildings immediately to hand. Normally the proper foci of one's observations might have been McCaig's Folly, looking like the Colosseum and dominating the town; or perhaps the fishing boats bobbing beside the pier; or, further south, the promontory of Pulpit Hill; or, west beyond Kerrera, the view towards Beinn Bhearnach and Sgurr Dearg. The fact that these tourist-attractions were hid from view made us look naturally towards each other. Thus a man with a craggy jib and seafarer's eyes shot me a gleyed and suspicious glance—a lass in denims, her hair *en brosse*, seemed to find in me someone she knew—while a man in a shop window squinnied surreptitiously and seemed for one moment on the point of crying out! I began to long for the sunshine. I wanted also to be quit of city clothes and to find something more suitable for a gentleman of the uplands. What took shape in my mind's eye looked sturdier and constituted a more traditional turn of dress. After all at some stage I might well require an outfit more suited to the hills.

Ruminating thus I came across one of those second-hand shops where the proceeds are intended for some charitable purpose. I went inside and began to riffle through a row of discarded suits. Soon I found an old waistcoat, some trousers of dungaree, and a heavily-worn homespun jacket: the ensemble was a bit of a mismatch but it would do for the wild steeps. Another find, and one which pleasantly surprised me, was that of a fine tweed suit, green in colour and to which time had patently been kind. Lastly, hanging on a peg was a faded cloth cap which bore a brown, chequered design and which had a small tear along its inside lining. I purchased the aforementioned items and then, realising I had no adequate means of transporting them, picked up an old rucksack—made out of canvas (I might add) and being set therefore in a frame which was robust rather than light. I changed at some public conveniences, there putting on the tweed suit and stuffing the raincoat and rest of my belongings into the newly acquired rucksack. Now I'd to decide on what to do next.

The best idea seemed to be to turn away from the town centre and to be rid of the tourists as quick as possible. I began to follow a road which was signposted to Gallanach but then after a short while struck out left towards Pulpit Hill. I came out eventually—after a somewhat circuitous route—at a gate beyond which a track led down to some houses. I felt better, I must own, when I had got past the latter and was walking alone along what looked to be an old drove road.

Beyond some ridges—through which I now passed—I could see the trail divided in two directions. I chose the right-hand track, the one which fell away sharply to the coast and joined the road near the Kerrera ferry. I was now rapidly finding my strength and felt fairly invigorated: the views of the sound were improving and I could even detect a smidgen of warmth from that northern sun; moreover, I'd made excellent progress so far and it was barely after noon. Deciding to cross over to the island I discovered that a boat was about to depart the jetty within a couple of minutes.

Quite soon I found I was looking back at the mainland toward the Ardbhan Craigs, lit up now by the first proper rays of sun we had seen so far. It was important, naturally, to keep my eyes alert to anyone who might be following: but neither on the road I had taken nor in the small company freshly assembling at the jetty could I observe anyone suspicious or ostensibly occupied in searching the waters. One man, it was true, was making use of binoculars, but he steadfastly directed them toward a luxury yacht: this stood off a long way away and appeared to be making for Colonsay down the Firth of Lorn. It was not until we had reached Kerrera, and had disembarked near the schoolhouse, that I chanced to spot amidst the island visitors that day a blackavised fellow with a pensive brow and furrowed countenance.

If ever a man felt stupefied at that moment, it was I. Had I not been congratulating myself on the bilking of my enemies, even beginning to dub myself the perfect fellow to aid Monty in whatever gambit he next chose to adopt? Now it seemed I myself was to be the victim of dupability and, were I not careful, should be out of the game before the first move had been contemplated. Yet the stockbroker-turned-tourist did not follow the main party but took instead the path that bore westward to the little hamlet of Balliemore. At first I was tempted to follow him, but the cover did not look promising and I might only draw attention to myself by separating from the rest.

The main group, I gathered, was intent upon reaching Gylen Castle to the south of the island. There they hoped to see the remnants of what had, till the seventeenth century, been an important stronghold for the clan MacDougal: until, that is, it had been burnt down by the Covenanters and left thereafter slowly to ruin.

The going was easy and we proceeded downwards to a smallish bay, declared by someone to be The Little Horse Shoe—an apt description, for it resembled just such a design. It was, incidentally, just as the party turned down to the shore that I began to notice the state of my footwear. Previous attempts to disguise the scuffing—to which I'd had recourse beside the Brighton skip—had quickly been reversed during my earlier tramp. I realised now it would be essential to obtain a proper pair of walking boots as soon as I'd reached Oban. What drew my attention to the ones I already had was a loose shoelace. As I bent down to tighten it I could hear from the corner behind someone coughing. Having deliberately dropped to the rear of the group, to be aware of interlopers from the back, I now became alert to the possibility of danger. I slipped into a small copse immediately to my right and waited to see who it was that was following.

I did not have long to wait. Within a matter of seconds there came into sight a man possessing the now familiar look of intent; hanging between his lips was the stub of a cigarette, smouldering fast in the prevailing breeze.

I stayed doggo for as long as it took him to come into easy reach of the main party. At that point the stockbroker slowed down whilst I myself advanced cautiously along the line of trees—all the time keeping him in sight. Very soon, however, was I obliged to depart the cover of the trees and to come out into the open. Then I found myself ducking and diving at every movement my opponent made: which indeed was as well—because on more than one occasion he glanced to his rear. Perhaps he'd noticed the company he followed was missing the very prey he himself sought: I opined him to be less sure, though, when he broke into a trot and linked up with one of the stragglers on the edge of the party. It seemed he was determined to draw sufficiently close to the other visitors to be certain of my presence. This at once gave his observer the upper hand.

While the others set off by Gylen Park—to explore the pillar of rock and single tower above the cliffs of Chroim—I took the shorter circular route via Lower Glen, across Gleann a Chaise, to Ardmore. This took me in a westerly direction. Glad to be in front I realised nonetheless I could not afford to waste time. Happily for me, though, the sun was once more a faded bezant behind wind and misty cloud.

Going at quite a speed I soon reached Ardmore whence the thinning track turned sharply to the north. It was now imperative I keep up the pace set so far. As soon as anyone rounded the corner at Ardmore I might quickly come into view, while I had good reason to think that the first person to find me should be an indignant financier. The thought rapidly enhanced my progress so that within a short space of time I had once again passed to a new direction, to wit, away from Barnabuck farmhouse and towards Oban.

By now the inferior path I'd lately followed had broadened out to become another drove road. As I'd not yet descried anyone approaching from behind I began to feel less of a fugitive and reduced my pace to meet the approaching gradient. I was, let it be said, walking in the midst of wild and beautiful terrain—an area made all the more magnificent by the inclusion of reddish bell-heather, purple ling, and by the sight of blue patches above widening in the haze. The sun was beginning to break through properly when I perceived I was in a veritable lather of vexation.

I stopped at once to regain my breath. Gladly did I draw in great gasps and lungsful of air. I began to feel better. Was I not after all in a kind of heaven? Views were opening up all across the Lorn, I had my enemy beat, and more and more did I feel envigorated by the notion of adventure. It was a crazy, outlandish affair, yet I seemed to be relishing every moment of it. As I stood there, dressed in my second-hand tweed and dusty, whitening shoes, I beheld the absurdity of it and could scarcely credit my own peregrinity. I laughed out loud and had the high exultant feeling of one dubbed monarch of all he surveys—of one grateful for the very gift of being alive at all.

But it is sometimes observed that pride comes before a fall. So it was with me. Even as I rejoiced in my strong and fortunate position did I notice across the colouring waters a single white yacht—no longer, as I'd thought, destined for Colonsay but making good speed now twixt Kerrera and the Isle of Mull, and to my surprise in a northerly direction.

In an instant I had my telescope focused on the plume of her sails; next, her silver enamelling. Beneath her starboard bows I was able to make out the gold letters of a name emblazoned on her bright and polished flank. She was called *Queen of Sheba*, and, in truth, looked every bit the regal lady. Moreover the resemblance lay not only in her opulent and powerful appearance; for, to my mind at least, she came also to test…with difficult questions. I do not say that what passed through my intelligence was in any way logical. Call it a fancy, if you will; yet I could not help but recall that other biblical figure, conjured up so recently by Montagu Fiennes—Ishbaal, scion of King Saul.

This association brought me round sharp, and with fresh clarity I began to review my position. Certain imponderables posed themselves awkwardly upon my troubled imagination. What might be the real identity of my pursuer? Why was he tracking me across the wastes of Scotland? What did he purpose to do in the event of my capture? It was hard to believe his intention was to do good. Then there was the man I'd seen standing at the jetty: his aim I'd taken to be harmless enough; yet, viewed in proximity to my persecutor, might not his objective transpire to be equally suspect? Moreover, he'd been carefully watching the progress of a yacht, the very vessel now sailing so speedily up the Firth of Lorn. Then again, what could be the significance of such a boat journeying to the north? Only one answer I could think of: namely, that the head of MQ1 was himself set in the same direction and that I was abetting him in whatever action he intended to take. Lastly, what kind of persons could there be on board such a fine-looking cruiser? In the frame of mind I then had, he would no more be a harmless holiday-maker than would he be an ordinary buccaneer. More and more, then, was I learning to fear the forces convened before me. That their ways were sinister I did not doubt. Neither did I hesitate in imputing to them the most vicious of purposes and the foulest of deeds. My one goal now was to get to the Regent Hotel as soon as I could.

Having so determined I set off down toward Balliemore at a fast canter and very soon found myself level with the school and away from high ground. At the jetty itself, though, dismay again clouded my hopes. There was no ferry and no boatman.

Then I recalled a yarn I'd once heard about getting to Cape Wrath—that northernmost point on Scotland's west coast. The most popular way was to be driven there from a dot-on-the-map called Achiemore. However, in order to do so anyone driving from Laxford or Smoo Cave had first to negotiate the Kyle of Durness, a substantial channel of water running between those land masses north of Strath Shinary and Strath Dionard. As the ferryman was based on the far side, and because on the whole visitors were few in number, anyone destined for the Cape had first to attract the former's attention. Only when that had been achieved, and overall conditions judged sufficiently clement, might further progress be made. I remembered at the time being heartily entertained by the picture conjured of impatient tourists frantically trying to signal in all manner of semaphore. No longer, alas! could I see the joke. Imagining there to be a cluster of onlookers gathered about the pier, I began to feel every kind of fool as I too waved my arms this way and that. To make matters worse, coils and dark swathes of mist were returning and threatened to obscure my objective. For one ghastly moment it looked as if my efforts must be in vain and that I must tarry helplessly for the return of my pursuer.

Then my luck changed. At last I heard the gradually-increasing drone of a small outboard. As its owner drew up to the jetty a glance behind revealed the extent of my good fortune. Smoking stockbroker or no, my opposite number was tearing down towards me at an alarming pace. Anticipating the inevitable reaction of the ferryman—who struck me as a typically dour character, done out in a pale blue cap, traditional jersey and serge trousers—I at once proffered a handful of notes. It was all to the good that I've long had the habit of carrying plenty of cash—although the fistful of green notes came in reality to less than it looked. Again to the good was my silver hip-flask—the last present ever given to me by my beloved parents—which I'd thoughtfully transferred from my former jacket to the present. I rather think it was the sight of that which did the trick.

It was not long before I was separated from my enemy by a sizeable stretch of water and only a little later before being landed safe and sound on terra firma.

You may well imagine I wasted no time at all in decamping to Oban. The boatman, thankful indeed to his solitary passenger, had commended me for my rapid tour of the isle. He would certainly have marvelled at the packman who jogged all the way back to town. Neither, moreover, did I forget to collect for myself a sturdy pair of boots before joining my companion at the Regent Hotel.

CHAPTER 5

A Small Packet Of Red Pepper

We found a seat in the lounge of the Regent Hotel far enough away from the window not to be seen from outside, yet affording Monty himself a prospect of the front and of any passers-by. His opening remark could have knocked me for six.

"And how did you enjoy your trip to Kerrera? I believe it was there King Haakon of Norway convened his fleet before being rousted at Largs."

"How in heaven's name did you know I went there?" I spoke with some asperity for I felt the rug drawn out from under my feet.

"I was the man," he continued, "whom you saw at the ferry beneath Gallanachbeg. At the time my attention was fixed on a smartly polished yacht heading for the Firth of Lorn. I'd made several telephone calls and had received a tip about a boat sailing north, which one of our chaps had spotted last year somewhere off Sardinia. It was thought at that juncture to be involved in a drug-running operation based in a suburb of Cagliari. Unfortunately the same informant lost the name of the vessel—which is why, of course, I was anxious to discover it. In the event the yacht appeared to be going south, and all I could get of her name in that infernal mist was *Queen*—or *Queenie*, perhaps. Then in an idle moment I glanced at a party which was already half way towards the jetty on the opposite side. I laughed when I saw you, for such an active excursion from the population struck me as highly predictable; it was just what I should've expected of you. I was glad, besides, that you were keeping out of Oban."

"So you were the man with the binoculars," I replied, feeling less nettled and in the knowledge that I had at least two cards to play. I decided to put them down both at once.

"Listen Monty, that yacht you mention is this very moment making for the sound of Mull. What's more, her brazen appellation is—of all things—the *Queen of Sheba*."

"Capital, Fred! Capital! You've lost none of your reconnoitring skills. But what exactly aroused your suspicion?"

"In the first place the change of direction—that struck me as odd. Why should a boat out of Oban making for Loch Linnhe—or more likely for the Sound—go via Kerrera, an island clearly not in her path and alongside of which she had sailed but hours beforehand? As to the name, though it may sound whimsical I connected it straightaway with that of Ishbaal. Moreover my observations were made not as a tourist but as a fugitive."

"What?" interjected my friend, "You were followed again?"

"Just so. Is it possible we were too quick in dismissing my earlier escapades in Brighton and in London?"

"Not we, Fred—I. It was I who did not treat your escape with the seriousness it deserved. I owe you an apology on that account."

"Accepted naturally. Besides, it was as crazy a tale as you could possibly hear. All the same, is there a connection here between this fellow—whom for want of a clearer denomination I call a stockbroker—and the business in hand?"

"I wish I knew the answer to that. At present I'm in the dark. You yourself, though, have inadvertently shed light on the cocaine delivery. The strands are coming together now and I begin to think we shall make a most timely intervention in the trading of narcotics.

That boat—*Queen of Sheba*, you say—she is thought to be carrying one of the largest hauls of illicit drugs known. Perhaps the biggest yet. We've already alerted the customs and excise people all the way from Ardrossan to Lerwick. Beyond there I do not think she will go. Moreover, we have reason to believe that the exchange will be made within the next seven days."

I poured for my friend a cup of deep-brown tea and took from an indifferent selection of biscuits a sliver of shortbread.

"An exchange?" I queried.

At once Monty's face darkened. His eyebrows lowered and the worried expression I'd earlier noticed on the train once more added to his face a handful of years. In the same instant I spotted a feature I'd not noticed before. There were flecks of grey adorning the sides of my friend's ebony hair. He looked at me grimly and began again.

"I told you before how I'm daily beset by coincidences. Some turn out to harbour a meaning which—if recognised—may be turned to useful effect. Others elude all understanding and serve merely to tantalise or to betoken to the more frustrated the handiwork of providence. Well, all that talk on the train this morning—I missed some of it, naturally; but that it centred on the Middle or Near East was clear. There's no doubting some very black deeds are afoot in that region and nowhere more so than in Iran and Iraq. Saddam's ongoing policy of *al-qiswa*—in which citizens both outwith and inside his territory are continually confronted by harshness and cruelty—persists, and it gives the governments of our day considerable cause for alarm. If relations between the land of the Ayatollah and the domain of Saddam deteriorate further, then the entire area could ignite. After that, heaven help us—as one country sides with another, as diplomatic common ground evaporates, and as each nation blindly defends its own quarter with the rhetoric of bravado or the menace of a pre-emptive strike. I dread to think what the boys in the Knesset or on Capitol Hill would come up with in the event of such a scenario."

I nodded my assent while my friend broke off for a draught of tea. I, too, took no pleasure in contemplating those eventualities that Monty described. With that peculiar combination of evangelism and consumerism, so typical of contemporary America, I shuddered to entertain what lunacy might prevail. Then again, the Israelis did not exactly court favour with the "doves." Moreover, speaking personally I'd always found it as hard to view dispassionately the plight of the Jew as I had the continuing difficulties of the Irish: both peoples appeared to suffer from the disease of intractability, and, say what one might of the peaceableness of the majority, it was hard sometimes to believe that such long standing hostility was not endemic to the whole. Still, it is possible that in this respect at least I have a tendency to be biased.

"Anyway," continued Monty, "the flashpoint could ignite sooner than we think. Although there's been much fortitude on the part of those trying to discern the purposes of the Arabs in Iraq, it's only recently that the full extent of the latter's mendacity and corruption has come to light. It is the ringleaders, of course, who are to blame. They and their foreign abettors. But now a devil has stepped into the arena—one who is able to introduce the lion tamer to the clown and the strong man to the fool. Such a circus could bring down the roof on the entire performance. I'm talking of Ishbaal, of course. It seems he and his henchmen have together devised what can only be described as an elixir of death. You've heard I dare say of the toxic element, thallium?"

"Yes," I concurred. "It's used in the poisoning of rats, isn't it—and the making of highly refractive glass?"

"That's the one. Mind you, under one guise it's been administered to humans and due to the delayed action of its effects has usually passed unnoticed. However, the men of shame have now devised a new weapon. They call it Devil's Redpepper—or, quite simply, Red Pepper—the most damnable invention yet concocted. I've never seen the stuff myself but am reliably informed the designation does it justice, for the powder is as fine as pepper and bright vermillion in appearance, the very colour of cinnabar. There, naturally, the similarity stops—though the gentlemen of dishonour point with glee to the effect of this condiment on its victims to affect a sneeze. But, I am jumping the gun. You see, Fred, when this powder is treated in a certain way and released into the atmosphere, it produces a virulent set of symptoms bringing about intense debility and sooner or later death itself."

"For the love of God," I cried, "we must stop such infamy! Is there no antidote to the substance?"

"None so far, and, till we can capture it to have it analysed by our experts, we can be sure neither of its chemical properties nor its molecular change on confronting the atmosphere. Furthermore, it seems it can be distributed in such a way as to alter the incubation period. It may vary in its range from a small pocket of a population to the dwellers of a capital the size of London. Regarding the symptoms, to begin with they look as much like a megrim as they do a fatal disease. There's a gradual nausea though which becomes the more unpleasant as the migrainous pain intensifies. Painkillers prove sufficient to ward off the distress only in the initial onslaught, thereafter becoming useless in mitigating what all too rapidly turns out to be sheer agony. I'm told victims become feverish in the penultimate stage of their deterioration and that this passes finally into what looks for all the world like delirium tremens—complete with violent shaking and paranoid hallucinations. It is not beyond the bounds of possibility that the patient now be judged to be suffering from the last stages of alcoholism. The brain damage has become irreversible and the inner wasting-away beyond repair. Death must follow."

"But Monty," I protested, "you speak as if this fiendish concoction has been used already."

"But it has, make no mistake. The wheels of corruption have been spinning in some pretty far-off places while the partners in ignominy have been inveigling officials in the highest of echelons. It seems permission was granted to have the invention tested in no fewer than four labour camps. One of our agents actually spoke to a survivor—not of the Red Pepper though, only the internment: the man was a scientist and highly respected by the experts in toxicology masterminding the trials. Anyhow, he was later able to report the consequences of the experiment—carried out on six men and women, all of varying ages and physical health—to a visiting party of journalists from the democratic west. Unfortunately he had great difficulty in convincing the reporters he encountered: the dangers in broadcasting the discovery were obvious, and, besides, we live in a decade when the Soviets are being accorded a new level of respect. It was fortunate for us the agent mentioned passed himself off as a reporter with a prestigious Sunday newspaper. He, in his turn, passed on his revelation to Malahide's second-in-command."

Monty paused. For several seconds he gazed through the large bay window. I knew what was going through his mind. He was revisiting the canal in Little Venice, hearing once more the blasting apart of the Eligibility and giving again the harrowing news to that poor, perplexed and grieving widow. Then he turned and resumed his account.

"Only quite recently has it been established that this execrable substance has moved to a new market whence it fell directly into the hands of Ishbaal. It seems that further refinements were called for in order to prevent its operation upon domestic animals; the idea was that any indiscriminate type of disease might be detected too readily as a form of chemical warfare. The intent of the men of shame is that this Devil's Redpepper be applied in ways that are both selective and subtle."

"And do we know," I queried, "what Ishbaal intends next?"

"Yes," replied my friend starkly. "You remember I left you in the carriage this morning? Well, I was putting a call through to Malahide. He gave me the worst possible news. It seems Ishbaal is to hand over a small packet of Red Pepper to the military in Iraq. My guess is he intends to fuel a covert but disastrous series of calamities, first in Iran and then in various headquarters throughout the Middle East. The ensuing mayhem, he hopes, will spark off a new level of international concern. When the time's ripe it's expected he'll inform various world leaders of the origin of such havoc—but then that he'll add a few invented threats of his own. For example, he'll persuade the ambassadors of certain major powers that the Iraqi government is planning a release of Red Pepper in their countries' capitals. It's then that the real chaos will begin."

"So we are doomed," I replied, miserably. "There's nothing to be done."

"Maybe. And yet…"

"There's hope?" I asked.

"Remember I said Ishbaal was having certain modifications carried out on his detestable product, to make the link with chemical warfare more elusive: that he wants to debilitate and to kill only those of our species. Well, the one good stroke dealt thus far—barring of course our own intelligence—has been that those modifications to Red Pepper have had to be carried out in Wiltshire, at Porton Down."

"That's impossible," I broke in. "The security's too strict. Besides, we no longer dabble in chemical warfare."

"That, dear Fred, is what you're supposed to think. The truth is rather different. First, we cannot afford not to, and second, some of our brightest protégés from the universities are employed on projects which, if push came to shove, could be adopted by the military. As to your other point, yes, the security is tight. But not long ago an American scientist was appointed about whom recent briefings had revealed several links with foreign espionage. It seems probable that it's this defector, hailing from the far side of the Pond and under the respectable guise of being a cousin of ours, who has been perpetrating this latest mischief. It just shows you, you can't trust anyone these days—not even the darned Yanks. However, I said *has been*, when what I really meant was *continues* to do so, for I'm afraid the deed's under way again."

"What? You mean you've been following this man's research, yet you've allowed him to escape!" I fear my exasperation was all too evident.

"We had to, you see, if ever we were going to bring in Ishbaal. Malahide had got word to us that it was Ishbaal who was going to oversee the final stages in the transfer of Red Pepper. If it was the case we'd been accorded a stroke of good fortune; it seems our enemy had been rendered no less a blow of bad fortune: Malahide was able to report that the bulk of the product had been spoilt through incorrect storage. There is, it appears, only the equivalent of a small packet left. It was this that had been so assiduously cared for by the American and then refined successfully along the lines I mentioned. Then, as I've said, the American escaped. He was soon enough captured, of course, and shortly afterwards—to speak euphemistically—disappeared. Unfortunately he'd got rid of the Red Pepper before we could arrest him. What we succeeded in discovering was the manner in which the consignment would be exported, namely, that it would be connected somehow with a trade-off in narcotics. Of the details, though, we remain unsure. That's the reason why our men are posted strategically along the western seaboard, for it's there we believe the next delivery of drugs—either as export or import, we know not which—is likely to take place."

"Even so, it all sounds a bit hit-or-miss."

"I guess you're right, Fred, but I have to retain a degree of optimism or else this fellow of the last disgrace will surely elude us. But yes, there are plenty hazards, plenty hunches, and plenty fathoms for error. And, though I may be wrong in my estimate of Ishbaal's intentions, in this business and with this man it is best to paint the darkest possible picture: there is place neither for chiaroscuro nor for luminarism of any kind, so I sketch in black while the only relief from monotony is the shifting outline of a demoniac's shadow. For all that, we must act as if illumination were possible: I am not talking bonfires or beacons or torches of flame; I am saying we are playing with matchsticks in a breezy, outlandish place, but that we must go on striking however futile the attempt looks, however faltering the uncertain flicker."

I could see, naturally, my friend was right. It was no use throwing in the towel. We must draw our bow at a venture and hope, like the legendary archer, to hit our mark. I asked Monty if there was anything else he needed to tell me.

"Only this, that Malahide's volunteers have linked the name of Ishbaal to that of Henrik Meyer—a giant of a man possessed of a broad skull that's badly scarred and devoid of hair: he's Norwegian and said to have been a spy—first for the British, then the Russians—though it's thought of late he may have gone freelance...which is why, presumably, he's been bought by Ishbaal. That said, I doubt he knows the latter's true colours or he would, I think, have had the sense to stand clear. You see he's not a villain in the same class as Ishbosheth. Even though he enjoys playing the game, the real fun for him lies in the hunt. An appropriate trophy at the end is but recompense for inconvenience caused. Anyhow, he can be a nasty customer and you would do well to look out for him. Finally, keep watching your back. The twins you speak of, they might well be onto us by now. Oh, and I've little doubt that before long her Highness from Sheba will once more be entering our sights."

"Do you think Ishbaal could be on board?"

"Possibly. Personally though, I believe he'll stay on the mainland—to keep an eye on his infamous cache."

"In the meantime," said I, nodding in the direction of a figure in black, "I think we'd better make our way back to the station. Unless I'm much mistaken, that gentleman over there is none other than our friend the chaplain. I should say he's not quite himself. Something vexes him."

"Quite so. Our train will reverse up the line in about thirty minutes."

Once outside the hotel I left my friend to join the chaplain, while I ambled along more slowly following at a distance. I could just hear him proclaim—"Well, Father, which of us chose the better part?"—when I happened to glance down at a window-display in a small bookshop. No less than twelve volumes had been put out with the controversial title—penned by the writer Samuel Rushton—*The Periscopes of Satan*. With all the tensions prevailing in the Middle East I couldn't help but judge its publication in paperback a most unnecessary gesture. Anything more to fuel the simmering oil of conflict was to my way of thinking as inopportune as it was regrettable. It was all very well to applaud the author's courage—and his arguments for freedom of expression—but were there not, I wondered, occasions when responsibilities and duties outweighed a person's rights? How important was a licence to offend when it so clearly exacerbated an already tense situation?

As I drew away my gaze fell to an adjacent newspaper-rack. Casually, I picked up a copy of *The Oban Times*. The first thing I saw in it was a red-printed item in the stop-press column. It read, "Arts Deal Scandal: Prominent Back-Bencher Arrested." True to his word Monty had not been idle. It seemed progress was being made even if the Devil's Redpepper remained in the hands of the enemy. I returned the paper to its rack and continued towards the station. In a matter of minutes I'd once more resumed my seat on board The West Highlander. Our next stop—some way off –would be Fort William.

CHAPTER 6

Across Rannoch Moor

As we settled down to enjoy the comfort of 'The West Highlander' it became apparent that the quartet on the other side of the aisle was engaged in some sort of dispute. I mention the fact because it was to be the prelude to an exhibition of memory that at the time was as typical as it was exasperating.

The comparatively successful visit to Iona had been displaced in discussion by a debate on the issue of land ownership. Sadly, though, the thing had become polarised between the rights of the laird versus those of the commoners over whom he governed. It had ended on the rather contentious query as to how much power the landed aristocracy was still entitled to claim; the point had been made that too much of the land was being sold—often for little more than a song—to acquisitive and foreign speculators, whilst the needs and interests of local people were continually being ignored. However, all the old myths and traditional divisions had once again emerged: the Scot was being exploited by the English as had the Highlander been by the Sassenach, the Whiggamore by the anti-covenanter, and the common man by his clan-chieftain; it seemed that even that old stalwart the Pretender Charles had found a place in their haverings and that the whole thing had degenerated into a perspective on history bedizened as usual by twilight and tartan. Anyhow the upshot of all this had been a lingering dissent on the matter of clan loyalty, with the physics teacher affirming the strength of kinship and with the minister impugning the chief as being little more than a "freebooting wastrel." It was at this point I myself had the temerity to intervene.

"But surely," I cried, "does not the whole edifice of the Mosaic Covenant rest on just such a system, with the part of the clan-chieftain being played by none other than Yahweh—the suzerain-deity—the God of Israel? I thought the work of Mendenhall in this area had proved to be decisive. Was it not an initial act of deliverance, brought about by a more potent chief in the pantheon, which not only bonded together the freed captives but required of them absolute loyalty to their God and tribal cohesion as a mark of their fealty?"

As I heard myself speak I had the curious sensation of a voice somehow detached from the one who had given it utterance. It could have been someone else talking in my stead. I rapidly became self-conscious and promptly lost the flow of the argument. What had happened was that my pre-Falkland's memory, so to speak, had pushed through into consciousness and had enabled the student of theology of a former day to find an unaccustomed tongue. Moreover, what happened next was not also without a certain strangeness. For the chaplain, seeing my stance of authority turn into a bemused expression of surprise, came back at me then with all the force of a theological gale.

"Philosophically speaking I must inform you your comparison is quite unwarranted. You argue from an overlay of religion upon event; I state merely the facts of history. Evangelically speaking, too, you are at fault. You talk as if the God of the Cosmos were an invention of man, a mere perspective on the accidents of fortune. Yet is not that which we dare to term God the great self-disclosure to mankind, the revealer of meaning to us mere mortals rather than some purpose unwittingly discerned? Hermeneutically speaking, you err again. Your exegesis contains an air of irreverence—it smacks of the Modernist heresy. What say you, now? Speak, speak. Let us hear more!"

But, as I have said, I was tongue-tied. I could make no further connection, and even though I suspected his reasoning to be fallacious it ill-behoved me at this point to take issue with a chaplain. In those few ghastly seconds I felt the silence weigh down upon me in a horrid admixture of expectancy and drawn-out discomfort. It was Monty who finally broke the tension, declaring with outrageous irony: "Like a lamb that is led to the slaughterhouse, dumb before its shearers. Still, was there not a powerful exemplar of such set by another? And long before now."

At that the chaplain averted his gaze and stared for a while through the grimy window.

When the train reached the station at Dalmally the staff began to serve us dinner. My adventures had made me hungry and I awaited with interest the details of the menu. All the same I declined the offer of Prime-Angus beef. It was not that I credited the BSC scare with more than a kernel of truth but that regulatory procedures should be tightened up in abattoirs seemed to me to be no bad thing and so I'd chosen to avoid beef for at least one year. Accordingly, while my thick-skinned companion now took revenge on my greed at breakfast I myself supped off chilled fruit juice, hot vegetables, and a modest slice of apple pie. And while Monty stayed on the Glenfiddich I settled for a Cotes du Rhone and ate with it a liberal quantity of unusual cheeses. Things were looking up and even the head boy wore an expression of approval.

It must have been a little later—at the Bridge of Orchy—when the physics teacher began to regale us with tales of how the Highland Line had been lain. I recall him pointing out how our route in pursuing a northerly direction would have to make an ascent of 1,347 feet, culminating eventually on the summit of Corrour. He commented again on how it would take 72 miles to affect the climb from sea-level, at a spot named Craigendoran, yet only 28 thereafter to descend from Corrour to Fort William. I remember, too, glancing out of the window and seeing through the clearing dusk a view of Loch Tulla—reaching out to the shadowy bulk of the Black Mount and to those riotous peaks of Glen Etive and beyond to the great Glencoe.

It was as the scenery became more and more denuded of vegetation, with the trees being replaced by heather and scrub and with bare rock now penetrating the thinning turf, that the account was told of how some twenty miles of moorland had been traversed by track. The area had been such a waste place of "bogs and hags and peaty pools" that the morass could only be crossed, here and there, by "floating" the line on a bulwark of turf and layer upon layer of brushwood. Where the bog had proved too deep the hardly less problematic task had been expedited of engineering a viaduct—steel structured and resting on solid piers of granite rock. Moreover, much of the work had been carried out during inclement weather and shortening days.

It was some three years before this and during the month of January that there took place the now legendary trip of the seven gentlemen of Spean across that same wild and scarce-frequented moor. Their purpose, to acquire information and to negotiate terms with the landlord, they had set out on a grey and windswept day and had spent that and two nights hazarding a journey to Inveroran, almost forty miles to the south. One only of that party had ever before been across that desolate space. Now, armed solely with umbrellas and a notion, they sallied and gibed into the driving rain and breezing sleet. Further and further, hopping over tufts and tussocks of bog, they floundered and fell and rose and dropped again. Only with the assistance of keepers and shepherds did they finally arrive in safety, while the wearying factor of the estate was himself bundled into a cart beside the welcoming haven of Inveroran Inn. The hero of the tale—if such indeed there was—appears to have been a fellow by the name of R. McAlpine, who, having at one juncture gone on ahead for help, endured fourteen hours alone on that moor before eventually reaching a cottage by Tulla Water. This adventurer—whose folly compared to the ineptitude of his companions seemed more like an achievement—was later to become Sir Robert McAlpine, and in view of his metier in engineering to acquire the novel sobriquet of "Concrete Bob." As I gazed out across the bleak and granite-studded landscape and imagined that importunate figure forging ahead over the roots and clumps of bog, trying to skirt the pools and icy lochans, I reckoned the nomenclature to have been well deserved.

Interesting though the teacher's commentary was, I'm afraid I began to experience it as the burden of a lecture: indeed, it has often seemed to me that people in the business of speaking do not always appreciate the no less onerous task of listening. Is it possible, perhaps, that after a while the performer of locution becomes as mesmerised by the tone of delivery as he is fired by the excitement of the brain? Or, on the other hand, may it be that a fellow is but a dunderhead when, poor soul, he cannot attach his mind to a single topic for more than twenty minutes? In any event I found my thoughts straying from the present field of discourse and my mind led back—by the young man's idiolect and absence of dialect—to his earlier comments on the monstrous Hussain.

In retrospect it seemed odd that our conversation had not included more recent developments. It was as if being held in some uneasy limbo between peace and war we had not dared to take our speculations further. Yet what we had said was barely the half of it; neither could I help but pall at the inexorable triumph that had taken place of pragmatism over idealism, how principles when voiced at last had been put merely to the service of expediency—though under the cover of rhetoric and the patent mock of an elevated morality. As all the world knew, Saddam Hussain had gone on to invade and colonise the kingdom of Kuwait. Shocking enough to Westerners though that was, how much more so surely to the inhabitants of Abu Dhabi or the hapless monarch of Jordan. And then there was all that devilish propaganda as viewers across the globe were entertained to a spectacle of concern over captive women and "pretty children." (When I'd first witnessed that broadcast, between cocktails at a party, the glass I'd held cracked under the pressure of my hand prompting my startled host to seek out bandaging.) There was, I began to think, sufficient to compare Saddam Hussain with Adolf Hitler so as not quite to blame the U.S. President for his forthright diplomacy.

At the same time I couldn't help but reflect it was now rather late in the day to be registering an effective protest. Earlier there had been no dearth of evidence of Saddam's insouciance and cold-blooded cruelty, yet the world had done little more than to watch events from a not inconvenient distance. Even the execution of Bazoft had not stirred our government to transcend financial considerations or her questionable influence over affairs in the Gulf. The prospect of an acceptable solution now seemed more remote than ever. Order might yet be restored, though any intervention from America must in the long run be difficult for the Arabs. Any backlash, moreover, was liable to spell even greater disaster. Against this background Ishbaal was like some crazy hobbledehoy armed with a lighter let loose in a petrol station. The whole lot could go up.

I couldn't on the other hand endorse entirely the scenario of my friend. Granted that Iran had proved herself to be no lamb-without-blemish—and that another war between her and Iraq would be no light matter—it still seemed to me that Monty was inclined to be a bit bogged down by historical precedent: give a dog a bad name and with him it would remain a most tenacious beast and vicious to the last; if it had happened once it could only be a matter of time before it must happen again. But with respect to the Great Bear of the Soviet Empire—that at times seemed more like an ageing grizzly armed with a zimmer-frame than any ferocious animal amok with swingeing paws. Regarding Iran, it might be true that any claim to respectability could not be made with fairness, yet relations between her and Iraq had seen a certain improvement since the ending of their hostilities—and most markedly by Saddam in the removal of forces from the purlieus of his borders. To my way of thinking those peripheral troops had constituted a kind of Berlin wall: they had been as a bulwark forbidding amity. Now that they had been withdrawn they could not only forgather to good effect elsewhere, but their shift of stance in the meantime must send surely a reconciliatory signal to Iran. Far from Ishbaal driving between those powers a wedge, might he not fuel an alignment and thereby weaken the vantage point of the western allies? Might not both the president and the ayatollah turn upon the Saudis? And might they not—in so doing—muster the Arab world in opposing the decadent West? In the teeth of such a possibility, what promise then for the children of Israel?

My unhappy reverie was broken by a cry from Monty.

"Look, Fred! Two stags and ten—no, eleven—hinds. What a sight, eh!"

Indeed it was. Through the dusky light we could make out a dozen or so animals, each bounding with a graceful yet angular movement over the broken reaches of the moor, their white rumps bouncing, hither, thither—over scrub, heather, and burn—while the antlers of the "monarchs" could be seen all at once etched black on a greying skyline. I had seen deer before, but of the Pere David variety, and in a southern landscape, where their passage was restricted to the confines of a park and where the beauty of the beast had a tame, even delicate quality. But there was nothing tame or delicate high up here upon Rannoch. These creatures were wild and majestic, inhabiting a remote and boggy vastness far removed from the tendrils of civilized occupation. Gazing out on the last to drop below the horizon I noticed it stop and turn, and in those few seconds of calm it was easy to credit it with an intelligence no less redoubtable than its outward form. In that pause—straining my head through the parted window—I felt a kind of wild excitement, as if my soul were being summoned to part from its normal course and to inhabit some primeval domain where conflict and beauty were atavistic, closer to nature in essence and design.

As I fell back in my seat I felt suddenly exhausted. I had no breath left for the common or the trivial. And there was, besides, more to marvel at than the simple fact of deer running from a train: for in watching those fugitives lope and scatter across the moor I had felt called to witness a phenomenon not new but seen already—in another existence perhaps or in former days. Monty, I knew, would tell me I'd already experienced something similar when he and I once had holidayed in the Highlands; for it seemed we'd sojourned so far on an earlier occasion. Alas! to such memories I had no access. Yet this thrill in my heart testified the claim to be no comforting lie but a matter of fact and blessed with all the urgency of some compelling truth.

The impress of the day however could not be forsworn. Suddenly the ethereal fancy was brought back down, back down to terra firma and the timeless itself scotched by time. It was the boy—he was speaking out loud after listening to a radio broadcast, his head positioned between two earphones. I'd been half expecting an announcement on the "footsie" or some speculation on a fall in shares, yet when he began a different kind of shock planted me most horribly in the present.

"Seems there's been some bother down in Brighton"—at once I was transfixed—"another plot to finish off the P.M. It was yesterday they found out and apparently no harm's been done…"

"Thank God," came in the civil servant. "But did they catch the blighter?"

"Hold on," whispered the prefect testily, attempting to adjust the wavelength. "Confound it, I've missed his name."

"But did they catch him?" repeated the interlocutor.

"Oh yes, only—would you believe it?—the silly fools, they've allowed him to escape. Now it seems he could be anywhere between there and John O' Groats!"

The allusion to that northernmost place did not amuse me. To speak plainly I felt terror-stricken, for my name at any moment might be uttered again on that infernal set. Then one of the party—for certain the boy—would pull the alarm. What then, I wondered?

After a couple of moments had passed, however, I noticed that all four were again in conversation and it occurred to me that for the time being at least none of them was actually aware of my identity. All that Monty had implied to the chaplain was that I was an old school mate of his. Notwithstanding that, it was Monty who now looked concerned.

For all his preoccupation, however, and seeing the train now speeding through the evening gloom and with only scant views left of Loch Treig, my companion began to busy himself with the latest crossword—a habit he assumed, incidentally, whenever his mind was particularly engrossed. After a while he held the paper out to me declaring sharply, "nine across!"

I looked at the clue. Seven letters—the fifth of which was a "c"—it read, "Take a leaf from the Haitian." I glanced up at Monty. He was gledging at me, bestowing a look that combined entreaty with despair.

"Why give it me, old chap? You know I'm no use at this sort of thing. My best advice is to follow the great detective and to smoke a pipe. I've a spare one here—and just the strong tobacco required to solve your puzzle. Let's step into the corridor."

Once in the space between carriages I turned to my friend. "What on earth," I queried, "was all that about?"

"Well done, Fred!" he replied, ignoring my question. "Better strike up though if we're to look the part. I knew I could rely on you to spot a ruse."

So saying, he began to inform his partner in detection of the proximity of Tulloch station, while next to speak highly of local farming methods north of the river Spean. I could only pray no-one was listening, for I was as certain that Montagu Fiennes knew nothing of farming as I was sure myself I couldn't conjure a souffle! Fortunately it wasn't long before our train entered the narrow defile which adjoins that most famous of the Spean chasms, the Monessie Gorge.

Monty opened the window and made as if to watch the dash of waters below, their fuming rapids now channelled, now falling between black granite walls. Then I perceived he was whispering hoarsely—over the din and chaos of the tumult—into that dark and airy thoroughfare. I drew nearer and could just make out what sounded like…"Vanish…disappear…if so—go to the hospital…senior citizen's ward…Bel—"

Just then one of the stewards came past commenting a touch pointedly on the freshness of the breeze. Perhaps we should like, he added, to order another drink before our arrival at "the Fort"? We gladly consented to this suggestion and prompted the fellow—who'd apparently done his homework more than most—to explain his curt description of our destination. The man—his name by the way was Archibald—was noteworthy not simply for his singular and upright stance, but also for a certain mischievous twinkle apparent in his eye: any attendant to his conversation was never quite sure as to whether the fellow was in earnest or in fun, and, if the latter, who was the proper object of his mirth; but, disconcerting though that proved, there was something most likeable both in his accent and bearing.

I cannot now recall everything he told us, but I do remember the names of Cameron of Lochiel and McKay of Killiecrankie. It was the latter who, seizing the opportunity of his foe's enforced convalescence, put up a series of fortifications on the landward side of Loch

Linnhe and managed to do so, it seemed, within the space of a fortnight.

"And then, sirs, d' ye ken what this fella McKay went and deid? Did he no name the blatty battlements after yon Orangeman? Aye, so he deid an' all. Now, beggin' ye pardon, was not that an awfu' thing tae dae? The devil's own name it be, and it sticks i' the thrapple like a bent o' hook. So up here it's a gearasdan—the Fort. Aye, the Fort."

And having put us right on that topic, the wistful Archibald left us to our dram.

When at length the train pulled in beneath Scotland's highest mountain there was nothing to be seen of the Ben itself, for by now night had fallen; nevertheless even the lights above the platform generated a kind of excitement. There was—let it be said—great comfort in the prospect of a proper bed and a hot bath. With some eagerness therefore did I reach up for my rucksack and, upon pulling it down, turn to Monty to observe that it had done little to enhance the furnishings of our carriage; but when I turned to the place where he'd been standing there was no sign of him. Montagu Fiennes had vanished.

CHAPTER 7

The Glenfinnan Viaduct

Immediate inquiries at the railway station revealed that travellers were booked in at one of two hotels—the Alexandra or the Milton. As I'd successfully been accommodated at the first, it appeared Monty might well be making his way to the second. It struck me as odd though that my friend should have departed so soon and I hastened therefore to see if he were on the transfer-coach before decamping myself. To my dismay it had already gone. Making the most of things and trying to be philosophical about this latest setback, I crossed the busy road outside the station and walked the short distance to the Alexandra Hotel.

My room, being neither specially modern nor yet decorated after the old style, was nevertheless serviceable for the occasion. I took my bath and was about to turn in when I noticed a telephone: it would be easy enough now to contact Monty, provided of course he had not gone out.

I got through to the Milton Hotel, spoke to a helpful if harassed receptionist, and was told that nobody under the name of Fiennes had been entered in the register. I tried Monty's favourite cover, that of Harold Hardanger, but that too failed to turn anything up. There was nothing for it but to get some sleep.

After the long and absorbing day I'd had respite came quickly and I slept soundly. I awoke, however, when it was still quite early. The red digits on the bedside clock signalled that it was just 6.00 a.m. My mind at once went back to our arrival in Fort William and to Monty's disappearance. I first telephoned the receptionist downstairs and then tried again at the Milton. Still there was no record of my companion having arrived: he had neither booked in that morning nor had he registered during the previous evening.

There seemed nothing else for it. I got up quickly, made a hasty toilet, and promptly returned to the station. 'The West Highlander' it transpired had in the meantime been shunted up a siding. When I caught up with her I found a young man there about to valet the interior.

"Anyone on board?" I queried

"None that I've seen, squire," the youth replied tartly.

"Mind if I have a look? Here's my ticket."

Then I remembered, I *had* no ticket. As my hand hovered about my jacket the boy let up though and allowed me to go inside. I reckon I made as thorough a search of that train as should the best of bloodhounds. But I found nothing—not even a cigarette-end in Monty's ashtray.

I stepped out into the fresh air and looked up at the massive shoulders of the great Ben. It was a cold and exhilarating autumnal day. Although there was a fair amount of cloud around it was mostly whitish stuff and there seemed little prospect of rain. I decided to return to the hotel and enjoy a three-course breakfast.

Proceeding to stroll down the deserted platform I became conscious of just how empty the station was. A second later there came to me one of those words that Monty had so queerly enunciated above the Monessie Falls,—"Vanish!" Was not that exactly what Monty had done? He had "vanished!" I tried to recall the rest of what I'd heard but could remember only the two nouns, "bell" and "hospital"—and neither of those seemed to connect. Perhaps a full stomach would assist me.

That morning I was the first person to take breakfast and the first to depart the hotel. I might never have got onto the trail were it not that I heard one of the waitresses call out, "I canna go this afternoon, dearie, I've to go to the Belford." The Belford, I at once inferred, must be the local hospital!

My destination proved to be only a stone's throw removed from the hotel itself. It wasn't till I was actually inside, however, that I realised the information my unconscious had surfaced was of little practical use. The hospital itself was a large one, and I myself had no idea what or whom I was supposed to be observing. Maybe Monty would greet me from some bed or wheelchair, or from a trolley being wheeled to the theatre. The notion was absurd, but then so was my predicament.

All the same a full hour remained to me and I was determined to use it. As I leapt up some stairs—two, three at a time—an elderly gentleman in striped pyjamas happened to pass by, teetering slightly as he made his own unsteady descent. Then it came back to me. Another part of the message had referred to a "senior citizens' ward." I asked the old gentleman which floor he was on and then, encouraged by this latest discovery, made directly for it.

Alas! When I reached the floor in question I was met by the word "Surgical," with not a prospect in sight of any senior citizen. I then approached a pretty young thing in a nurse's uniform and was told I should try downstairs. Just as I was leaving, however, she called out to me: "Or else you could try the Belhaven."

Fort William, it seemed, had more than the one hospital, and of the two the second not only specialised in geriatrics but harboured in its name a sound, by now familiar, of a tintinnabulum. The coincidence struck me as a trifle bizarre, while it served as the prelude to a series of scenarios I can only describe as "surreal."

I should inform the reader first that the Belhaven Ward (to give it its full title) comprised a square, single-floor unit accommodating about thirty patients. Like so many modern constructions it was of a functional design, although it appeared less of a blot on the landscape owing to its reduced height. It was surrounded by a low brick wall, and between that and the hospital there ran a peripheral path of mixed gravel.

On the Sunday morning I arrived there the person I first chanced to meet was a workman. He was clad in green and held in his outstretched hand the not altogether likely object of a flame-torch. His purpose was to burn away the occasional growth of weed spoiling the path.

In my approach to the main entrance—between this viridescent personage and myself—there passed a collared gentleman in black and grey whom I opined to be a member of the clergy. He made some remark in Gaelic to which the worker replied with a grin and a friendly wave of the hand. I confess I couldn't resist making a quip to this irregular "gardener" upon his obvious good fortune—in not receiving a sermon, bearing in mind that this was the Sabbath.

"No, no," he replied softly. "Wass that not Father John? It is all the same to him. Besides, am I not going to see to the man's driveway chusst as soon as I haf finished here?" With the lilt of that broadcast in my ears I pushed the doors open to the Belhaven Ward.

My first impression on entering was that everything seemed unusually quiet. There was a communal lounge to my right and through its glass doors I was able to see the priest in the process of talking to an elderly patient—the latter hunched forward and evidently confined to a wheelchair. I myself naturally wondered if I was not missing the full shilling: for I had no notion as to what I was about. Still, at least I couldn't spot Monty anywhere in the residents' lounge and there were no nurses waiting in attendance.

Turning to my left I made in the direction of a small group of minor wards. Holding my breath—as if somehow to make my progress less visible—I passed by an office with its doors partly opened: it was to be hoped the echoing laughter from within signalled occupants too distracted to notice my presence. I remained in luck, but drawing closer to the penultimate ward got the shock of my life.

Just inside the doorway, and sitting up and completely filling the bed, was the biggest man I'd ever had the misfortune to contemplate. He must have measured every inch of seven feet and in an upstanding position might well have seemed taller. As to his girth, though it was considerable, and though the general impression was certainly one of weight and of size, a word like "fat" would not have been apposite to denote his overall appearance. Rather, he seemed to be so much muscle and brawn that I wondered how he could have been invalided at all. In addition it was difficult to determine the fellow's age, for his scalp boasted not a shred of hair. Allowing for the trouble I have in guessing a person's age when so afflicted, I should have said of this Brobdingnagian that his years were numbered somewhere between fifty and seventy—presumably nearer the latter, given his current confinement. Yet it was not the mere fact of his size which staggered me so much as the sight of a multiple scar—stitched unevenly across his crown—one single ramification of which ran all the way down to his left eyebrow. The man's injury—together with the surgery subsequently required—had had the effect of slightly raising that hairless brow, giving to that part of his visage a wide-eyed, almost lunatic aspect. Then again it was also the case the man had a nose that seemed disproportionately large (not to mention hooked) while his lips appeared unusually broad. His identity was obvious. This strange personage was none other than Henrik Meyer about whom Monty had so judiciously warned me.

Neither, moreover, was the patient alone. Standing at his bedside was a slimly-built, towheaded youth with a look on his face I took to be fear masquerading as amicability. The boy himself was comely-looking and had his elegant hand firmly and incongruously held, grasped (it looked) by his companion's fist. Then as my gaze settled on the youth's demeanour there was that about him which made me wonder whether I had not seen him before. Certainly I'd seen others like him during my afternoon in Brighton. He could, I reflected, have been any one of those joggers I'd seen on that day. The thought seemed improbable, though, and I soon dismissed it.

I was awoken from my reflections by a corpulent, middle-aged nurse. "Yes, sir. How may I help you? You are looking for someone?"

However I did not tarry to make a reply anymore than I allowed myself to be detained further in watching Henrik Meyer sitting with his boy. I rushed to the front door, flung myself through it and subsequently almost collided into the man in green. The latter—holding finger to lips—made a vigorous whisper of "*Ssht!*" before dropping out of sight behind some elevated railings. A rather thin, elderly minister, whose sober mien affected a sharp contrast with that of his co-religionist, followed him almost at once. Indeed he looked as if he might belong to a rival denomination, for he wore a jacket whereas the priest had merely sported a pale, short-sleeved shirt. He greeted me formally and at once passed into the hospital.

Almost immediately the "gardener" reappeared, calling out jovially, "You will be thinking me daft, but that one is on the other side. I shall not be mowing his lawns until the morrow."

So saying the fellow took himself off in the direction of the presbytery, leaving me—not without relief—to check out at the Alexandra and board the train at around two minutes to ten. It had been the queerest kind of morning I could recollect and it was not over yet.

By the time I looked back to the departing platform I realised with nauseous certainty that Montagu Fiennes had indeed "vanished." The sad truth of it could no longer be gainsaid and even my companions of the way began to remark upon his absence: it was all I could do to assure them that Monty would be joining us later. Deep down it was I who had the greatest cause for worry; for, though I might know a little of what lay ahead, of the details of any of Monty's stratagems I was supremely ignorant. There was left to me now only one course of action: I should have to devise a set of tactics myself. I confess I was about as happy at doing that as would be a one-eyed batsman poised against a googlie and last in for the series. Nothing less than a century would do. Frankly I didn't think I stood a cat-in-hell's chance of succeeding.

Weary of mind I let my eyes close and with the seeming inconsequence of a hawk-moth allowed my thoughts to flit madly from one image to another: Monty—bound and gagged in some dark subterranean chamber; the sinister and foreign-sounding twins—one possibly off my trail, but the other hounding me remorselessly down the iron line; Henrik Meyer—sitting handicapped in a hospital, yet without a trace of weakness to his mighty frame; the fair-haired youth—strangely beholden to an invalided giant; a party of joggers—first running beside the Thames, next along a shingle beach, then up Brighton's high street; the well-known face of an M.P.—shielded beneath his forearm while under the stubborn glare of a scrutinising press; the Old Etonian—one minute distinguished and courteous, the next a chameleon, extending his hand to Saddam Hussein; Ishbosheth—a limping demon, half-crazed and in the grasp of his hand a condiment of shame. It was, bar one of them, the best, a gallery of nondescripts and rogues: the only good man had been robbed from the show. Then I tried to imagine Malahide, but it was difficult to find an image that would stay: the poor figure conjured by my imagination began to blur around the edges, first looking uncomfortably like a smaller version of Meyer, then like the Etonian but bereft of hair. Finally I thought of Freya. I hadn't, I admit, hitherto allowed myself that indulgence—and even now I felt unable to permit it.

Instead I opened my eyes and saw standing along the last stretch of Locheilside three solitary herons: the nearest of them exhibited a stance of precarious elegance, for it stood tall upon a single leg; the second was dipping its beak into the quiet sheen of water—its neck one long smooth and graceful curve; the last was poised on a stump of wood and was engaged in adroit dodges as it sought to fend off a black-headed gull that rounded and fell, circled and fell again.

Perhaps it was simply my mood, only truth to tell I did not at the time feel enamoured of the landscape. Although the wide and silvery loch had about it an agreeable appearance, and on the far side was flanked by a low ridge of hills—and while in the foreground a variety of trees gave added interest to the scene as a whole—there was something about it which failed to excite admiration and which tended to rob it of its anticipated cynosural appeal. Once Ben Nevis had retreated into the distance the view certainly became more far-reaching, though it offered neither the exhilarating expansiveness of an English vale nor yet the inspiring majesty of singular yet proximately-ranging summits. In addition to which the sky above was almost completely overcast: having lost the blue and brightness of early morning it had acquired a texture that appeared curiously dark—ominous, even; I would not depart from the truth if I were to say it had an air almost of menace.

The threat of a storm increased as the train began to push its way, now more laboriously, gradually up the glen. Then all of a sudden the indifferent landscape narrowed and seemed as such to grow by leaps and bounds in splendour and height, while on a deep green knoll a lone stag stood attentively as if guarding the threshold. As we passed beneath this creature the train broke out of the pass to give views of such glory and grandeur as to render the onlooker nigh o'erwhelmed. The eyes darted rapidly—left, right, this way, that—but all the time trying to take in the whole: the long sweep of Loch Shiel with its towering, engulfing hills; the massive valley and rearing summit at its head; the great crescent of a viaduct spanning the way forward. The physics teacher—his name by the way was Stalbridge—had, it was true, been in raptures of anticipation for the previous quarter of an hour. We had heard already the story of the viaduct's construction: how its pillars of concrete had been fortified with crushed rock and of its radius of twelve chains; how a horse had fallen a distance of a hundred feet down an empty column—and of how railway workers speak of the viaduct moving and of the dead horse neighing there on a winter's night. But all of that, fascinating though it had sounded, had done little to prepare one for the spectacle encountered now in the moment of experience. To be a witness to this hidden domain, to come across the kingdom of the hawk and the stag, as it were unawares, to break forth into this territory for the first time: such an experience was breathtaking, measurelessly exciting, and in the end seemed to defy description. Perhaps one must go to Glenfinnan personally, cross over its great viaduct and so relish for oneself this wondrous place.

Half way across the elevated course of track the train came slowly to a halt allowing its passengers to admire the panorama spread out before them. Soon aching necks were craned from parted windows and spectators made bold to open wide the coach doors. An assortment of cameras began to click and to flash, and this too was something to behold. As for myself I was as much struck by the splendid valley to the north as I was by the views framed to the south and the west. The tops of Beinn and Tuim and Fraoch-bheinn incorporated the same call-of-the-wild experience that had so excited me upon Rannoch Moor. The waterfalls, too, evoked a drama of complementary power as they plunged seething-white down the mountainsides to join at last the rich chaos of river below. At the foot of the viaduct Glen House seemed but a child's model, way beneath, while we ourselves were poised magically—the airy heavens above with far below the lesser work of human hands.

After a few minutes I turned to contemplate the vast spread of Loch Shiel—from its distant reaches to the south to its return close at hand and to where stood that most illustrious of Scottish monuments: rising magnificently between the wave-lapped shore and the green field of Glenfinnan towered the great memorial column of the Highlander; kilted, indomitable, loyal forever to the Prince's Standard, to the colours enduring of blue and white and red.

A less famous if annual "gathering" had taken place there but weeks beforehand in the form of the Glenfinnan Games. I was about to observe to Stalbridge that the pitch used for its location had not yet recovered, when I caught sight of something which fixed my attention not with delight but with horror: for a hundred yards down the line stood two men engaged in what appeared to be mortal combat.

As I looked on, incredulous and amazed, it seemed as if the taller assailant were being pinned to the side by a man dressed in a cape. The outfit of the latter seemed remarkable in itself, for a railway viaduct is hardly the most promising route even for a wayward cyclist: that such he was I'd already decided, even though at the time I'd failed to discern any clips attached to his trousers. As to the identity of the victim, I'd no idea.

Then all at once it was obvious. I was a fool not to have seen it before. The man was wearing a green waxed anorak with black markings down each sleeve. I'd know that garment anywhere. It belonged to none other than to Montagu Fiennes. With this realisation all sense of caution left me—as did no less the anticipated vertigo of my jump to the sleepers. I landed awkwardly, but was soon on my feet.

For an instant it looked as if Monty might invert the status quo, for he had the demonic cyclist pushed half way from him. I yelled out encouragement as I rushed to assist him. Then just as hope was kindled—and to my utter astonishment—his opponent seemed to pick up my friend, manhandling his tall frame like a limp marionette, and hurl him forcibly into the giddy reaches below.

I had then to witness my friend's body drop—like some puppet carelessly discarded—into that awful and empty silence. There was no cry, no clamour, only an angular movement of limbs. Time for a while stood still. Then it was all over—just a muffled *dunt* far beneath and with it the absolute certainty of death.

I had only one objective now, to get my hands around the neck of that murderer and to cast him into the very same eternity. Thenceforward God could dispose as God deemed fit, and thereafter at least I'd have the cold comfort of commination, of a revenge carried out in a most timely manner.

Yet already my enemy was tearing down the line to make good his escape. He had shown no interest at all in the outcome of his act and those precious seconds gained afforded him the advantage. Where now, I wondered, were my military training, my sharp wits, my readiness to react? Even so I might have reached him—for as I've said I am quick on my feet and not easily outrun—only as fate would have it there was to be no race, and bitter though the pill be my act of revenge would have to be postponed.

Other people had begun alas to converge on the line. Whatever their intentions might be they constituted nothing but an impediment. Even poor Stalbridge got in the way, so by the time I'd caught up with the engine driver the caped maniac who'd killed my friend was nowhere to be seen. Then a voice loudly called out insisting I return. Blinded by rage I refused to accept the injunction and held back in a vain attempt to seek out the assassin. I reckoned he'd probably departed the viaduct whence it adjoined the hill. Certainly there was no sign of him on the railway track. As the train pulled out though—and I cast madly about—not a single trace of him could I detect. I was in a worse funk now than before.

There occurred to me then a further possibility—suppose he had managed to board the train? In a dreadful fury I began to race towards the station. I knew I had to get there before its departure at eleven o'clock. A glance at my watch indicated it was nearly that already.

As I bounded down the track towards the station, however, I could see that the doughty Stalbridge was engaged in delaying tactics at the start of the platform. Railway enthusiast that he was, he had noticed that this stop housed a museum and was now roundly questioning why they might not waive the schedule and go inside. As I drew closer though the manager urged him to join his companions, promising that they should still have an hour there on their journey back. He made as if satisfied, but then turned round and called in my direction—in a tone of some urgency—"My God, man, thank heavens you made it! Do you know that fellow, the poor devil that was thrown?"

"Did I, I think you mean," I replied tartly. "No, no, it's just I can never comprehend how the Great British Public can stand calmly by as one of its members is robbed or beaten!"

"We've rung for the police, of course. I thought maybe you'd recognised him."

The temptation to enlist help at this juncture was enormous. I had not a friend in the world to whom I could turn, added to which I was acutely conscious both of my own vulnerability and the hopelessness of my task. I had, moreover, already warmed to this teacher and, as I've said, sympathised with his feelings. What worried me most was he wasn't alone. I might trust him, but could I trust his companions? I decided I couldn't take that risk.

"No, no. But I'm pleased somebody's phoned for the police. Thanks for your help, Stalbridge. It's much appreciated."

"No problem, old chap, no problem. Best step up though, we're due to depart."

On the point of reviewing the decision I'd made there then occurred an incident to confirm me in my caution. I'd no sooner sat down than the chaplain—who was moving forward down the aisle—suddenly stood back, looked me in the eye, and with the expression of a Punchinello pronounced in triumphant voice: "I know who you are. You're Major Delman...Major Frederick Delman! It's been bothering me a while. You see, I met you at Lady Salaston's tea party."

The echo of this announcement was just beginning to sink in when the stationary train started to move. In an instant I seized my rucksack from the luggage rack, pushed the chaplain aside and made a prompt dive for the nearest exit. As 'The West Highlander' pulled out of Glenfinnan I found myself for the second time that day lying amongst the sleepers.

This time I was more bruised. Shakily getting to my feet I was aghast to discover a policeman pacing down the line in the direction of the viaduct. To my alarm, another officer appeared in the museum doorway and was attempting to light up a cigarette. By now a fresh north-westerly was blowing so that the first match went out before its work had been done. Here was my chance. Over to my right stood a low fence containing a makeshift style. Without a moment's delay I nipped smartly over its step and dropped down to the lee of an adjacent cottage: the latter, I recall, was a tidy-looking affair recently extended to blend-in with the original. (I presumed it must once have belonged to the stationmaster in the days before cuts and redundancies had forced him, prematurely, to retire from his post. Perhaps the keeper of the museum now lived there, while the extension provided a facility of 'Bed and Breakfast' for stopover tourists.)

Below the cottage was a narrow access-road, while situated opposite was a small car park lain out in pink gravel. Stationed under a row of pines stood a highly polished automobile of pre-war vintage—a shining black Lanchester, no less. With little in my mind just then I wandered over to the car and saw the passenger door was open—and there, lying on the seat, were three copies of the *Glasgow Herald*.

Just then it began to rain—an expression which does scant justice to the streaming torrent of water which then began to pour in solid sheets over the road ahead. Rather than dig out my mackintosh I opted to get into the car and to hide behind a newspaper. The driver could not be far away and I had decided that there was nothing else for it but to surrender my trust to the anticipated hospitality of an invisible highlander.

My notional man of the highlands was soon substantiated—with an outlandishness, moreover, I had not imagined. Standing at just beneath six feet, he possessed a girth that appeared at first glance only a fraction dissimilar. But, if his physique was formidable, so too was his outfit outrageous. Granted, his calf muscles made a manly foil to his *skene-dhu* and his lower torso was respectably hid beneath a magnificent kilt of the clan MacDonald. Nor was there anything wrong with the tartan he wore, nor yet with his equally splendid and pendant sporran. The problem, alas, lay with his tight-fitting jacket, suggesting as it did either a mischievous tailor or an oleaginous diet: for it was a Prince Charles *coat'ee*—apt for our location but not at all wise for this particular soul. In addition, he wore at the neck of his shirt a curiously chequered bow tie done out in some horridly queer and misfit design. As to the man's face, he had the head of a Teuton but the hair and beard of a Nordic warrior.

He was also surprisingly nimble. Ignoring my presence entirely, and opening the door to retrieve from beneath my legs a well-preserved crank, he began to zigzag the automobile into action with the seeming ease of a decathlon-athlete. Within seconds we were accelerating down the access-way to the main road and within minutes had left behind Glenfinnan and were going at a royal pace in the direction of Loch Eilt. And all the while he showed not the slightest interest in his uninvited passenger!

Neither, let it be said, was I anxious to communicate myself. Nonetheless, I felt the bizarre nature of this episode could not long be contained in silence. The Lanchester was speeding towards the first reach of rain-pitted loch when I opened my mouth to speak.

"Ye need say nothing, laddie. I ken fine yer in trouble. Ye dinna haf tae explain yirsel'."

"Walter Makin is my name. I can't say I would be so sympathetic if our roles were reversed."

"It's nae bother tae me what folks does or doesna dae, sae lang as I'm left tae missel'. Mind, I notice yer wearin' good cloth, even if it dinna match wi' yon rucksack. Ye boots, too, they're sorely scrappit."

It was tempting then and there to take this Scotsman (highlander or no) into my confidence. The burden of my isolation was wearisome, and there was in any case something about the fellow that suggested I might say what I would and it would go no further. On the other hand, why put the man at risk? He was already doing me a favour. It would be unreasonable to place him in further danger.

"I could comment you're wearing a fine and noble costume yourself. Unless I'm much mistaken, it's that of the MacDonalds."

"Aye, sae it is, laddie, sae it is. I've been tae a wedding. A local lass has landed hirsel' some queer Adonis from the city, a Glasgow yuppy. Nae guid'll come offit, but it were a grand sight at the kirk of St. May and St. Finnan. It wasna a bad reception, either. Noo, I must ask ye te stay kinda quiet. I've only a lend o' this beauty and mi heid's nae sae clear jus' noo. Them folk back there, they put owre muckle peaty juices into yon wee drams."

I was not entirely comforted by this last admission. To be caught by the police in the act of aiding a drunken driver would hardly be to have one's cares alleviated. On the other hand, the heavens were still teeming their worst and I was making good progress in the right direction. I had not yet devised a plan, but to make for the coast made every bit of sense. After all it was there that the *Queen of Sheba* must surely be found and I might well determine her intended rendezvous. Besides, there was no point looking a gift Scotsman in the mouth. I decided to settle back and trust my fate to this tartan but friendly inebriate.

The Lanchester continued to do her work against all the odds. The road turned and twisted beneath the gloom of the hills and followed closely the perimeter of the loch as well as mirroring the railway track on the opposite side. A stuffed culvert at one point set the streaming belt of a burn overflowing our way and made my companion roar above the din of the rain: "Losh! But what a stramash o' watta!"

By contrast, I myself—being simply the passenger—had the enviable prospect of the panorama as a whole and did not need to concentrate on the swivel of the road. I could admire the pouring white cataracts, the broad glens with their dark cauldrons, the massive hill-structures and disappearing ridges; or marvel at islands in the loch beneath—their ancient pines straggling athwart the rough, blackish mounds—each lodged in a compass of waves. More than once did we set up a startled hind to dash through a brake or run up a bank. I recall at one stage seeing a particularly powerful stag held in *meditatione fugae* as the car splashed past with all the while its driver as silent as a dream—*muet comme un poisson.*

The calm of the motorist was interrupted, however, at the place where his automobile sped past the inn at Lochailort, sending spray tossing towards the beach at Camas Driseach: "Damn! ... damn! ... damn! Damn—damn—DAMN!!"

"Good Lord, man, whatever is it?"

"Ach, it's just the polis, laddie. I'd caught sight o' one uvem as he made quit o' the Glenfinnan Hotel. I didna bother much because he looked ha'-cut hissel'. Al' the same, I jaloused his game fine. He must have phoned aheid, away up t' Arisaig. Ye see, we have just left another back at the car park at Lochailort."

I slewed round. Through the now thinning veil of drizzle I could make out a speeding white car intent on our arrest.

"Can we lose him?" I cried.

"No afore Arisaig, that's one thing definite sure. Yud better start praying, laddie. I canna go much faster than this!"

So saying, my friend grimaced ferociously, hunching himself up close to the wheel as if by dint of pure concentration he could extend the car's maximum speed. Initially, and in the face of credulity, the tactic seemed to work, for we did indeed appear to gain ground. Then, after a few minutes, the inevitable happened and the gap between pursuer and pursued got shorter and shorter. By the time we'd broken through to the shore-side of Loch Nan Uamh—and were getting our first misty glimpses of the Inner Hebrides—the game, all bar the shouting, seemed well and truly up.

Then Lady Fortune smiled once more. Her timely intervention was a touring caravan—the very bane of motorists in a territory blessed only by a single, sinewy and uneven road. Even then the trick could have been lost: if the police had been the first to overtake that trailer our card would surely have been trumped. As it was our man at the wheel put his best foot down, muttered something under his breath, and pushed forward past the dilatory vehicle in front.

We had done it! At least for the time being we had put a barrier between ourselves and the bobby. The look of relief on my magnificent chauffeur was evident as he settled back again into a more comfortable posture. Even better, the road itself continued to narrow. Try as he might our pursuer would be hard pushed now to overtake either the caravan or the Lanchester. All the same I could yet make out the shrill whine of his alarm exhorting the holiday-makers to draw into the verge. It seemed this reprieve bespoke the one noble fellow in our hand; the rest was dross.

We made Beasdale, nonetheless, and there caught sight of 'The West Highlander' on her journey to Mallaig. It was not long before we'd passed the driveway to Arisaig House and were then all set for the clachan itself. But it was just then that our fortunes were once more reversed. A curse from the stalwart driver to my side gave the signal that the caravan had pulled in at the driveway: the policeman any second now must make good the setback.

Then, drawing closer to Arisaig, the Lanchester suddenly slowed down. I turned to my partner-in-flight, about to exclaim my horror, when he crooned softly to me, "Dinna worry, laddie, dinna worry."

My lack of faith ill became me. Almost as the police car caught up with us—at the very point of overtaking—the Lanchester swung violently to the right, there to pursue a new course down a small side-road. The latter, ironically, led both to the local police station and the nearest stop on the railway line. However, we were not long detained in that direction. Very soon we rounded a bend to the right and cruised down a slight incline till we came upon a handful of small villas. There, somewhat to my surprise, we came to a halt.

"Noo, laddie, wud ye taak a wee stravaig up to the crossroads? I'd like tae know what ye can see."

I was not entirely content at the prospect: it did not make me invulnerable—yet since on the whole it seemed I'd fallen into capable hands I wasted little time in decamping to where the roads in question intersected. Almost immediately the police vehicle came into view. I promptly dived for cover but saw to my relief the car, instead of following a course to the right, had chosen to corner to the left and moved quickly out of sight. I ran back to the Lanchester and informed my anonymous friend of what I'd seen.

"Chusst as I kenned, chusst as I kenned. It is bluff and counter-bluff that is needed with the likes o' him."

"What was your strategy?" I roared, in no way disguising my pleasure.

"Well, ye see I reckoned he'd be thinkin' we'd most likely make for Mallaig—a no unreasonable assumption. But by comin' quit o' the main road I made it look as though wi' were headin' for yon train. But then again, and at the same time, he kent—and I kent—that that were only a diversion. I never had any intention o' doin' that. But ye see, whereas he thought I'd be headin' still for Mallaig, I kenned fine I wass not. Instead, I slipped doon this wee sideroad, tae give us a few extra minutes. Hop in though, laddie, he'll soon turn back."

"Where to now?" I asked.

"Tae Rhu. Doon to-warrads the Point and there tae an auld boatshed by the pier. I'll stow this beauty away there and then pass the night at the Porter's Lodge. But no you, laddie, though there's a muckle o' places tae hide in. That's if ye've a mind tae. Else ye can abscond—right'way."

The truth of the matter was even now was I had little notion as to where we were actually heading, while it looked as if the hospitality so far afforded was shortly to come to an end. But—in for a groat, in for a guinea—I decided to continue in the Lanchester and to give the enforcers of the law a run for their money.

As we double-backed veering south onto the Rhu road I noticed for the first time that the rain had stopped. As our route looped and wound its way to the west, a brighter aspect of white and cream-coloured cloud started to unfold. And as the sky lightened, so too did the pewter glaze of the sea begin to dissolve. Moreover, as the single track we were on followed the line of the coast from time to time we were able to see colonies of gulls rise up or disperse airborne in a tumult of wings. Occasionally a handful of oystercatchers would dart across an ebbing bay—their angular designs etched sharply in black, their beaks a vivid red. To the landward side the terrain was rough though mostly low-lying, with bright outcrops of heather pitched between broad swathes of bracken. I thought then of the lines of the poet:

> O let them be left, wildness and wet;
> Long live the weeds and the wilderness yet.

Earlier on I'd been too preoccupied with escape to confuse any darksome Ben with Liakoura. Now poetic sentiments made a welcome intrusion into my troubled imaginings.

They were, however, to be short-lived. As we dropped beneath Torr Mor my companion vented an unexpected poser:

"Ye'll be keepin' an eye on Maggie, the week?"

The reference to the P.M. was unmistakeable. Temporarily nonplussed, I failed to make reply to the question and was promptly confronted by another:

"Is it no in Bournemouth this year?"

I was about to babble something about Brighton when I remembered Monty's tirade on my confused and aberrant thinking. Fortunately I was not required to answer.

"Aye, sae it is, sae it is. I ken fine as mi' ain dear mother—she that spirited hirsel' that very same way but four months back—wass she no tellin' me that they were te foregather at Bournemouth? Ye'll be one o' the same crood, I shouldna wonda."

Even as he spoke we passed a house on our left which turned out to be the aforementioned Porter's Lodge. It seemed that this road, with its mean ornament of grass running down the middle, had at one time provided a regular access to an established pier. Sea ferries had travelled all the way from Glasgow and Strathclyde and had transported passengers and cargo to this improbable peninsula. It was, in truth, a remote spot, being far removed from the main thoroughfares. In due course the link had been lost, but the dignified home of the porter still testified to its former importance.

As if without warning we drew up before an empty and decrepit boathouse. I got out and swung each door wide. In no time at all the Lanchester was hid from view. The last thing its temporary possessor did was to chuck over to me a pork pie; while the last thing he uttered was, "Sorry, laddie, but I haf nae a dram. Maybe I'll be seein' ye again." With that my nonesuch friend made bulky but confident progress back towards the lodge.

As for me, I stared bleakly all around and felt as bereft as a child lost in the wilderness.

CHAPTER 8

A Long Way To Mallaig

Standing alone in that silent quarter of Arisaig my first thought was to find sanctuary till the local police had abandoned their search. With this in mind—and seeing before me a wide track winding about the headland—I determined to set out in the direction of Rhu Farm at the southern tip of the peninsula. Once there I might find some pound or disused shieling to furnish me with sufficient accommodation in the immediate term. In the event, however, the place was so clearly outlandish—and my mission no less patently important—that I could no more pursue that path in reality than I could forbear the highway. The plain truth was I needed to return to the village and thence continue north until I had come to the end of the line; until, that is, I had arrived in Mallaig.

With this realisation I turned to retrace my steps and began disconsolately to make my promenade in the direction of the clachan. I recall that both of my feet felt like lead while my heart seemed burdened by the weight of a depression. My pace slackened and I soon began to imitate the proverbial tortoise. At first I could make no sense of this mood, but when the road once more abutted the shore—and I sat down to eat the food I'd been given—it was not long before I discerned my predicament.

The simple fact was that until this moment I had had no time at all to consider Monty's demise—untimely, premature—at the Glenfinnan viaduct. My best friend had been summarily despatched—with a violence and total absence of ruth—and yet here I was like a manic desperado chasing the midday air. I had to allow my heart to grieve, to let in some of the sorrow. Still, endeavour as I might, perched on that insensate boulder in that anonymous bay, I simply could not. Instead, a rising indignation was all that would surface, while to attain relief I found myself hurling pebbles into the indifferent sea. Then at last the tears came and with them the remorseless impact of a man's unwanted solitude.

After some time had passed I spotted in the shallows of the water a sudden movement—supple, elegant, sinewy—and saw a small, whiskered head poke up into the air. I knew the outline of a seal but opined this animal to be of quite a different species. What I was observing was that most enchanting of aqua-faring mammals to grace our western coastline—the by now all-too-rare otter.

In its paws the creature held a dab which, periodically, it would let fall into a plash of water. The poor flounder had become the plaything of the otter, though the latter was engaged in such semblance of innocent amusement that it seemed unfair to impute to it anything other than mild mischief-making. In any case, there was something about its wistful and carefree movement which infused my sad temper with happier feeling. I laughed at the sheer nonchalance of the animal. It must have heard me, though, for all at once my lutrine companion had the fluke in its jaws while in an instant it had bolted back into the titubant waves. All too quickly, it seemed, had my otter vanished. Yet so too had the worst of my indulgence.

I glanced at my watch. It was 12.00 noon. If I delayed no further I might be able to board a certain steam train of which I'd heard Stalbridge boast and which at one time had conveyed the passengers of 'The West Highlander' on their journey beyond Fort William. Realising it would have departed Glenfinnan around this time I calculated it must leave Arisaig between one and a quarter past. I finished off my pie and struck out vigorously along the switchback road.

The reader may wonder at my boldness when but moments beforehand the sole intention had been to remain unnoticed. Now, however, I reckoned I might pass in the locality for an itinerant rambler and that the police should have better things to do with their time than to bother with an inebriate wedding guest in charge of a motorcar. Moreover, I had no good reason to imagine that they would associate me with my kickshaw friend. On the other hand, I couldn't be sure the chaplain wouldn't identify me on his arrival in Mallaig. Yet, why should he bother to link me with a failed assassin? The importunate prefect, so far as I was aware, had not picked up my name on the radio, and in any case—and to my embarrassment—my late friend had been entirely correct in placing the Tory Conference not in Brighton but in Bournemouth.

Two things, however, continued to perplex me. If the man with the gun—apparently the Etonian—was not rehearsing a shot at the P.M., then who did he have in his sights to be the recipient of a bullet? It seemed as if some foul play were afoot, while it looked as if the sham flautist had made the same mistake about Brighton as I had. And that, in truth, was passing strange. The other thing to vex me was the way in which the chaplain had declared my identity. It was the manner in which he'd done so: it had been confrontational; almost as if the pronouncement had amounted to an accusation. Still, it remained the case that any terrorist pursuing the Prime Minister would hardly head for the wilds of Scotland on the eve of the conference. That would make no sense at all.

So it was my thoughts increasingly turned away from my own safety and towards the business in hand. Somewhere in the ocean to my left was a boat called *Queen of Sheba;* somewhere an exchange would have to be made between an illicit cache of drugs and a small deposit of Red Pepper; and somewhere out there—or perhaps already on the mainland—was the arch villain of the piece, Ishbaal, the master of shame.

I wondered, too, about the situation in the Gulf, although it was hard to link the peaceable grazings of Rhu—full of sweet and honey-scented heather—to the stark reality of arms-proliferation in Southern Arabia and along the Kuwaiti border. Yet if ever Saddam was to do a deal with Ishbaal there could be no doubt of the dire consequences that would follow. The powers of the U.N. must surely rally in the teeth of an invasion, while the use of chemical bombs might well demand a heavy counter-attack. But were the allies ready? It would take time to obtain the full complement of arms needed and our military would require weeks of training to become fully acclimatised. What if the Kuwaitis were to become victims of an unknown plague? The application of Red Pepper, remember, did not have to be carried out wholesale; it could be implemented surreptitiously and strategically in piecemeal fashion. And all the while time would be on the Iraqi leader's side, his conquest no doubt consolidated through Western acquiescence. The thought was intolerable, and despite my pack I broke into a fair imitation of a canter.

As a matter of fact I reached Arisaig station several minutes before one o'clock. I had then some quarter of an hour to endure and chided myself on my haste. I stood there, I recall, looking out toward the distinctive horizon of Eigg—*le lion couchant at regardant*—with its neighbouring isle of Muck a prey at its feet: while stationed to the right of these there reared the mighty shoulders of the Rum Cuillins.

Gazing out across Arisaig channel, its islets and wrack-strewn shore and beyond to Sleat Sound and Hebridean Sea—then back to the cincture of hills all about—I found this place to be in one of the loveliest settings I'd ever beheld. Such favourable judgement, moreover, was not lessened by the change in the weather: though change there now was as the day itself turned grey and a chill north-westerly once more put spots of rain into the dampening air. It was jolly to imagine, all the same, what this might have looked like on a summer's eve: the water of the bay going gradually a tranquil black, the hills still clear in a manifold green, and around the dark islands the sky going gold or flushed with pink.

In the meantime, however, it was necessary to ground my fancies to the hour in hand. Approaching the station at a spirited pace appeared an elderly couple—each of whom was kitted out in an olive-stained anorak—while following behind was an eager triumvirate of hardy hikers. I strolled off the platform to a disused siding and hid myself behind a corrugated shed till the train should arrive. Though I could already hear the yelp and shriek of its whistle I opined it to be some way off. I waited: two minutes, three minutes, four minutes.

Then it came: solid, proud, magnificent in its advance, puffing and chuntering down the line till it gasped to a halt wheezing between the platforms. I dived in at the first doorway and had the immediate good fortune to alight upon a seat. The reverse to this farthing of luck was still I had no ticket. It was beginning to look as if I was making a habit of dodging my fare.

Presently from the other side of the aisle I caught a child quizzing its mother on the location of the next tunnel. That would be handy I thought—I could do with a measure of darkness. Then back came the response: "No more tunnels now, Clive. Just you settle down and watch the view, and see if you can't give your mother a few minutes peace."

Strange to say the injunction to the small boy was less easy to obey than one might have imagined. For one thing, a widespread drizzle seemed to have closed in—thereby limiting our prospect—and for another, the windows of the train were hopelessly dirty. In addition to which the actual carriages were devoid of comfort, which prompted me to wonder what exactly these enthusiasts might be getting for their money. I couldn't help but reflect it was I who had had the best of it, for not having been on the train I'd been able to witness the great engine as it had steamed its way down the track before huffing and exhaling to a halt. Periodically, it was true, there was the scream and shriek of the whistle. But after a while even that began to pall, and what at first seemed novel soon became an irritant.

Nonetheless occasional views of interest were still to be had. By looking downward, for example, I could make out a flat area of farmland with here and there broad bundles of gathered hay—each stack being trussed in what resembled some gigantic dustbin-liner. I could make out several piles of peat, too, the mounds themselves being staggered and assembled to almost mathematical proportions. Between them there lay wide troughs dug deep into the soil: these last, no doubt, to improve pasture and to increase the souming. To the other side the terrain rose sheer and steep and forbade the train further access inland.

Attempts to engage my mind on the scenery of our passage were soon interrupted by the approach of a uniformed railway official. I noticed, however, he was answering queries about the route ahead as well as collecting tickets. As he got nearer I felt myself breaking out into a lather of vexation and heard the sound of my heart pounding. Closer and closer he moved towards me. Again the engine emitted its fateful whistle. What was I to do? I looked studiously through the impervious glass.

"Your ticket, sir?"

I reached into my jacket.

"Of course. When are we due in?"

Tempting the fellow to conversation might, I considered, delay the moment of realisation; it might even—the chance was remote—win him to my side: he could afford perhaps to indulge at least one absent-minded passenger.

"Sorry. Must be the other pocket. I should think you're pretty tired of all this by now, Sunday an' all."

In terms of ingenuity I had arrived well and truly at the bottom of the barrel.

Then came the boy Clive to my rescue. Just as I was on the point of giving up, he exclaimed singularly and enigmatically, "Gotcha!"—and proceeded to make a harish dash down the length of the aisle. The person who had been "got" was the dutiful guard, while the manner by which he had been "gotten" was the subtle interweaving of two shoelaces. The prestidigitation of the juvenile in my hour of need appeared most promising.

It was not, I think, that the official himself would have wanted to make a fuss. Rather, it was the mother of that mercifully delinquent child who felt compelled to intervene and thereby—as they say—"save my bacon." In a fluster of blouse and embarrassment the dismayed woman got to her feet and confronted the situation. Unfortunately in so doing she attempted to do two things at once—a fact which soon proved to be her undoing. Or rather that of the guard. That she should have wished to chide the fleeing miscreant was understandable. Intelligible, too, was that she should have wished to apologise to the victim. Less comprehensible was that she should have tried to do both at one and the same time. The net result of her endeavours was that a high degree of commotion ensued during which time the aforementioned lady not only attempted to placate the guard but also tried to push herself past him to apprehend her son. Alas! the balance of the official was lost, leaving the hapless parent to turn first to the stricken collector, then to the boy, next to the supine guard, and so on. At the end of this episode the goal of acquiring tickets was temporarily abandoned, while both adults marched up the aisle in a state of mutual harassment. My own sympathies were all for the boy. I quite pitied this perpetrator of mischief and should have liked then and there to have pinned a badge to his breast. I thought it improbable, however, that a medal would be the likely outcome for all Clive's pains.

I decided to get out of the train at the first opportunity. I made for the nearest door and opened the window. Below was a churning spate of water which I knew from Stalbridge to be Scotland's shortest river and which linked Morar's loch to its legendary coastline. I had no time, however, to contemplate the adjacent silver-sands, nor to attest local reports of any deep-fathomed monster—this last, a cousin of Nessie's and Morag by name. For by now the train was drawing close to a level-crossing and slowing down sufficiently to make a jump to the ground void of danger. I threw out my pack and myself after it, rolling as I fell through a thicket of bracken and reeds and heather. There was nothing to impede the engine from its crossing so I was able to watch the train—to my immense relief—pass by the station platform and carry on up the line. At the same time I happened to notice a little way to the right the familiar sign of a Post Office. If my judgement were correct that would also mean a village store and a place to purchase a map.

Seeing my fall had done me no harm I wasted little time in donning my rucksack and making for the sign. I was correct in my judgement about a neighbouring shop and it was not long before I had in my possession an ample supply of chocolate, some cartons of long-life milk, and an all-purpose Ordnance Survey map. The latter was of the area surrounding Loch Shiel extending as far north as the shores of Loch Nevis. On the front of it was a picture of the Glenfinnan Monument: an ill-needed reminder of my friend's demise.

Opening the map I became more convinced than ever of my need to reach Mallaig. It was clear its harbour constituted a major focal point with the town itself being a convenient centre for all communications. The *Queen of Sheba* might put in there for supplies, whilst news concerning her movements might be had either from village bars or from local fishing-boats. Equally apparent was the inadvisability of pursuing the main road. Not only might I be spotted by a traveller along the adjacent railway line, but any passing motorist might blanche at my progress or venture so far as to offer me a lift. By now I had determined that my disappearance from 'The West Highlander' must surely create a stir, while the hasty manner of my exit must have aroused the suspicions of passengers in general and of the chaplain in particular. I had also been trying to recall Lady Sunningdale and on what occasion I might have encountered the clergyman. Presently it came to me; it had been during a money-raising function held in a stately home on the outskirts of Plymouth. I could not, however, recall the presence of any chaplain. This was all the more worrying as we'd apparently been introduced. Then it struck me—could he have been in mufti? I think that worried me even more, for it suggested in a way I didn't need that this chaplain might not be everything he seemed. I could not, it appeared, risk further exposure. I should have to make my way to Mallaig by stealth.

Examining the map more carefully I found there to be a single-track road which followed the northern edge of Loch Morar for about four miles: thereafter the main route appeared to peter out, becoming southward an unmetalled way along the side of the loch, or, to the north, a steep proclivity hillward to a croft denominated Stoul. However, I did not wish to be so far removed from Mallaig itself. Fortunately, about half way along the minor road there looked to be another and narrower path to the north, terminating between two small lochs: Loch a' Ghillie Ghobaich and Loch an Nostarie. At the head of the latter a fresh track was marked: this took an eastward turn on the one hand, towards an imposing and massif-type structure, while on the other debouched seaward to a hamlet called Glasnacardoch. The village of Mallaig appeared to be only about a mile beyond and could be reached by an elevated, subsidiary road. I therefore judged I might risk the last few minutes of my journey without fear of being apprehended. After all, a person indigenous to the area could hardly be expected to take notice of a wayward Sassenach, and in any case I should sooner or later need to establish contact with members of the community. I made up my mind there and then to follow the path to the two lochans and thence to turn westward towards Glasnacardoch.

By now it was mid-afternoon and despite the drizzle and the dampness I was beginning to enjoy myself. The moist air, the lapping lochside, the swirling ribbons of cloud, the grandeur of the high environs—all lent new vigour to my limbs and to my mind a fresh temper. Whatever the odds I remained free and was ready for adventure.

It was not long before I had passed the drive beside Morar Lodge and shortly afterwards spied the rough track leading to the north. The way to begin with led alongside a fast-flowing river, whilst the surrounding terrain appeared surprisingly fertile with fine outcrops of trees and plenty of vegetation—south-facing slopes and a gradual declination of the land to the edge of the loch, no doubt, comprising the cause. After a while, however, the path pressed upwards and came out onto a broad reach of land consisting mainly of bog, myrtle and benty grass. It was then that I began to wonder whether Wellington boots might not have served me better than the sturdy walking ones that I'd elected to buy and which barely protected my ankles. It was then, too, I began to feel the impress of my pack as it jostled and bumped against my aching back.

Gradually, however, the path was lost to sight and I had only my wits with which to govern my course. I kept bearing slightly to the west and attempted to adopt a middle route between the one lochan and the other. I became occasionally disorientated while in addition there was always the temptation to pursue one of the several sheep-tracks which, with a perplexing logic, crisscrossed this confusing territory. Then, just when I might have turned too soon for the correct detour to the road, I chanced to come across a group of twenty or so cows looming large and solid through the shifting vapours. Ranged beside these beasts—rough and stolid-looking creatures that they were—was stationed a vast black bull. I determined that now was not the time to put to the test any potential I might have for diplomatic engagement and so gave the entire herd a suitably wide berth. This in turn fetched me to the east and almost beside Loch an Nostarie. I topped a slight ridge and found myself standing above a swathe of peaty mire, highlighted here and there by strategically-placed stones. Happily for me this thin sleeve of steps soon became a more or less visible path; so, having first taken a wash at the skirt of the lochan, I opted for this way and struck out jauntily towards Glasnacardoch.

At one point in my progress the sun overhead put in a brief, wistful appearance. It almost marked the end of me: for the abrupt illumination caused me to turn round—being curious as I was to see something of the mountain steeps which, till then, had been hid from view. A rare spectacle now confronted me. A sharp, castellated ridge rose up behind a broad neighbouring crest, conveying to the onlooker an impression of menace coupled to formidable height. A staggered summit, this, it stood out hard against the sun-splintered mist, with the granite rock and veins of water momentarily held in a glittering coruscation—as if somehow all four elements were colluding to manifest the numinous.

Neither was this particular locus devoid of its daemon. Some fifty yards away a tall man emerged limping determinedly towards the broken hill. What fair took away the breath and froze the blood was the manner of his going, for it seemed to combine solid strength with an almost maniacal agility. There was something else, too. At the foot of the man's left leg was a black, cumbersome boot, the elevated stump of which was four or five inches higher than its appropriate counterpart. There could be no other explanation for it but that this queer, dancing figure was the very archetype of shame, Ishbosheth himself.

Rooted to that spot, gazing upon Ishbaal—watching his curious, demon-like progress—I now found to my alarm I was, quite literally, unable to move. It was as if I was in the thrall of some fiendish spell. Even though the devil had his back to me—and was making off in completely the opposite direction—I simply could not move one foot forward or backward. At any moment this evil avatar might turn round, look my way, and—such was my panic—be sure to recognise me.

Still I could not move. I knew I needed to pursue my quarry at once and, what with the fellow being crippled, should surely overcome him. On the other hand I had also the option to retreat, conscious that I had discovered him and that I could accost him forcibly at a later date. But for the present at least it seemed I was unable to do either. I simply could not move.

Then slowly the sun began to retreat, the spectacle to diminish and that eerie wetness to close in around me. I started to shiver and became aware of an ever-thickening darkness. Then I began to tremble more strongly—as if I were being subjected to a fit of dementia. Looking before me over the distant sgurr I could make out a set of inky black clouds; they were spiking upwards, unnervingly, fantastically, and I could hear a sound accompanying them as of some deafening roar: a sound, it was, like shells exploding. And with this there came red tracer fire shooting across the heavens, a fearsome blaze tearing apart the dark with staccato brilliance. Suddenly the noise, too, was everywhere around me, hard, fearful, dreadful noise, a noise which shot or spat or roared in echoing, ebony realms. My legs, they were growing weak; my head, it was beginning to spin. I was snared within the web of his spell, yielding to the handiwork even of my foe. Was I not, after all, but Ishbaal's plaything? Then the noise stopped and I collapsed into a blank, silent world.

I suppose I must have been unconscious for over an hour, as when I awoke it was already twilight and I found myself in such a dusky, spectral place that it seemed I'd entered a domain inhabited by trolls or strayed into a mythic abode of hobgoblins. I was soaked to the skin and my clenched teeth chattered. It took several minutes, moreover, to recall what had happened, and several more to regain my bearings. One thing though was clear: fortune was no strumpet but a lady gracious and protective toward her stubborn charge. How else had I come back to consciousness and Ishbaal failed to see me?

I retrieved from my pack a slab of chocolate and proceeded to wolf down several chunks of it before stumbling forward in what I presumed to be the right direction. As I still felt chilled, cadaverously and to the marrow, I forced myself to jog-along almost at a trot. This did the trick splendidly: for the mist by then had become so thick that I took a number of nasty falls; the constant effort required to pull myself up—combined with the concentration demanded in keeping to the higher ground—soon made me forget the cold and fix my attention firmly on securing the highway. I began to wake up properly, however, when a canine half-breed leapt from the back of a farmhouse and began to stir the heavens, nipping and nagging at my ankles. That made me put on a fair turn of speed and I soon bypassed the entire complex of buildings: only when I looked behind—toward the glare of lights illuminating the frontage—did I discover that what I'd taken to be some sort of homestead was in reality an hotel. It was a smallish affair, but the cars parked at its entrance indicated I should soon be quit of this infernal sump.

With not a little relief then did I come at last to the metalled road, finding to my satisfaction that the way ahead was forked—the nearer branch dropping to a course between the sea and the railway, the other comprising a more discreet entrance to the periphery of the village. Very soon did I put Glasnacardoch behind me and before long was able to make out the lights of another and much larger hotel—the West Highland—perched high above me on my right. I proceeded down the main street as far as the pier but could not, at that hour—and with the mist prevailing—make out much of Mallaig itself. What I needed now more than anything else was a hot bath, a square meal, and somewhere to lay my head.

By chance I happened to notice at that moment a big shambling fellow walking up the road. He was going round the bay and was pushing what for all the world looked like a shopping trolley. This irregular form of conveying portage was apparently being employed on behalf of an elderly couple in search of accommodation: for after a few seconds the party stopped outside a house where their bags were duly delivered and the occupier of the trolley—to judge by his gladsome proclamation—became the recipient of a welcome gratuity. Not being short of a bob or two myself I strolled over to the delighted porter and made some inquiries.

For a moment I thought I was going to have my belongings forcibly detached from my person. It seemed that there was no end to the gratefulness of my newfound "pal"—nor either to what he was capable of doing. However, on my assuming a more military tone he promptly straightened up and pointed me in the direction of a neat-looking cottage at the corner of the bay.

Inhaling the fresh sea air and delighting in the handful of lights jewelling in the mist, I made my way next to a small painted gateway beyond which I hoped sanctuary might be found. At first there was no answer, but, since there was smoke piling from the chimney and lights shone downstairs, I rapped my knuckle against the door and held my breath.

Quite soon a frail but courteous old gentleman opened the door. He looked at me with some surprise—and, no wonder, for I was older than your average hiker, oddly dressed for such, and here and there dripping wet.

"Good evening," I said. "I fear I'm living proof that City gents should stick to their offices and not venture beyond where wheels will take them. I've had a most alarming excursion, nearly drowned in a bog, and I've never been to Mallaig in my life. Rufus Gormally is my name, and I'm in need of a bed."

CHAPTER 9

Storm Force Ten

My hosts, it turned out, were both elderly, had been married to one another for the best part of forty years, and had, though only recently retired, been the proud occupants of Rum View for nearly two decades. The name of the cottage, incidentally, was quirky in the extreme: the view could hardly be said to be "rum"—and, while on a clear day it incorporated the island of Skye, it did not include the one bearing the appropriate eponym. Indeed, perhaps only the sobriquet deserved the description. However, the present tenants had known their predecessors and so had decided to keep the epithet, playful though it was.

The head of the house, Dougie Robertson, was a fisherman who hailed from the distant port of Stornoway. His wife, Madge, was one of the few surviving old-style "herring girls" from the tiny Isle of Barra. It was, as they were later to tell me, a pretty queer mix: he from Protestant Lewis and she from Castlebay, he from the north and she from the south; they'd met halfway during the course of a ceilidh, at Uiskevaig on Benbecula's east coast; thereafter they'd been inseparable—save that Madge herself had never set foot on Dougie's boat, for according to Hebridean lore that was not to court romance but to spell disaster. Anyhow, they had left behind them the chain of the Outer Isles and had eventually settled in Mallaig on the Scottish mainland.

To me on the evening of my arrival they accorded a degree of hospitality that was as undiluted as their whisky was strong. I got my hot bath; dined off Scotch broth, mutton stew, and as many potatoes as I could manage; drank as potent a tea as you could hope to sup; sampled a collection of homemade biscuits; and, to crown it all, accepted a fistful of shag from the man of the house. I tell you, when I sat back at last by the fire to relax and to light up a pipe I felt I had not an iota to complain of: rather, I'd discovered a hearth as might befit a lord.

That said, I myself felt a complete cad—returning their compliments with a diet of lies and a spurious appellation. I was appalled at my capacity for ambagious thinking. Just the same it would be patently unfair to expose them to any risk. It seemed better all round, then, if they remained ignorant of my identity and of the mess I was in.

At around eleven o'clock I went upstairs to my room. There, through the parted curtains, I looked out onto a moon three-quarters full and a night sky devoid of mist: the heavens themselves, though had an odd, cloudy appearance, with the milky moon set in a strange, luminous halo.

I slept soundly and awoke refreshed. I pulled back a pair of pink, floral drapes and looked out onto a fresh windswept vista of sea-swell and rolling cloud. Beyond the pewter-coloured waves lay the island of Skye, with the Cuillin Range and Red Hills rising prominent above the Sleat Peninsula. In the foreground a debacle of gulls shrieked and yelped over a remnant of the tide, while a young mother battled with her pushchair against a hard confronting breeze.

Downstairs Dougie and Madge had already prepared a welcoming fire at the hearth and a no less inviting spread on the dining-room table. I breakfasted well and—having glanced at the newspapers—decided to go out: from the press columns it appeared there had been no follow-up to the incident in Brighton, while with the Tory conference proceeding in Bournemouth and with the situation in the Gulf akin to a stalemate there seemed little cause for a lone and muddle-headed assassin to occupy any journalist. I should still need to go cautiously, but at least I'd not stumbled into the headlines.

I stepped down to the roadside and straightaway realised I'd no idea yet as to what course to follow, nor indeed any notion of what to do next—a by now all too lamentable state of affairs. Glancing at a nearby sign I perceived that an alternative to my going directly to the village—a cluster of shops and bars, nothing more—was to pursue a rough-looking track to the rear of Rum View and thereafter to wander once more upon a Scottish hill. Although my clothes had barely had time to dry I still favoured the latter course for it would give me a better opportunity to reflect, and—what was more—freed of my rucksack I might set the kind of pace best calculated to invigorate a man's mind.

I set off up by the side of a burn pushing my way between a riot of privet-hedge, late honeysuckle, and a mass of mauve and crimson fuchsia. Up several flagstones and onto a dirt and gravel track I began to review my present position. To begin with there was a fair chance that the *Queen of Sheba* would pass up the Sound of Sleat, the more so now that the wind was rising and, if I judged right, a storm lay in the offing. Next, a large haul of drugs was about to be switched—maybe to be taken on board—while it was likely that a small packet of Red Pepper would be passed into enemy hands, in all probability for Saddam Hussein. On the other hand, Ishbaal himself might adopt the leading part, seeing money was not so much his aim as bloodshed and destruction. A nihilist and a megalomaniac—that was the combination—and when the dual purpose had been achieved he would proclaim far and wide his inglorious triumph. To think I'd seen the villain even yesterday parading the hills! Such meditation fairly "stiffened the sinews" and "summoned the blood."

Though when it occurred to me I might at any moment bump into him I confess I shuddered at the prospect. All the same it was heartening to reflect that I was clearly in the right locale. The problem now centred on how soon matters would come to a head and on whether I alone could do anything to prevent them. Monty was dead and Malahide—ah yes, if only Malahide were with me. But the matter of the fact was simple: the fellow was not, and I should therefore have to manage without him.

Furthermore, as far as the drugs were concerned, Monty had speculated the connection would take place within the next seven days—now less than a week's time. It appeared, too, a most opportune moment. A bleak bit of mountain loch was hardly the focus of attention even in the most halcyon of seasons. Right now it must seem supremely irrelevant. Ought I to try directly to contact MQ1? I thought of it, certainly. But I'd no idea how to go about it while—in the light of my earlier escapade—my credentials seemed meagre indeed. The only tangible curiosity was one at least of the two brothers had been tracking me down apparently intent on doing me harm. Yet even that I couldn't prove though consciousness of it underscored the need to remain vigilant. I had to admit to myself over the past twenty-four hours I had given to that danger not a second's thought. I took out my telescope to scour the landscape and beyond the wide menacing swell. No suspicious yacht, no short-legged villains, no queer men from the City. The truth was the whole thing seemed utterly preposterous. With the wind in my face and the sound of bleating in my ears I had to concentrate even to convince myself.

By this stage I'd reached the summit of a crest and was looking down on a scattering of homes tucked into the sides of a poorly cultivated glen. Three or four of the residences were traditionally built, while about the same number were timber-built, being constructed from kits. One of the latter seemed to entertain pretensions towards styling itself a ranch, though in reality it stood out incongruously between a ruined cottage, a derelict caravan, and a scar of cliffside track around the glen's eastward flank. Actually the whole place had about it an air of desolation, much like a ghost town in a certain kind of Western.

I had turned to go back when my gaze alighted on a small gate standing a short distance to my right. From there there seemed to be a subsidiary pathway climbing higher and further away from the habitation below. If Ishbaal were determined to go to ground then this might well be the route to his hideaway. I jumped the gate and took to the high places.

To begin with I pursued a gradient along the top of the aforementioned clachan; then I struck further inland, moving along a narrow pass and being careful as I went to check the steeper terrain above me. Now and then would I hobble or stumble among the ubiquitous wiry roots, in the boulders and in the fading bracken. At length I came out at a vantage point some half a mile to the north of Loch an Nostarie. I had rounded the breast of a hill and could see several knolls and staggered features to the ground further east. Cheerless and inhospitable though the place seemed, the air itself was so sharp, the remoteness such an intoxicant to my spirits, that I was treasuring every minute of it.

I decided to bear more to the north and so retain a measure of height above the sodden floor of the mire. I zigzagged between sheep-tracks, finding before long I was wading through a patch of heather as rich in pinks and purples as ever I'd seen. There was the wild Irish heath, bundle after bundle of common ling, and here and there a broad swathe of bell heather. Occasionally I would stoop down to inspect the variety of the species apparently without colour, bearing the quality of white. In most cases, though, this signalled merely the plant's immature growth, and, on closer viewing, revealed the colour purple lower down: and, on at least one occasion, some invasive euphrasy likewise distracted me. I did alight on the genuine thing eventually, however, and pushed a tuft of it in my pocket as a harbinger of good fortune.

After a while, I found myself looking down toward a large, square, sheep pound—over the walls of which several fleeces had been strewn in piles. Then I heard a dog begin to bark and noticed subsequently it was racing towards me. The occasion seemed ripe to retrace my steps.

It was not long before I'd once more made my way to the original path—designated "The Circular Walk"—and was heading back in the direction of the Robertsons' cottage. There were some far-reaching views to be had of both Rum and Eigg as well as of a number of fishing boats struggling against the wind. Just beginning to spit in my face were the first few drops of rain. All in all I judged there to be a fair old gale brewing up and I started to contemplate a hearty lunch with increasing devotion.

After the meal was done Dougie switched on his radio to obtain the latest shipping forecast. It was an ancient instrument—an old "wireless" from the fifties I should say—which, from the bright sheen of its casing, had clearly been well maintained. Even so it crackled and whistled erratically, so that making out the broadcast was not at all easy. This did not trouble the seasoned fisherman, who in any case tuned in to seek verification rather than obtain information having already determined the prospective conditions from his own appraisal of the elements. According to Madge, Dougie had only ever erred once, and that was on the day the lifeboat had been summoned to Inverie during an inclement Hogmanay: even then he'd simply miscalculated on the side of caution, predicting a severe gale when the most that ensued was a measure on the Beaufort scale of force five. We listened intently: westerly, seven to force nine; later, north, storm force ten; rain—visibility, moderate to poor.

"Wass I no telling you?" commented my host. "It is not a day at all to go to the fishing. Indeed it is not. No, no. No fishing boats today.

And not for a few days yet, if I be the judge of it. You were the wise one, Mr. Gormally, when you stravaiged afore noon."

Incidentally, Dougie Robertson, besides being a skilled prognosticator of the weather, was also something of an expert in the game of chess. This I was to find to my cost on three separate occasions—during which time the storm outside blackened the sky while the wind rose rattling the glass window, blowing tiny gobs of soot down into the fireplace. I had once been a fair player myself, so it was fun to be reminded of how to "skewer" one's opponent or to make "forks" or to position one's knights to command the maximum of squares; that, as well as such arcane facts as not being able to "castle" if one's king traversed a square "checked" by one's adversary, or, again, the sometimes forgotten trick of *en passant*. This last, as the reader shall discover, was to be of special value when later I took on an opponent of more sinister persuasion. For the present I was reassured by Dougie's insistence that my game was improving, though also relieved when his attention came to be demanded elsewhere.

Before he left, however, I found myself in an idle moment standing by the window, and there –in a slight interlude in the weather's deterioration—looking out towards the harbour. The wash at the sea's edge had lost its smooth coalescence and slopped and broke heavily on the shore with increasing persistence. Some of the smaller boats and craft were starting to buck and bounce on the choppy waves, while beyond the breakwater the wind blew spindrift across scudding crests and the sea's current seemed set in a powerful race down the long dark sound.

Somewhere in the foreground, the mail boat, *The Little Hebrides*, was still at anchor. It would need to be tied up beside the fishing vessels closer to the pier. I watched a man on its decks, busy with the boat's gear and with tackle for the dinghy. He was a tallish fellow dressed in an oversuit and with a blue woollen bobble-hat planted on his head. He moved about the boat, for all the urgency of the hour, with such deft grace and such sureness of purpose that he seemed to be less the vessel's temporary attendant than some integral and moving part, as if somehow his absorption in the task made him belong to the very identity of the boat itself: its soul or vital spark.

I chanced to observe something of the kind to my host, but was suddenly taken aback when he spat vigorously into the burning coals. Seeing the look on my face he promptly explained himself.

"Ach well, Mr. Gormally, you will haf to forgiff me. The man you speak of, he that is seeing to *The Little Hebrides*, Angus John is his name. Effery-time I sets eyes on him I thinks of his daughter, the youngest—Catriona—and effery-time I thinks on her I remembers my age and that neffer again will I enjoy such beauty. If only I was younger, eh? Ach, but what's the use o' speakin'?"

"Now, Dougie, I hope you are not pestering poor Mr. Gormally with all that awfu' talk o' yours. There's important paperwork for you to see to, as I think you well know."

"Aye, aye, woman. I know, right enough."

So saying the not-entirely penitent husband repaired, hesitatingly, to the back room. Madge, meanwhile, had begun to ply me with tea and scones and—having eyed me with an unnervingly knowing look—put it to me straight: "You're not married, are you, Mr. Gormally? You will be going to the ceilidh, then?"

Quite apart from the obvious mess I was in, I am bound to say the prospect of a large and noisy gathering in a smoke-filled hall—with inebriate revellers making whoopee in dervish-like and esoteric reels, adrift in alcohol-induced mirth—did absolutely nothing to uplift me. Quite the reverse, it depressed me. I should be the proverbial "duck out of water," for I have no patience with that sort of thing.

"What time will it begin?" I queried.

"Oh, not till the bars have closed. Eleven thirty will be soon enough."

The advice duly given, I was left alone with my thoughts. They quickly turned to Freya. I knew it was ludicrous but how I wished she were here, here to remind me of my more familiar world, here to talk to, here...oh simply to *be* with. Then I decided to parcel-up the book on flowers I'd bought the previous Friday. After all, my niece's birthday was in two days' time. I should not, naturally, indicate my identity by putting a signature to it. On the other hand, by underlining certain letters I could convey the simple message, "Unavoidably detained. Do nothing." They themselves doubtless would guess the sender, though I reckoned I could count on their having enough wisdom to comply with the stricture. If the package fell into enemy hands—and there was no reason to suppose it would—no connection should be made between its source and a certain absent-minded major.

At the hour of six o'clock I resolved to go out. *The Little Hebrides* had by now disappeared from her earlier moorings and the evening itself was cast in as dirty a mixture of dun and grey as a person could imagine. It was horribly wet and an atrocious gale was blowing from the west. Yet the truth of the matter was that I welcomed the distraction of having a task—however mundane or prosaic—that I could actually perform; besides, I could not at this juncture envisage even so much as a thimbleful of soup.

By the way, the blind man's greatcoat turned out to be a great godsend; for, by wearing it and by hanging ferociously onto my cloth cap, I made the Post Office more or less devoid of the anticipated soaking. Afterwards I found my way into one of Mallaig's ubiquitous bars. It was, considering the evening, surprisingly full. About ten men stood at the counter, another dozen or so were sitting in twos and threes round tables, and a couple of visitors in the centre were watching an unusually tedious game of pool. On the wall opposite the bar hung a huge glass case in which was pinioned impressively a stuffed and open-winged gannet.

I walked over to a space at the bar and there ordered a large whisky mac. Above me in the opposite corner was a television set emitting a barely audible broadcast. By the sombre look on the diplomat's face, not to say impassioned countenance on the American President's, I judged there to be no let up in the crisis in the Gulf. It looked as if war was inevitable. Only a certain and former Prime Minister seemed truly intent on preserving the peace; for, as he seemed to be saying, it was impossible to engage diplomatically with one's adversaries if no negotiations were to be permitted. Besides, to my way of thinking the world's acquiescence in Saddam Hussein's fearful reign—and in particular his protracted build-up of weaponry—allowed the allies only the most tenuous of footing on any higher moral ground. An inveterate smoker might plead his cancer be removed promptly, yet even he—tragic enough though his plight was—had often to take some measure of responsibility for the genesis of his illness. Perhaps the valuable lesson had to be learned at last—that prevention, in matters military as well as personal, is always better than some prodigal or piecemeal cure. That said, if the conflict came I had no doubt that any operation would be brought about through surgical precision and an immensity of courage.

Yet how ill it behoved me at this stage to entertain such thoughts. I would have been better off acknowledging my former penchant for the grape and the grain, the more so as on three or four occasions at Axminster I'd discovered to my amazement—not to mention that of my colleagues—that I'd a capacity to consume alcohol which verged on the reckless. How this came about I couldn't say, though Monty had advised me I'd no difficulty in holding my own at undergraduate parties, whilst it seemed in Northern Ireland—after defusing a bomb—I'd downed a gill-bottle in one go! But on that evening in Mallaig, with a reminder of Saddam's intent constantly to hand, and with the knowledge I bore of Ishbaal and his henchmen, I should surely have known better.

Alas, I did not. As the evening wore on I began to fall in with some of the regulars, a less and less stable set of cronies anxious to argue about everything save, surprisingly, whose turn it was next to purchase a drink. Their talk at the outset was about fishing areas off

Rum and around Sleat Point; then it changed to a discussion on depleted fishing stocks in the Minches, took in en route environmental protection-measures against oil spillages, returned to the possibility of a new roll-on-roll-off ferry, became a trifle misty as someone recalled a former cook aboard the Loch Bheag, and lastly, while the semblance of sense still obtained, the probable construction company of the proposed Skye Bridge. (Although not everyone agreed on the latter's design, it appeared at the time that the tender was to go to the firm Morrisons & Co.) At one point in the colloquy I became distracted by a youth standing at the pool table: he was boasting how he had spotted the royal yacht sailing into a neighbouring sea-loch; but, as his friend chipped in with the aside—"So, what's new then?"—I let it pass.

There were also that night two exchanges of a rather heated kind that threatened to disrupt proceedings and to bring matters to a close through an out-an'-out brawl. One of these quarrels had to do with regulations governing the mesh-size of a certain kind of fishing net, while the other centred on whether or not pollution was being caused by placing fish cages off Stoul bay. (I recognised this last place from my initial scrutiny of the local map.) However on neither of these occasions did an actual fight take place. It transpired that the down-in-the-mouth publican—who happened to be on duty at that hour—was better acquainted with his clientele than is many a physician with his registered patients. In the first instance, he simply desisted from polishing the glass he was holding—whilst at the same time muttering inaudibly under his breath—and in the second, dourly and casually spoke out at the offender, "Duncan, are you going to pay for this round?" It seemed a most impressive performance, calling to mind the conductor of some large symphony orchestra who is able to halt the progress of his players with a mere tap of his baton.

Only at a little before eleven did I hear anything said about a ceilidh. It was around then one or two of the younger element began to depart the premises—each holding in his hand a clutch of cans or a hefty half-bottle. It was around then, too, that I became aware of what one might put on record as the most infectious and consuming laughter that anyone could hear. It testified so completely to the enjoyment of the yarn—and was so delightfully complemented by a creasing of torso and face—that it seemed the entire person was in utter transport at the joke being told. The man himself was standing beside another for whom a certain epithet, depicting the state of intoxication—to wit, "steaming"—was patently, if amusingly, appropriate. When the first of these, the taller, eventually stood up properly I saw it was none other than Angus John of *The Little Hebrides*. By contrast, a man I'd espied earlier—sitting by himself and drinking a steady stream of brandies—remained as grave and sober-looking as an aphoristic judge. The same one was wearing a small, close-fitting balaclava rolled up over his eyes. Before I should take my leave of the western seaboard that same grim figure would attempt to exterminate me with the seven-point-six-two-millimetre fire of a "gimpy" machine gun.

For the present I had a different problem to tackle in the person of Henrik Meyer. At some time after eleven I'd procured a half bottle of a well-known whisky and had more or less made up my mind to attend the ceilidh. I confess I had found my tongue, regained my confidence and now was game not merely for a dalliance with tartan but even, wondrous to admit, a highland jig. I got as far as the door. Only it was not the door that was filling the frame but a bald-headed giant. His hands, moreover, were like shanks of mutton and he had a scar on his forehead like the brand of Cain.

He flung his arms round me as if he'd found a long lost friend whilst declaiming to all and sundry that I was his "bosom buddy." I don't know if it was apparent to my erstwhile companions, but I had the distinct impression that the soles of my feet were no longer adhering to the floor of the establishment. Once outside the Norwegian steered me away from the thin trek to the hall and with the aid of a friend manhandled me speedily in the direction of the pier. I caught a glimpse of the latter in a shaft of lamplight: he had the face of a taxi-driver I'd recently had cause to remember, for he had a slightly rivelled countenance with thick, silver sideburns.

Now that I was in the cold night air with my face to the wind I found I was surprisingly alert for one who'd just downed the better part of a bottle of "the cratur." The sight of my new companions, moreover, wonderfully concentrated the mind. I decided to go along peacefully—in so far as I could be said to decide anything—and see whether I couldn't turn this remarkable event to my own advantage. Exactly what notion I had in view I no longer comprehend. I imagine I hoped—if I were fortunate—to elicit further information regarding the intentions of my adversary.

With hindsight I perceive my judgement was reckless and my thinking without sense. What sobered me up at last was the moment the twin took my half-bottle from me, smashed it against a piece of railing and then advanced its glassy remnants in the direction of my face. I squinted to right and to left but could see nothing but piles of fish boxes stacked higher than a man standing. With the Norwegian behind me I was well and truly trapped.

Fortunately for me it wasn't Henrik Meyer's style to savage an opponent's countenance. Instead he beckoned to his aid to drop his provisional weapon and commanded the man in halting English that he empty a share of the contents of a nearby crate. This turned out to be a square box crammed to the top with chips of ice. The Norwegian—who by now had his forefinger and thumb pressed firmly upon my scalene muscle—pushed me to my knees and swiped me heavily across my dextral jaw. Momentarily stunned, I was then unable to prevent the twin from kicking me forcibly into the discarded ice; thereupon almost without realising it I found I'd been stuffed into the upturned container like a cargo of fish. It was black, freezing—almost impossible to breathe. I tried to shift the thing but had somehow not the strength. I fancied that those two men—whose total weight probably lay between thirty and forty stones—must be seated squarely atop the container.

They had done their job well, moreover, because I had ice in my mouth and ice up my nose. I had just begun to push upward however—for a last do-or-die attempt to get free—when I found myself rolling backwards through a debacle of icy splinters and an uncomfortable imbroglio of clattering boxes. What was more it was no alien thug I discovered then standing by, but a familiar looking figure from the evening of my arrival. He was looking at me with a whimsical mixture of mischief and concern.

"Are y'al-reecht, pal? Ye two friends, they haf made off. And ye know all I did here wass to push this wee trolley into yon waal o' boxes—though granted, I pushed kinda hard!"

My saviour was none other than the self-styled porter-cum-tourist-officer who had so helpfully assisted me in securing accommodation. Without thinking I pulled from my pocket a wet clump of bank notes and insisted he accept it. He did not quarrel with this but gave a nod in the direction of the station, "The big fella—he went that way."

"The other?" I gasped.

"It wass to the pier. Ach well, now, but it iss a shame, a shame I haf not the strength that I used to. Ye'll pardon me—these days though I take a wee half o' something first thing—in preference to mi porringer o' meal. Ye best leef mi the while. Cheerio the now."

So saying my earthly redeemer went hobbling off to proffer his weight to the scrum at the bar. For my part I staggered similarly towards the end of the pier.

Mercifully the storm had by now much abated, though the wind remained blustery and the tide's ebb complete signalled the commencement of a fresh flow. The masts of the sailing boats still tilted sharply whilst the waters below looked far from steady. I myself was feeling more determined than ever and what with that and my undeserved reprieve I launched myself forward with an absurd vigour.

Besides, as my rescuer had so starkly put it, the "big fella," had moved off.

I caught sight of my foe as he disappeared over the end of the jetty. I hurried towards the same point and stood for a moment directly above him. He had loitered though in his descent of a set of steps—a series of iron rungs projecting sharply from the wall—and was only now setting foot to the gunwale of the nearest trawler. I reckoned it was a drop of some eighteen feet to the deck, yet I'd the curious sensation I'd done the thing before—though not, I grant, onto a potentially slippery camber motioning in a swell.

I took a chance. I think if I'd been sober I should never have tried it. As it was, I barely missed the bulwark and crashed awkwardly into the boat's main hatch. It must have looked bad, too, for my opponent stopped a second to see if I would get up. But I did, and was soon after him.

We lumbered forward as best we could crossing decks and jumping hastily from one boat to the next. It was a comfort to recall that most of the respective crews were preoccupied at the ceilidh: hopefully we would not be observed and could sort things out by ourselves. I remained anxious all the same as to what the swarthy fellow in front intended to do.

When I found out moreover I felt every bit the fool. For just as I lunged towards him—he was standing with his back to the fo'c'sle—he produced from his right-hand pocket a Browning automatic. So, I was to be shot—clean, simple, effective. I need anticipate none of the scrupulous refinements of Henrik Meyer. That this fellow meant it was quite evident.

At the same time, however, he had positioned himself badly for the balance required, his soles resting on a loose piece of board on which I too had set foot. I was now about a metre away from the man and was certain that the wood beneath us had been unevenly secured. Accordingly, as I stepped back—slightly and to one corner—my adversary was just sufficiently startled to lose for a second his fixity of purpose. In that same instant I swung my left foot into action and the deadly pistol went flying through the air. It dropped with a splash into the turn of the tide and so put an end to an easy victory. For my part I should after all need to grapple with my foe.

To my surprise, however, the wretched fellow stole the initiative: he raised himself over the rim of the bulwark and dropped forthwith to the sea. This was a nuisance: I was no swimmer and quite terrified of drowning. I'd no choice therefore but to watch my first real success dwindle by degrees, each fall of my opponent's hand increasing the distance between us. Then I noticed a dinghy.

It was a smallish affair tied up astern the last boat as if intended to trail it. I swung myself onto the rope and eased my way down towards it. Very soon I was rowing towards my enemy. Though progress be haphazard I'd little doubt I'd reach him before long.

It was at that moment of presumed victory I noticed something was wrong. The man was not making for the nearest section of shore but striking out for the rocks on the far side of the bay. For the first time I was forced to admire the sheer pluck of this rough dastard. The shifting current would be difficult to negotiate and the water itself shockingly cold.

I was only about six yards off when I saw to my alarm the fellow was not so much swimming as threshing about aimlessly in the deeper water. He was having trouble, too, in keeping his head above the waves.

"Hold on, man!" I yelled into the wind. "I am right behind you! I'll be with you in a second!"

I am not a weak person and can say that despite the rigours of the evening I put my best efforts into hastening that dinghy towards my hapless foe. Yet, when I turned round next there was not a sign of him. I searched and searched in every direction. But there was nothing—not a head, not a hand, not a rumour of life.

My feelings were strangely mixed: I'd lost an enemy it was true, but on the other hand I'd also lost the chance to gain further information on the *Sheba's* whereabouts. Moreover, as I looked all about me into the roll and pitch of the tide neither was my regret devoid of pity. He would have killed me, I know. Yet I could not envy him the manner of his going.

For the moment, however, I became anxious to secure my own safety lest the truculent sea claim her second victim. Her mood, indeed, was fast returning to an earlier, wilder temper that made the rowing of the dinghy an increasingly cumbersome matter. A mishap of some sort seemed ever more likely.

When eventually it came I'd been striving hard to keep the tiny craft afloat the crests but had suddenly drawn back too forcibly and missed entirely the surface of the water. The right oar produced a horrible juddering sound and before I'd resumed my position slipped the rowlock to become one more piece of flotsam redundant in the sea. At the same moment the boat's stem caught such a switch that it got drawn into a trough, while with the next rise I myself was rolled over under the weight of the dinghy. To my considerable amazement I came out of that crashing chaos standing bruised but shoulder high and with all the force of the tide propelling me to the shore. I was half-hurtled onto the shingle and for a brief while lay stunned and scratched on that broken beach. When I had my wits collected and my legs sufficiently planted I endeavoured to reach the road encircling the bay. I found—again to my astonishment—that I was staring straight into the face of Rum View, with its two firelit windows peering at me as might a pair of welcoming eyes.

I've little personal recollection of what happened thereafter, but as far as I can tell it ran something like this. For a start, when the door opened it was not face to face that I confronted the gaze of Madge Robertson, but upwards from the doorstep of her cottage. Next, I woke up in a room where shadows flickered around the walls and where a roaring fire was ablaze in the hearth. Dougie was dozing in a chair by the window, while I myself lay supine in some sort of truckle bed. Beside me was a table—carefully set out with a cloth of white linen, a jug of water, a glass of the same, a tot of whisky and the rest of the gill in an adjacent bottle.

I woke again when the shadows had slowed and the blaze dimmed. I could hear the roar of wind in the funnel of the chimney, and, on propping myself up for a drink, noticed a piece of old carpet and a pair of discarded slates had been placed there in front of the grate: that indeed was just as well as several bits of ember and soot lay here and there about the open fire. When I next awoke the curtains had been drawn and the glass slab in the window was being spattered, in fits and starts, by dollops of rain. The pane had a bright greyness to it and occasionally a pair of wings would pass its corner and I would hear the squawk of a frightened gull. Once I dreamt that Freya Boyesen came towards me in a nurse's uniform and that she bore in her arms a bowl of fruit: but, in the next second, the bowl was a bright platter bearing a silver, dome-like cover; yet, when the leaning surgeon—whose bare scalp was badly scarred—removed the top, there like the head of John the Baptist stared the face of my drowned opponent, bloodied and dripping wet.

When I was eventually able to manage some food, Madge prepared for me a portion of steamed fish and with it offered chunks of bread in boiled milk. It was invalid's fare, food fit for a child, but for the first thirty-six hours better suited than a king's ransom. To cheer me up, moreover, I remember being given advocaat—when I declined to take the whisky. Not once can I recall being interrogated. I do not believe the Robertsons put to me a single question.

On Wednesday morning, before Dougie came in to see to the fire, I sat up in bed listening to the gale. My head was clear, and I felt totally alert. However, Mr. Rufus Gormally, alias Walter Makin, alias Major Delman, had this further admission to make: he felt very guilty and very, very foolish.

CHAPTER 10

I Take The Burma Road

Not till I attempted to walk again did I realise the extent of my affliction. My right ankle was giving me gyp, my knees were swollen, my shoulder blades felt as though they'd been swiped by an iron bar, my ribs ached and my head swam. It was high time, all the same, to straighten the back and to keep a stiff upper lip. These people, the Robertsons, had put up a splendid show and I did not wish to disappoint them.

I decided to offer them at least an inkling of the truth. Yet I'd hardly delivered my first sentence when the man of the house interjected:

"Look now, Mr. Gormally. Yer business is yer own. We haf said nothink, and do not intend to."

He continued his theme slowly, with increasing deliberation.

"It is clear you got yersel' inna mess. But as a matter of fact I haf been in a few scraps missel' and neffer did take kindly to them that asked me why. Ye seem tae haf come through, and of that we're glad. And then there's our son, Ruairidh, he's awfu' like yersel' to look at. And he's somewhere—we dinna ken precisely where—somewhere in the Gulf. He's a pilot. Ye may be a Sassenach, Mr. Gormally, and he—I'm bound to say it—of the stronger blood, but I think that you and he wud hit it off chusst fine."

I could detect the emotion in his voice and felt right then I'd have given the world to have swapped places with his son. I felt an out and out cad. I looked him straight in the eye, put it to him bluntly that he and Madge deserved my genuine admiration and indeed that they'd every right to know more than I'd told them. To begin with my real name was Delman, Major Delman.

"There!" said Madge, as if she'd scored a bull's-eye. "Wass I no telling you? I said you were military, Mr. Delman—that is, I mean, Major. Well, well, now isn't that the thing."

"There's something else though," I put in, "which you also need to know. I'm wanted by the police. I'll not expose you to the risk of knowing why or what my purpose is or who's for or against. Only don't believe everything you read or hear and trust me when I say that my mission is vital and that you do a service not just for me but for the nation—for those like Ruairidh in fact who are ranged against Hussein."

That, as they say, fairly took the biscuit and the good wife in front of me had a handkerchief at her eyes. Her husband meanwhile spoke for them both.

"Well, Maechur, ye mus' stay chusst as long as ye need. Now, then, you will surely taak a dram."

I obliged the old gentleman and indeed felt the better for it. Then I fell to thinking about what my next move should be. It was clear I couldn't do anything very difficult or demanding for at least another day, and, since the weather was so atrocious, there could be little afoot on either Ishbaal's part or that of his cronies: they too would be delayed by the same severe gale, the same biting hail. On the other hand the *Queen of Sheba* would have to find shelter: in the prevailing conditions—with the storm now in the north—it was likely she would steer for a sheltered location somewhere between Mallaig and Lochalsh. I got out my map and soon decided she would not risk the waters of Sleat Sound but would make in all probability for Tarbert—lying on the south side of Loch Nevis—or else pass through the kyles there towards Camusrory. As long as the barometer gave its present reading neither side need make a move—although when things improved it was obvious my adversaries would waste little time. I should be ill advised, therefore, to be caught napping.

Ideally, what I should liked to have done was to make for the hills and there to follow the high ground abutting Loch Nevis. From such a vantage point I should have a fair prospect of any boats passing by and might even encounter my shameful foe. The drawback would be I should be adopting—in the face of a wise saw—only a single basket: if it fell my plans would be smashed and my mission come to naught. For all that, that was the case whereby I endeavoured to keep alight the flicker of hope. Had I not seen Ishbaal in this very vicinity? Had I not conquered at least one of my enemies? There was still, of course, the Norwegian to fear as well perhaps as the remaining twin. Hope I should have kindled into optimism if only I'd had a companion. It was the fact I was entirely on my own—and incommunicado accordingly—that was the chief bother. If I proved unsuccessful who would replace me? I and Malahide together might stand some chance, but working alone the task seemed set to defeat me.

There were moments, indeed, when the smouldering flax seemed well nigh quenched. The more so when I attempted to exercise my ankle. What if I were not—when the storm abated and the clouds shifted—sufficiently recovered? Of what use would I be tramping over the sort of ground designed to test even an Achilles perfected? Then again, how many would there be on board the *Queen of Sheba*? And how many would be posted to bring about the connection? What on earth did I consider one individual to be able to do?

At such times I would stare blankly into the hearth drawing comfort from its hypnotic effect and from the smoked narcotic of strong tobacco. Flames would twist and distort into a thousand shapes while my own imaginings rose and fell in fanciful conflicts or in a host of perceived encounters.

On Thursday morning it was clear that Dougie Robertson was worried. He was pacing up and down the hallway starting to get in Madge's way and tugging at his shocks of grey hair.

"What is it, Dougie?" I asked.

"Ach, it is nothing…"

"Nonsense, man. Out with it—"

"Ach well, Maechur, it is simple enough. This house of ours, the truth is, it is not our own. Yet, in another way, it iss. Ye see it stands on croft-land, and the generations of crofters whose patch includes our solum here, they haf come to an end. The last tenant died intestate a full six months back. Beliefin' it then to be our entitlement, we wrote to the landlord and asked him if we could purchase the site. Ye see, we neffer paid anythink. No, no rent, nothink at all like that. We wass secure in an accepted tradition. But the landlord, he hass refused. Aye, and he is going to put in one of his factor's stoogies, and very like it is that he'll buy up the place lock, stock and barrel. And then, ye see—and this is really the point—we'll no be able to leave the house to Ruairidh. And then there's Madge, poor dear; she does not take kindly to this at all. It's a sign, says she—a portent. We're no going to get our house because there will be no-one to inherit it after wiff gone. Aye, that's watt she says! That Ruairidh's no comin' back!"

My brave host faltered. For a moment I thought he had finished, but then he picked up a pile of papers from the table and resumed his lament with renewed vigour.

"And the shame of it iss, ye see, that Ruairidh wass workin' on these here peppers. He said we must write to the Land Court. He got forums—and docoo-ments—and this new book here. Then he got called, and the next day wass gone. I thought I could see to it missel', but I wass foolish to think that. I canna. Really, Maechur, I dinna ken what tae dae."

I could have howled when I looked at that proud fisherman: he bore the scandal of his suffering with a courage and a dignity I have seldom met. I answered him immediately.

"Now look here, Dougie, this is what's to be done. You must let me go through these papers and permit me to see what case you have in law. I must warn you though, if there isn't a legal case to be made then by itself the principle of fairness will not be sufficient. Your accepted tradition may not be enough, either. On the other hand, it seems your son knew what he was about and he believed you had a chance. So, there's hope. Now then, with your permission I'm going to take this material to the back room and there go through it with a fine-tooth comb. If there's writing to be done it may be I could—again if you'll allow me—lend a hand in whatever application you need to submit. All right then, I don't want to hear another word about this until I've had at least six hours. Madge can bring me some tea and biscuits, but apart from that I'll brook no interruptions. Is that understood? Good. Then I'll see what's to be done."

On an occasion such as this—when it's the despair of the other person that's the problem—I often find it easier to be hopeful. Maybe I have a tendency too to confront difficulty with a certain boldness. All the same the truth of the matter was I didn't know whether my hosts had a valid case or merely wished that they had. Still, I'd had to deal with some tricky customers at Axminster and was no stranger myself to the mumbo-jumbo of litigation. Besides I owed the Robertsons a not inconsiderable debt and believed in their integrity one hundred per cent. Maybe I was applying a salve to my conscience too, because instead of carrying the flag in the Gulf here was I nursing a few bruises and more or less falling asleep on the job. It came as a relief and a distraction then to be dutifully employed.

At first I could make nothing of it. It was easy enough to determine the grounds of the application: the Robertsons' status constituted that of non-rent paying cottars and the Crofting Reform (Scotland) Act of 1976 outlined their right to a conveyancing. The problem lay in proving their occupation of the cottage was carried out with the due knowledge and consent of the landlord. That the latter was necessary was clearly indicated in the latest textbook (by MacCuish and Flyn) which dealt with the subject. The authors referred the reader to various test cases which made this apparent. Ruairidh had done his homework well, for he'd obtained copies of these from the Scottish National Library in Edinburgh.

I worried poor Madge in the late afternoon by asking whether or not she had consulted with a solicitor. It evidenced my own increasing anxiety.

"Solicitors, is it? Indeed! The problem ye see, Major, is this. Any solicitor at the Fort—or at Portree; it's nae different on Skye—is beholden tae the estate. If it's business they be wantin', they canna go against the factor. Still, Dougie tried one poor cretur, but he only says at the end of an hour that we might be squatters. Squatters! I ask ye now, Major—what kinda help is that? Solicitor! Ha! Some solicitor that!"

Unfortunately, if the Robertsons' occupation of their cottage was—so to speak—in the face of the landowner, squatters might well have been the appropriate term. Furthermore, it seemed the only correspondence they'd had with the estate was two years earlier when they'd requested financial help for the erection of a fence. This had been turned down, while the factor himself had categorically stated that they were not "tenants."

However, the more I read over the wording of the statute—and subsequent judgements of the Land Court—the more persuaded I became that there existed a distinction between "tenancy" and "occupancy," and that the latter was not in fact being denied by the estate. Was it possible, I wondered, to contend that the estate had "acquiesced"? After all, the Robertsons' position had not been properly clarified. But it wasn't until I'd come across a case that was rather obscure—it dealt with different types of "disposition" and, in particular, the two designated feu and simpliciter—that a speck of light began to dawn at the end of the tunnel. It seemed from this hearing—held by the way before an assembly of the Full Court—that, in the light of the 1976 Act already mentioned, the status of the crofter had changed in one significant sense: that, whereas prior to this date it had appeared to be that of a vassal within a feuing system, it had now been upgraded to that of "part-owner" with the system itself being deemed outmoded and emasculated; it seemed the main argument centred on the new right of the crofter to purchase his croft, thereby putting him on a stronger footing with regard to the landlord; again, the latter had little to do with permanent improvements whilst the former was now entitled to a share in any development value.

You may take it from all this that my tea went cold and any biscuits chiefly acted as an aid to concentration. The long and short of it, after much rumination, was the owner to whom the "crave" had to be made was not simply the landlord but also the tenant of the croft. It was clear in the Robertsons' case that the latter had approved the occupancy for many years—had, to use the jargon, "known and consented"—that there could be no question therefore of Dougie and Madge being mere "squatters." In their favour, again, was the fact that their application had been made relatively early; before, that is, any executor had been appointed to transfer the tenancy.

All in all things were looking up, and sometime after ten at night I joined Dougie for a pipe and a dram and conveyed to him my thoughts. I shall not embarrass myself by setting forth his effusive response. Let us just say it did me more credit than I deserved and that the Land Court had still to approve my argument. Neither of us hurried to our beds, but when we turned in at last for the night we both slept well.

The next day the storm diminished somewhat with the wind dying down to a modest gale. Even beyond the harbour the prospect was improving with the Isle of Skye now standing forth more darkly—a solid grey under the blanketing of umbrageous cloud stretched above. Then sometime around noon a thin blaze of sunlight shot through the heavy nimbus and gave to the mercurial wash of sea a stroke of sage. I nodded towards the barometer—the instrument was registering a minor change—and the chief forecaster in the house was inclined to agree. It looked as if the wind was dropping and that a drier spell would shortly ensue.

"Aye, and more than that, Maechur," my host added grimly, "I should say we're in for a fine and bonny autumn, leastwise for a week or two."

"You don't sound too pleased, all the same. I should say it's been long enough in the coming."

"Na, na, it's yersel' I'm thinkin' of. I heard news this mornin' which may not be tae ye likin'. I wass taaking to the diver's son, early on an' doon at the pier. He wass tellin' me that a dour-lookin' fella in a jersey-hat had been snoopin' aboot, and not by hissel', either. Seems an' all there wass sam sort of o-fishal. He didna think it wass the polis, but he wassna sure."

My face, I fear, blanched at the information, while the bearer of the tidings grew more solemn yet.

"Aye, I'm afeard so, Maechur. Ye see—though ye may no agree with the point of my phew—I'd say until now ye haf bin kinda lucky. No man wanna gets soakit to the skin if he can helpit! For you though this weather's been chusst fine. But it's changin' now, and to speak mi mind I dinna think it's tae y' advantage. Folk'll be comin' and goin' and then chusst think about all the visitors here. Aye, think on that. There's Peggy next door, she's no been round for full six days. That's another peace that'll break! Ye ken that yer welcome, Maechur, but it's yersel' I'm thinkin' of."

He was right, of course. As soon as the weather lifted it would be business as usual. Although I could not know the identity of those two men it was not improbable that they had been told to observe me, and, then again, it was not impossible that their orders contained some other, more severe stricture: once they knew my whereabouts my own lot would look increasingly forlorn. In any case I needed to progress further up the loch, for it was unlikely my enemies would rendezvous in Mallaig itself.

In the afternoon I again got out my map and pointed to a tiny square located in a bay; it was situated about a mile east of the hamlet of Mallaig Bheag that I'd earlier seen from the higher terrain. Apart from what I took to be a nearby outhouse—a barn or boatshed—there appeared to be very little there. It was connected to its neighbouring bay by what looked like a hillward-track or cliff-side path: either way it appeared to traverse a steep section of the two hundred and three metre uprise of Ben Cruach. I guessed I'd seen its approach when I'd spotted a way carved out along the skirt of the hill—above what had struck me as a disproportionately sized villa.

My host informed me I was pointing to Aridhghlinne, or, in English, the Shieling in the Glen. The track itself—known locally as the Burma Road—had been blasted out of the rock in the early sixties, an undertaking carried out by the military. Soldiers had encamped about the eastern side of the valley, and for days on end the whole glen had reverberated with noise while great explosions—one after the other—had been expertly detonated. At the end it had fallen to a former occupant, one Ecky Donaldson, to translate the rudimentary way into a proper path. This he had done through the construction of low walls, the digging-in of drains and the tunnelling of culverts in strategic places. He had carried out the venture, moreover, single-handedly. Even before that he had devised a mile-long footpath of stones set to follow the shoreline some hundreds of feet below—but where users here and there today were left to the mercy of the tides. Before that Ecky Donaldson had tramped his journey the hard way, trudging manfully high over the gaunt ridge of the hill. The army's visit certainly proved to be a great blessing—and one not simply restricted to the forging of a track, for when they had departed the engineers left behind them sheet upon sheet of corrugated iron: what had temporarily been employed for the soldiers' accommodation would henceforward be taken by local crofters for their own use—whether to give roof to a byre, restore a broken pen or block an awkward hole under a wire fence. And all the while the way to Aridhghlinne would lie open to both keen walker and casual visitor.

This last point did not, naturally, escape my attention. Taken as a whole though I felt drawn to Aridhghlinne, for it would provide me with an easy access to Mallaig—should I require it—while at the same time permit me to make whatever sorties necessary along the southern flank of the loch. I could, I told myself, successfully remain out of sight during the day while at night stow away unnoticed in one of the nearby outhouses. I asked Dougie if he knew who inhabited the main dwelling.

"As queer a customer as ye could hope tae find. He iss Scottish, but he's no one of us—that's one think definite sure. He is cleffer, too, one o' yer in-telly-gentsia. Aye, so he iss. But man, he's daft as a coot! He's fond of the uisge beatha, an' all. Yet he's kind too, I'd say that for 'im. He wouldna see anyone stuck. As a matter of fact he might be of help to yersel, Maechur—if ye haf a mind to trust 'im."

"His name?" I queried

"There's no many that knows for sure. Ye cud try Roderick Farquhar Mackinnon, and ye cud be right an' all. But round here he goes by the name of Mac. Aye, that's all."

I made no decision then but asked Dougie if I might borrow a couple of blankets were the need to arise. In the event he found me a sleeping bag stashed away near the eaves of the roof. That would suit me even better since I could properly trust then to my own resources. However there was no question whatever of my going immediately. I had first to put my knee and ankle to the test.

Later that afternoon I put myself through some exercises in the back room. I found that while my shoulders still ached I had not overall lost much of my strength: indeed, I was feeling in my muscles a growing need for exertion. I decided to go out when it grew dark and to make tentative steps along the road to Mallaig Bheag.

After I'd dined that evening I took from my rucksack the cap, jacket and trousers that lay folded within and added to these an old but still thick sweater which Madge had insisted was fit "chusst for chumpple." Then, when darkness had fallen, I set off under strict instructions to return by nine-thirty and on no account to be later than that: thereafter I should encounter members of the village community making for one or other of Mallaig's bars. This was after all a Friday night and so a traditional time to quench a man's thirst.

I recall a blackish evening that night with the bay still mirroring an ominous sky and with it a cold breeze stiffening from the north. All the same it had at least stopped raining. I looked towards the pier and there noticed a considerable display of lights shining over the ferry-terminal and over the serried vessels of the local fishing fleet. On the road itself a few street lamps illumined the way as I turned my back on the village and ascended a gentle slope along the eastern side of the bay.

I came out eventually beside a row of semi-detached bungalows, the uniformity of which suggested initial ownership by the Council. Smoke issued forth from several of the chimneys and in the garden of one of them a housewife was taking in her washing; in another, a sheep was nibbling at some grass—the front gate lying loose on its hinges: at the door of that dwelling three scrawny cats were quarrelling over a tin of fish.

The air was wondrously clear and fresh while mixed in with the heady odour of ozone was that thick, oily smell which tells of the return of boats to the harbour pier. It was an intoxicating combination. Having been cooped up for the past four days I felt the sudden thrill of freedom and had a compulsion to break out into a dash. However, I remembered that this was (so to speak) a test run only and so duly disciplined myself to a steady, careful promenade.

It was not long before I'd left behind the houses and was stomping methodically up a tall and surprisingly severe brae. I had put behind me the last of the street lamps and now passed into almost total darkness. When I reached the top I could make out a narrow strip of lights on the far side of the loch. This I knew from Dougie to be the small habitation of Inverie. It looked quiet and remote, tucked fast beneath Knoydart's deep and towering hills.

The near half of the hamlet of Mallaig Bheag was concealed in the pitch of night, but on the other side a garish dazzle of light blazed about the hillside and I could make out the beginning of the track to Aridhghlinne which I knew now to be the Burma Road. Above the receding hill a patch of sky opened in the cloud and in it a single star winked and shone. I took it as a good omen and might then and there have continued my progress. The sound of a dog barking and the noise of a nearby motor, however, brought me to my senses. I turned round and made my way back slowly in the direction of Rum View.

I was pleased all the while to discover my ankle caused me only the slightest difficulty, and, as for my knee, I was scarcely sure which one had prompted the pain. Twice during my return I passed a lone inhabitant sloping quietly down the road; in each case I contrived to walk along the opposite pavement, though in the instance of the second—a lanky fellow with the stub of a cigarette cowled in his hand—I grunted an echo to his salutatory, "Ay, ay," before quickening my pace.

My hosts were keen, naturally, to hear how I'd fared. It seemed that Peggy their neighbour had called in and that earlier she'd seen somebody leaving the house. Madge'd maintained it had only been a stranger, but it had prompted a probing and persistent line of questioning. Peggy was only persuaded at last after four cups of tea and an imaginary long-distance call of Dougie's due "any minute the now." They were relieved to hear all had gone well and were reassured both my legs were in good working order.

That night I dreamt of Freya. I was again strolling up the slope of the brae, only this time it was during daylight and there were primroses in the verges and tiny birds calling in an ampersand of newly-planted trees. Coming down the hill—in a style that was almost slow-motion—was a bright red bicycle with a young woman sitting astride its saddle. She wore a loose flower-patterned dress with a blouson of brown velvet. Her hair was flaxen and blowing in the wind. She had the refined and slightly angular countenance of the woman I most admired and to whom I felt increasingly attached. On the way up the gradient grew more difficult and I found myself pausing in the middle of the climb. It was then that she cycled by, Freya, giving me the sweetest possible smile. My heart began to beat with a strange heaviness; then I had the weird feeling of drowning in some unfathomable sadness. I turned. She had stopped at the bottom of the hill. She was waving goodbye. I turned once more to the front, to look ahead. At the top stood the limping figure of Ishbaal summoning me with a long, twisted finger. I spun round. Freya had gone. Then Ishbaal too disappeared and suddenly the brae was a gradient by Leighton Moss, and Monty was there diving for cover. A gun fired. Then I awoke.

I sat up in bed. My heart was pounding. How I detested this whole damnable affair. What in heaven's name was I doing up here? I should have been with my aunt at Winchester and by Freya's side—not here: here with these strange people in a rough landscape of sea and rock and in a dour, depressing climate. Freya! Freya! What could she be thinking? We had planned this holiday long ago. What was more—were I to be truthful—I'd even considered making a proposal! Damn Ishbaal, damn his henchmen, damn the whole sorry, sordid affair. Why was I allowing Saddam to interfere with my life? Maybe the world would never change. Supposing I recaptured either the drugs or Devil's Redpepper, they would soon enough be replaced. It was all a game and, in such fearful, fateful play what was I bar an unwitting pawn in a dead man's strategy?

Yet as I continued to think of Freya I knew in my heart of hearts that had I shunned Monty's challenge I could never again have looked her in the face. If she would have me at all it had to be me as I was, the genuine me—and that meant also the conscientious me. All of a sudden it seemed the ludicrous business in Brighton had somehow been planned, predestined even. I'd turned down Monty to begin with but circumstances had reversed that decision. Then again, maybe I'd also to prove to myself I was worthy of such a one as Freya Boyesen, and worthy too of her wondrous loving.

I slept poorly and fitfully and so before breakfast took a cold bath. That fairly put the sense back in me: indeed, I was able to eat a morning meal that might, I fear, have scandalized even the redoubtable Madge. Outside, and fortunately—for it might enhance my present cover—it was once again raining. I was impatient as it was, but had the sun been shining the delay would have seemed intolerable. Even so, by early afternoon I was pacing the floor of the house like a wolf in captivity.

I decided in the evening to announce my departure so that I might slip away early the following day. We'd determined already that Sunday morning would be the safest time to negotiate the Burma Road: locals at that hour should either be in bed or else contemplating church, while visitors to the area would be taking a late breakfast or—observed Madge—suffering a hangover! However, when I tried to recompense them for their hospitality the Robertsons would have none of it. When I began to persist their refusal took on a note of annoyance and so I was obliged—with not a little gratitude—to accept their kindness.

Then Madge intervened. "We do this for Ruairidh, too, you know."

"Then likewise I shall do whatever I'm called upon for Ruairidh also."

With that we each took a smidgen-and-a-half from of a bottle of One Hundred and retired to bed. I slept, I recall, surprisingly well.

I rose early the next day and anxious to depart found I could eat only a little of what Madge had put out for me. She'd also, I noticed, placed on the table various tins of luncheon meat, half a fruit cake as well as an assortment of chocolate bars. Next to these was a flask, a packet of long-life milk, and a clutch of tea bags. I shoved all these into my backpack, pulled on my boots, and opening the rear door of the house made a quiet exit onto the aptly named "Circular Walk." As I did so I felt at last I was truly on my way, the next episode in the hunt for Red Pepper now properly begun.

Not for the first time did Dougie's weather prediction prove to be correct. There were the makings of a fine day ahead: only meagre quantities of lumpy cloud remained which were already disappearing from the horizon or edging away from the higher ground. The breeze—about force three on the Beaufort Scale and blowing from the north—was just sufficient to make the going pleasant, the air itself agreeably invigorating. I stepped forward with a sense of excitement, fully anticipating adventure.

All was quiet and I covered quickly the ground to Mallaig Bheag. Eventually the zigzag route came out onto a well-made gravel road and this took me near to the vantage point I'd occupied the previous Friday. Here the vivid morning sunlight shone down on the tall grass, onto the scattered and cut-down rushes and onto the brown and broken bracken; it coloured the sea a deep and brilliant blue. Amen, I thought, to a bright autumnal Sabbath! Yet, as soon as I walked within the mantle of shadow then hanging from the hill the wind seemed once more to harbour a chill, making me glad of the jersey beneath my homespun jacket. Neither was I displeased by the weight of that ancient rucksack.

Drawing near to the ranch-styled villa I believed I had the hamlet to myself. The place was still and the curtains of the bungalow opposite were not yet parted. But glancing about me, to my alarm, I saw high on the outline of an adjacent ridge there strode a rugged fellow walking with a stick: he was going along at a most ferocious pace and had with him two dogs bounding by his side; he hailed me from afar and I waved nervously back in his direction.

It was all too easy, I opined, to imagine I might pass undetected. These hills had eyes. Where there were sheep or cattle so also must there be herdsmen. I should have to go forth as a rambler exploring the Highlands, or, as a geologist perhaps, collecting rock samples for a foreign university.

Negotiating the start of the ascent reaching out of the glen, I realised that the so-called Burma Road ought better to be defined as an upland stream: all the rain of the previous week had set earthy overhangs or pelmets of heather awash and a-drip with water, rivulets into madcap watercourses, and the rough track as a whole into a streaming debacle of root, weed, and rolling stone; I jumped and splashed from one wobbly rock to another. Now and then I would surprise a coterie of black-faced sheep, the startled creatures giving me a sharp, insolent stare before tittupping over the edge. Twice I came across a tiny frog, forging little leaps from puddle to mud to verge, while once I put up a small flock of greenfinches to dip and dart erratically before me.

Where the Burma Road evened out it turned a corner to the east, and I fairly soon found myself looking out onto the bright waters of Loch Nevis and to the rampart heights of Knoydart. Yet owing to the winding nature of the road and the rising gradient to my right, much of my progress remained in shadow. The way itself now became thinner, being transformed into a narrow and waterlogged path. There were silver birches and mountain ash clinging to the sides, with sharp falls of scree to one flank or steep drops of broken ground to the other. The berries of the rowans appeared scarlet and caught the eye again and again. Small bonnets of heather gave added interest and were interspersed with green spongy moss and leftover scabious.

Out at sea a slight swell motioned between the mouth of the loch and the cobalt sound.

About half way round the cliff-side the land fell away completely and was broken in two by a narrow gorge. All along this defile a riot of debris had been sent plummeting to the shore. The breach had been traversed, however, by an iron bridge fastened to two buttressing walls of concrete. Nonetheless, the massive timber sleepers which lay across the top had been badly damaged by some animal or vandal; rotten sections of it were stove in entirely and gaps opened up in the yawning chasm. Someone had put down a few strips of wood to the landward side, and it was over these that I trod my way gingerly across.

The path then sloped downwards and curved gradually into what was virtually a semicircle. At one point I spotted a splendidly constructed stone culvert, with the remains of the circular outlet still protruding over the shoreline below. It was quite dry, however, and had missed altogether either the manic rush of waters or any of the steadily collecting pools. Not all of Ecky Donaldson's interventions, then, had turned out to be tactical, and I wondered what it would take to bring his labour of love into line with his purpose.

The track lifted slightly and once more drew to a corner. Even before I'd reached that gazebo I had stepped out again into the warmth of the sun and spied there, far above me to my right, the rugged and ravined outcrop of the majestic Sgurr Eireagoraidh. Now, as I stepped along the edge, I caught my first glimpse of the bay below and of the beauty and splendour that was Aridhghlinne.

CHAPTER 11

Aridhghlinne

Unknown to me at the time, pausing to survey the early morning shade withdrawing from the glen and lost in admiration at the secluded bay beneath, there had been added to as keen a pair of eyes as one might fear to find the artifice of a lens, allowing thereby its owner inspection from below. But, as I say, I suspected nothing staring long at the proud frontage of a single, whitewashed house, imagining its occupant either to be in bed or barely up and in *déshabillé*. Even the window at the gable end did not alert my suspicion, for the impress of nature had for a while eclipsed any wariness I might have over the presence of man.

Taking in the view now before me I could make out on the far side—above the green sward separating house from tide—a ruining cottage complete with tilted stack and network of loose sarking and exposed timbers. A hundred yards to its right stood a building of not dissimilar size, but the rusted roof of which was corrugated and which I took to be a byre. These appeared to be the only buildings that remained, other than the house itself. According to the map, however, there also existed a boatshed to the west end of the bay, so I presumed that its location must lie under the skirt of the hill, for I could get no view of it from where I'd temporarily halted.

What I could see clearly, though, was the lower course of the burn: this bisected the small valley and appeared to loop around the far side of the dwelling, partly enfolding it before it broadened out and spread thence through arable to a ravelment of stone and incoming sea. The beach itself seemed to consist mainly of shingle, with a raised line of weed and debris at the high tide mark and with formations of boulder and wrack at either flank. Only at some distance into the bay was any sand observable, although through the turquoise deeps there then appeared a sizeable stretch of it spanning the cove. Further out at sea a chaos of gulls was caterwauling over a shoal of fish, while above, a determined gannet drew back its wings and plunged keenly ocean-ward.

I began to descend the waterlogged track. The latter followed the perimeter of the bay like an angled horseshoe, and it soon gave me sightings of both the shed-roof to my left and a large sheepcote to the right. This last was situated at the far end of an area of grazing comprising about one hectare in total and with the park itself lying athwart the stream, although (to tell the truth) it had been spoilt at the fringes by the unfortunate but permitted infiltration of bracken and rushes. About twenty or so sheep of the blackheaded, moorland type had nibbled their way into sunlight, while two or three of them were now sitting sideways in an attitude of rest.

Although an air of quiet permeated this landscape I soon became aware of a sound that was alien to the place, a sound almost like music; different from any sough of wind or occasional bleating, it reached me intermittently and was not clearly audible but served as an irregular counterpoint to the more elemental melodies of the morning so far. At the point at which I chose to take the lower margin of the park, and thereby descend to a path by the burn, it seemed to acquire the quality of a rallentando and afterwards indeed actually to stop. Then, quite abruptly, as the sound returned to me and as I was brushing from my face a cloud of midges there was the unmistakable intrusion of a human voice.

By now I'd come within view of the back of the house and, catching there a glimpse of the kitchen window, dropped down in order to remain hidden. The voice was evidently that of an accomplished singer, his tone and timbre being rich and persuasive. Because there was no face at the glass pane, and because I hadn't seen even a wisp of grey at the chimney, I crossed over the small bridge before me and crept towards a pebbledashed wall which gave out onto the south. By this time I was sure the voice was Italian and the melody familiar. Slowly I began to move along the far side of the house. I became aware of the sun's warmth—and then, where the light was filtered by a line of trees, of the cool of the shade. The volume of the singing grew. I turned the corner of the house and there, instead of facing the closed side of the porch, found myself looking directly toward an open doorway and—even as I stood in disbelief before it—being loudly regaled by a melody more usually associated with the city of Naples. So there was I but three miles from the village of Mallaig and being entertained to a performance of *O Sole Mio* by perhaps the best—surely the most formidable—of our great Italian tenors!

I had no time to take stock of this marvel before I was met by another. A monumental cry from behind veritably sent the stumps flying.

"Mr. Make-in it iss, Mr. Waal-ter Make-in. Well, laddie, dinna stan' there gawpin', get yersel in ma hoose: the kippers are gannin' cauld!"

The man, of course, was none other than Roderick Farquhar Mackinnon, about whom Dougie had earlier spoken; but, unknown to the Robertsons, he was also my quondam companion on the road from Glenfinnan.

"Yon jaw'll fairly hit the floor, laddie. Come inn…come inn…come inn."

Thus echoing his invitation, the corpulent Mac swept deftly past me, instructing me to follow him to the kitchen-dining room.

There—and again to my surprise—was a table stationed at the window at which two places had been carefully set.

"I'll chust say ta-ta to Fat Lucy and then we can start."

The music stopped and as the master of ceremonies busied himself with the serving I had occasion to note both the window in the gable end and the prospect afforded thereby of the road above. That explained how I'd so easily been discovered. Unbeknown to me my progress had been most assiduously attended and the owner of Aridhghlinne had stolen the initiative. He was about to steal it again.

"Sit doon, laddie. I see there is chusst the one of ye. It wass a trinity I wass hecks-pecting. Waal-ter Make-in, Roofuss Gormlessly, and Major Delman. But ye haf only brung yersel'!"

With this expos, of identities assumed—not to mention the mischievous inclusion of my real name—the whole barrel-and-a-half of the man slapped down his cutlery, tilted back his chair and laughed out loud till he was crimson in the face and wet about the eyes. Still he kept the initiative.

"Let me venture, Major, you're a touch taken aback. I mean by all this wisdom on a Sabbath morn."

With the sudden dropping of the far-flung idiom—which until then he had dutifully espoused—and with the adoption of a more carefully modulated accent of some Edinburgh solicitor, Mac recommenced his laughter—and with all the unbridled enthusiasm of some gigantic infant. As for myself, I may indeed have been a "touch taken aback" but I was also thoroughly nettled by a sense of powerlessness, to say nothing of embarrassment. I believe it was when Mac detected this that he quietened somewhat, altering his discourse to match the suit he wore. This, by the by, was a smartish three-piece affair, which unlike his earlier kilt cast him more in the role of the magnificent than the absurd-but-splendid. Mac had not as yet put on a tie and his top-shirt button remained undone.

"First things first, " he began. "I'm Scottish, yes, but all that twanging nonsense of the Lallans and queer turns and twists of phrase, not to mention the occasional concession to the mild Hebridean, all of that's by way of being—through fact or fiction—an inveterate traveller. It also provides me with a cover and now and then a means of keeping amused the local people. In reality, though, I was educated in Oxford, moved on to Paris, and thereafter spent a goodish while in Geneva. I became one of your high-ranking civil servants and for four years was attached to the European secretariat at Lausanne. After that I made the kind of blunder which everyone can afford to make at least once in his life. I shot someone..."

"You did what!" I exclaimed, desisting momentarily from eating the food in front of me.

"Yes, I shot someone. In cold blood, too. Mind you, she'd been tailing me for weeks and I can't say I'm best pleased when my every move is being watched and my calls being tapped. Yes, I did say *she*. As a matter of fact she was an undercover agent for the C.I.A. Have you ever had dealings with that organisation? Nope? Well, neither should you. I don't rate the Yank all that highly to begin with, though I grant if he chooses to he can be as friendly and honourable as you could hope to find. But listen here, all the worst excesses of that nation—I mean the bureaucrats who serve expediency, the restless entrepreneurs, the hard-boiled capitalists, the cynical manipulators—they're all of them to be found in that agency. Add to that the fact it's riddled with paranoia—beset with suspicion at every turn—and you have the makings of a first-class megalomaniac institution capable of infinite harm and mindless cruelty: and all under a veneer of patriotism, a mock of diplomacy, and an inglorious connivance from the boys at the top.

"But, to return to my story. This hapless female, well, she pushed me into a corner one day and the only way out of it was a scrap. I didn't like it, of course, and my deference to her sex was nearly my undoing. Employing kid-glove tactics, I'd allowed her to recapture the gun I'd previously put out of reach. You know, I'd swear that woman was some sort of expert in martial arts. Anyhow, she soon had me creased on the floor and with the pistol to my head. Then it was time for a little rough play of my own. However the wretched gun suddenly went off resulting in the agent taking a mortal shot somewhere about the midriff. Then, as if from nowhere, there appeared some dozen policemen. The next thing I knew I'd been banged up in a blasted cell and a deal was being offered to me by a lawyer as seedy in manner as were his clothes grimy and his pate greasy. The upshot—nice and simple it was too—was apparently no less than five of those cops had seen me shoot the woman in cold blood. Yep, that's right. While I myself was for the chair—for sure—unless I agreed to enlist personally with the very same bunch. How could I refuse such an offer? Well now, Major, did you ever hear the like?"

It was at this juncture, perceiving an altogether different "Mac"—and one now staring me earnestly in the face—that I may have been guilty of committing an error. The truth of the matter was that my newfound host was of both grander stature and more heroic lineage than I had hitherto imagined.

"Look, Mac—if you don't mind me calling you that—there's no need to bother with the title. I've not seen active service now for some while. Fred will do fine."

"Okay, laddie, so be it."

And, from that moment on, whenever we were alone I became relegated to the junior rank of the diminutive boy! But then again my ally in the making did not stand on ceremony any more than did he limit himself to any single style. Indeed, in the matter of speech he could at times be highly irregular, shifting from one accent to another and slipping in dialect as might a ferret from a man's hand. It was perhaps to maintain a feeling of control—of needing to keep the upper hand—that he resorted to this preferred form of address; for he was, like many another magnificent soul, all heart beneath and a softie for whom the worst form of abuse was negative criticism. Later I was to appreciate this trait for what it was, but I confess on the occasion of my first breakfast with him to having been a touch put out by his continued familiarity. Anyhow, my interlocutor resumed his tale.

"Well, laddie, the next thing I knew I'd become a defector to the Ruskies, stationed in Leningrad and slumming it—but and ben—with a queer red prole uncertain of his gender. You might well wonder by now I had any friends at all. Certainly their efforts were to no avail and all I could do was to play the rotten game. It was that wretched transvestite, incidentally, who told me about the woman I'd shot. It seemed she'd just about finished her working life and was on the point of opting for a late marriage somewhere in Sweden. Well laddie, that was altogether too much for the loveless boffins of the agency. They had her consigned to a task that was to end both in her own death and in the recruitment of yours truly. Moreover if I myself had not shot the woman one of the others had been told to do so. It transpired that the C.I.A. had singled me out ever since my early promotion to the department in Lausanne. And as if that were no bad enough, laddie, ye ken what they went and did next? No? Then I'll tell thee. When I discovered one day that a certain person—awfu' high up, min' ye—was hissel' a traitor and a conspirator, and when I then alerted his second-in-command: that being the second of those blunders which, you remember, everyman is entitled to make at least once in his life—well, I was then smuggled into the Kremlin and there arrested on a charge that I'd infiltrated the propaganda programme of the Communist party. And d' ye ken how it was they nobbled me? I'll tell thee, laddie, I'll tell thee. Wass it no the Americans? Aye, so it wass..."

For a moment my host stopped his narrative to gaze up at the ceiling, as if the contemplation of our cousins' perfidy was enough to silence even his voluble outpourings.

"Aye, it was those damned Yanks. It was they who put me in, you see, and who telephoned to the Soviets then and reported I'd been passing on information, even if it was out of date. It was true, of course, I had been passing on information, although none of it to my way of thinking seemed particularly sensitive—and, mark you, only because I'd been forced to do so by the Americans. Now the very same people were blowing my cover! They dropped me—and some plonk it was too—into a seething broth, a most horrendous brew. I should have been bled, starved, and driven mad to death were it not for that frightful little man—Minnie, I called him—who hastened to my aid. It seemed that Minnie had taken to our flat a rather senior official of the Soviet hierarchy. It was he who got wind of my arrest and who subsequently advised us that the Ruskies had never heard of me prior to that event: nor could they uncover any of my operations. It appeared they were nearly as bamboozled by the agency's revelations as I was by Minnie's solicitude. Anyway, there was—as they say—more to Minnie than meets the eye. Furthermore, his contacts extended to the purlieus of the prison. Added to which he was able to suggest a new identity and obtain a passport to go along with it. It was during that year's May Day parade an escape was effected and that yours truly—Roderick Farquhar Mackinnon, a computer salesperson from Fife—made his egress from the U.S.S.R."

There then followed a silence, during which time my host paused for breath and made eager inroads into his bread and kippers and during which time I strove to muster some sort of pertinent reply. The main response to surface lay between a feeling of admiration and a temptation to disbelieve. It was as crazy a yarn as I could possibly have heard. I attempted to fill in the rest of the story myself.

"Presumably your present location indicates a fear of reprisals against either yourself or your friends. If the C.I.A. can get you once it must be anticipated they may try a second time—as often in fact as it takes to dispose of you."

"That's about the size of it, laddie, I've been obliged to adopt an outlandish character in an out-of-the-way place. The beauty of this spot is that it's right on the periphery. Mind you, at the outset I'd determined to go even further and began by sampling a somewhat precarious existence on the remote island of Mingulay—away out there to the west: then again, in a northerly direction, I rather fancied the island of Bressay, for it lies only a few minutes sea-passage from the capital of Shetland. The problem, however, was I felt so darned cut off from the main world that my earlier life seemed to have come to a halt. At least here there are railway connections to London and to Glasgow. That's allowed me to regain some of the stimulus and variety my temperament demands. All the same I continue to avoid former friends and remain in contact—via a P.O. box-number—with just two of the oldest. One day perhaps—as the good song says—we'll meet again. In the meantime my best disguise has proved to be my rotund figure. Aye, laddie, and dinna be grinnin' noo…I've put on six stones in the past few years and have grown a beard to satisfy a Viking. As to my name, hardly anyone up here knows what it is; the banks are happy with 'R.F.M.' and the natives with 'Mac.' So, there you have it. One other thing, I'm fifty-seven and no mean chicken. Now, will that do you?"

What could I say? Clearly Mac had kept his ear to the ground and had discovered both of my pseudonyms as well as my identity. That he'd kept abreast of the news was patent; neither had he done so with the one ear only. He had obviously picked up the fiasco down in Brighton, seen through my ruse at Glenfinnan, put two and two together and decided I must be the major the Yard were investigating. More than that, he had decided he could trust me, confiding in me all but his name. Why he had done so I couldn't say. Nonetheless, two questions remained unanswered.

"It will do very well, Mac. Only, how did you find out about my second alias? And, why did you not turn me in? I must tell you, I'm a staunch defender of our democratic processes."

"Oh so am I, laddie, so am I. Believe you me, when you've seen what I've seen—down and up this naughty world—you begin to treasure this system of ours even if it be on occasion antiquated or on others adorned with many a wart and unwholesome carbuncle. You know all of my travels and dealings, they've left me a pretty fair judge of character. Your own escape for example, it had a quality about it that was almost naïve, while you yourself bore that curious combination of the ordinary and the imaginative. As to Rufus Gormally, I'm afraid you can put that one down to good luck and the strength of Madge Robertson's voice. I had cause, you see, to call in upon Dougie—we were following some correspondence in *The Church Times*—and I happened to hear his good lady call out to the back room. When I questioned Dougie, honest man that he is, he appeared more flummoxed than he should and disputed my hearing. I let it pass, naturally, but I have better hearing than most and trust entirely Dougie's integrity. Ach, it was easy, laddie. No problem at all."

The difficulty, alas, was all my own. Granted Mac was everything he said—and on the whole I was inclined to think so—to what extent could I reciprocate with an apologia of my own and how much of the Red Pepper business could I afford to lay bare? I came in at a tangent.

"Ever heard of M.Q.1.?"

"Nope, can't say I have. That doesn't mean it doesn't exist, of course. Could be one of those old-world clubs of the ancient aristocracy, a genteel venue with an espial brief beneath the sporting façade. Good food, good sport, and good anecdotes of foreign parts. No women mind you! Typical of the tight-lipped brigade, all wind and pips but now and then a savour of the truth, a hint of a crisis. On the other hand there's not much of the kind in these pared-down days of the functional, tightly fiscal, and astringently entrepreneurial."

I wondered what poor Monty would have thought about his highly specialized and honourable colleagues being dubbed old-fashioned, self-indulgent, and chauvinistic. Yet for all his style I couldn't help but warm to Mac. If the going got nasty he could turn out to be a most useful ally.

It would help, in any event, to let him know about both Henrik Meyer and the remaining twin. Of the existence of Ishbaal and the scandal of Red Pepper I was more cautious. I had not so long kept quiet to be pushed now into declaring my hand for a pair of smoked herring. So having informed him to the degree I considered prudent I again fell silent.

"There's more to it, laddie, isn't there? You're keeping back the worst of it. Maybe that's for the best. It's one of those fine and fickling verdicts, the sort honest thinking persons struggle to make. Aye, so it iss. Tell thee what..."—and with that the mighty figure before me rose and began to busy himself once more—"I've something left at the foot of a bottle and having had that and a glance at the Broons I'm for taakin' a wee nap. You get yersel' away oot and taak a bit of a waak. When ye get back I'll do us a fry-up and a pot o' the Souchong. See how the world looks then."

I felt a touch guilty I'd not inspanned Mac to a greater share of my secret—the weight of which had scarcely diminished—yet I was relieved to have imparted at least something and pleased again to have an opportunity of exploring the terrain. Before I left it was decided I should sleep at Aridhghlinne, thereby adding my own presence to the tidal flow of waifs, strays, and eccentrics that regularly fell at its doors. I retrieved from my pack the flask and chocolate, crossed the planks at the rear of the house and, on finding myself on the correct side of the burn, began the gradual ascent of the adjacent hill.

The start of my walk took in both outbuildings serving formerly as home to man and beast. Behind the ruining house—with its vacant windows and unbroken views of the Cuillins—I discovered a narrow sheep-track winding steeply through the firm but fading bracken. I followed this path and after a while came out onto a green and purple knoll. There I was able to glimpse once more the homesteads of Inverie and, to my delight, found at my feet a handful of Orchidaceae. At this juncture the going to the left—which led down to the shoreline—looked to deteriorate to a rather awkward and fruitless exercise. I was inclined to bear more to the right and to surmount thereby the ridge which even then hung before me. I stayed with the latter and found myself gaining height all the while. It wasn't long before I was standing next to one of those ubiquitous tooth-like rocks that seem to litter that difficult and monticulous landscape—a quirky remnant perhaps of the distant glacial period and with no more purpose than to tease the imagination with intimations of an enigma. Nevertheless individually they might serve as markers if I was to lose track upon the return. Putting behind me both the diminutive house below and the ribbon of road above, I pressed on till I'd gained a broad, grassy tract. Through this patch there now coursed the same burn I'd had to cross when joining the sheep-track and which would eventually influence the separate spate of waterfall below.

It was at this point I was faced with a choice. Either I could make directly for the nearest summit or I could remain on the near side of the burn and climb up beside its downward course. The decision was made for me by the sudden appearance of a party of walkers. Having come via a different route—one that passed above the shore—they had opted for the first of these alternatives and appeared to be making steady progress. Not wishing to be seen I myself bore well to the right, taking whatever cover available from the gully of the stream or from the birch and alders accompanying its flow. By now (I might add) the weather had come on pretty hot and the way up was increasingly assuming the nature of an assault course—though it was none the less invigorating for being so. After a while, though, the stream levelled out and I came to a vantage point well to the side of the walkers and some little distance from what looked to be the first true summit. It was to the latter that the others were making—their bright reds, oranges and blues standing out well against the greens and browns of the hill.

Again I became confronted by the problem of being seen. About a thousand yards in front of me lay the next and final ascent of Sgurr Eireagoraidgh proper. It's broken and tortuous ridge I'd already spotted on my earlier forays; now it rose before me a great triangulated curtain of scree and rock here and there ravined by veins of water. I noticed at the end furthest from me that there existed a green gully and that it appeared to betoken a more acceptable approach. Unfortunately it was sited at a greater distance inland than I'd originally intended to secure. What I needed was access nearer the shoreward side, and there then as a matter of fact stood before me one which looked sufficiently promising—though as any seasoned walker will aver what seems negotiable from afar often appears daunting in the approach. Fortunately my telescope confirmed that it would indeed go without difficulty. All the same I felt I'd journeyed long and far from the riant and rolling pasturelands of the Southern Downs.

Seeing no alternative for it I decided to head for the nearer of the two ways that adorned the Sgurr, trusting I should occasion neither surprise nor suspicion to my fellow ramblers. I crossed the rough ground that intervened and then paused at the foot of the partly-cropped channel which I intended to climb. I looked behind and glimpsed the last of the walkers slipping beneath the horizon. It became clear to me then that they themselves were no more interested in going on than they were in the identity of the one in front. All of a sudden I felt stupid and alone. Why on earth should I be of any interest to them? Besides, seeing they'd gone, did I not now feel more lonely than ever? Still, there was no point in indulging in any interior harangue, so I put my best foot forward and hastened to the ascent.

The first reach of the summit came sooner than expected, for I suddenly found myself standing in a cooling breeze with nothing but a gimmer and a buzzard for company. The view itself was breathtaking—a mountainous vista of blues and browns, an airy pavilion whose wide sweeping domain had the effect of lifting the heart and of bestowing on a man feelings both royal and rare. I drew in lungful after lungful of that blessed air and could have wished for no better tonic. Neither was that the only prospect to gladden me, for towards the narrows of Loch Nevis there could now be seen a small white dot. In a trice I had my telescope trained on it and lo! discovered a yacht. I could not at that remove be certain it was the *Queen of Sheba*, yet the fact the main season had passed—together with the usual disinclination of the holiday-maker to stay for too long in one place—suggested to my eager senses that it was indeed so. I sat down on a rock, drank tea from my flask, and devoured a goodish quantity of thick milk chocolate.

Glancing then at my watch I noted the entire expedition had taken but an hour and a half to accomplish. It was too soon to return to the house. In any case I'd made no plan and had not decided yet on what to tell Mac. I felt in such a jolly, exultant mood that I opted next to continue my climb, failing thereby to notice that the then changing wind must facilitate the *Sheba's* return towards the mouth of the loch. It was such a glorious location and such a splendid day that it was difficult to keep my mind on the task in hand. If I had been less intoxicated I should have realised it was not so much my foes who were like a dot on a surface as it was I who was like a mere pinprick on an horizon—far removed from that shameful vessel and utterly outside the confidence of its crew. Neither had I the freedom of movement of the hawk, nor yet its keen capacity to see. Maybe I had a little of the sheep's stubbornness and must hope to God rather less of its proverbial woolly-mindedness.

I part scaled, part scrambled the remaining way to the top and settled then for the furthest of the green gullies observed earlier in the day. The trouble lay in determining where precisely it began: though a variety of ways presented themselves none of them looked safe enough actually to pursue. At length I dropped into a trough between two large boulders and began slowly to engage in making my descent. Unfortunately the narrow ravine into which I had stepped harboured little of the turf I'd presumed to exist: rather it consisted mostly of rock and to my surprise turned sharply to the right instead of the left. I had too soon veered from the top and had therefore to regain my earlier stance, continue walking on for a few more yards and only then enter the more passable declination of grass, heather, and stone. This took me to a level coterminous with the point whence the ramblers had decamped. To my left there now lay a deep gorge eventually broadening into a wide pass between hummocks and hollows and which contained a dark, peaty burn. To the front there stretched a large tract of bog embellished here and there with myrtle and asphodel and decorated with white cotton-grass and tilting wreaths of bent. I made a stick of a broken branch and determined to risk the sodden floor of the mire. The latter's sweet pungencies and aromatic scents began rapidly to assail me as I trailed on doggedly under the hot blaze of the early afternoon.

Beyond a lengthy set of ridges delineating the far skirting of peat there was a wire fence standing some little way above the widening gorge. I surmounted this and made a steep descent into the pass below. On the map a small lochan was indicated, but I could get no sign of it, scan the ground as I might. A striking prominence rose upward, though, on the other side of the defile. I nipped smartly to the top of that and, looking back down, could see I'd narrowly missed what appeared to be a miniature reservoir—only it could not be seen from the route I'd followed, sunk as it was below the surrounding peatland. I decided to wander over to take a look.

As I neared the edge of the reservoir, trudging through the purplish bell heather and clumps of vegetation, I became aware that the pleasant breeze had all but died down. Standing at the pool's sandy perimeter I was struck by how calm this place appeared to be. The sun shone directly on the water and its rays sent jewels of light sparkling over the surface. I sat against a rock angled beside a tinkling rivulet, the better positioned to observe this scintillant rhapsody. In the hush of that spot, with only the purling of the stream to distract, I gazed upon that dancing brilliance mesmerised, my mind numb in the dizzy scented heat, in the warm mellifluous air. For a second, I closed my eyes.

When I looked up I could see a youth of perhaps eighteen to twenty years. He was stripped to the waist and bending down to the edge of the water. Cupping his hands he drank freely several draughts from the shimmering surface. Then he splashed some of the liquid over his head and face and flaxen hair. I called out to him lest he suddenly discover his ablutions were being observed and be irritated by the intrusion. He stood up and remained motionless, so I strode over to his side. He was in good trim and boasted a lithe, sinewy figure as well as being patently sunburnt. It may have been this fact that triggered an experience of *déja vu*, although I did not think before I'd ventured so far. Perhaps it was just that the boy resembled one of the runners off the Brighton waterfront, or maybe again he simply looked like an adolescent companion of my lost years. Anyhow, his reaction surprised me for he did not appear to be vexed or embarrassed but held his ground instead, droplets of water running down his forehead. He smiled broadly and extended his hand.

He was just about to say something when a shot rang out. I swung round immediately but could see not a soul—only a sheep bolting in amazement, its noisy bleat sounding over the moor. When I turned back the boy in front of me almost fell into my arms. A blot of blood was opening up about his right temple. A thin issue of red trickled towards his mouth and large drops fell from his lips.

I picked up the youth in my arms and carried him to a nearby trough abandoned from the old peat-cutting days. I stared in horror at his frozen face. Fearing the worst I held his limp wrist in my hand and waited for a pulse. Not a tremor of life quickened beneath my thumb. The boy was dead. He had been murdered without mercy. I rose up then in a rage, imbued with all the fearlessness of a madman and with about as much common sense. Instantly a bullet whizzed about my ear and ricocheted off the rock, off the very spot in fact where I'd earlier lain.

I dropped for cover beside the dead youth. I appeared to be horribly exposed with no means of escape. If I stayed where I was it would only be a short while before the assassin—whoever that might be—succeeded in catching me. At the same time I couldn't be sure it was me whom the assailant was seeking. It was the boy who had been killed. I couldn't see any reason to connect him with myself. On the other hand, it seemed likelier I was the intended victim of so dire an assault. Moreover I could not at first see how I might avoid further attack. It wasn't long, however, before an idea occurred to me.

Provided I was prepared to crawl and push my way through a minimum of cover I might retrieve successfully the higher ground I'd previously abandoned. Furthermore, if I could put some distance between myself and my assailant—between, that is, myself and Ish-baal; for I could no longer refrain from making that connection—then I could afford to reveal myself to him: indeed, it would be part of my plan so to do.

What I had in mind was to return to the nearest part of the Sgurr and to re-ascend the last of the grass-adorned gullies. It would be a risky business because there was little by way of shelter to conceal me. On the credit side I could accomplish the task with a degree of celerity and could then pass to the penultimate and mistaken route I'd previously been obliged to ignore. In the meantime, my opponent must surely opine my intention to be a retreat beyond the Sgurr. In fact, I should drop into the more difficult passage, the one initially I'd had to discard. My one ace was that I'd spotted—in my chosen descent—a more viable means of access, one which swung to the side rather than passing down directly to the mire below. I'd spied at that juncture a stout boulder and a small rowan; but beneath these obstacles there lay another offshoot which, whilst exceedingly thin, eventually lined up with the foot of the original gully. I hoped thus to deceive my accursed follower and to return diagonally to Aridhghlinne.

Three times I deliberately revealed my position while once—by accident—I prematurely broke free from the channel of a stream. On all four occasions a shot was fired—though none in my judgement came close to its mark. The worst stretch was when I was obliged to traverse a large portion of bog towards the start of the ascent. Here, had I delayed long, I should surely have allowed my predator to bring down his prey. Instead I wormed and writhed my way unseen through the first section and not until I'd stolen the moment of surprise did I dare finally get to my feet and flee like a madman to the base of the Sgurr. In so doing I was forced to trust to the poor aim of Ishbaal and to the hope that his disability might slow him down. Oddly though—after the fourth shot had been fired—there were no further reports to alarm me

As a matter of fact I'd still not spotted my adversary when I entered at last the penultimate gully and thus had the distinct impression I was no longer being pursued. I'd nonetheless given little time to observation and this meant I felt vulnerable in the extreme as I set my foot to that narrow offshoot. Suppose Ishbaal be no marksman, he must—if he was to tarry rather than give chase—have the perfect opportunity to bring me down from a single shot. I wondered where it would hit me.

The minutes passed and I became increasingly agitated. I confess I expected my life to end at any moment. I became seized by something like terror and began suddenly to run—in the reckless fashion of a nightmare—in the direction of Aridhghlinne. I traversed two or three ridges, set a lone deer fleeing across the heath and then scrambled down to a watershed at the top of a glen overlooking the sea.

Striving eagerly to cover the ground before me, again and again I witnessed those stone shapes which in the morning had so intrigued me. Their sheer number, however, made identification impossible. If only I had taken note of their outline and location! But alas, I had not. Now they merely confused and intimidated, like so many blocks of ice bobbing in uncharted waters. It was the sight of a familiar patch of ling—whence earlier I'd extracted a fistful of white heather—together with a glimpse of Nevis loch, that brought to an end my undignified sprint. I halted in my tracks and took stock of my position.

I was dripping wet from my thoroughfare in bog and burn, my face felt flushed and burnt and my heart and head hammered ferociously. I had seen the life of an innocent youth extinguished in front of me, had barely hung onto my own life's breath and even now had not settled on what to tell Mac. Well, I should have to pitch him a yarn about stumbling in the mire and falling in a burn. I reflected with a smile that that indeed was the truth.

I descended the glen slowly, momentarily pausing above a stone-built cell—an ancient shieling, perhaps, or the corner of a pound—in case it should house my hirpling but fleet-of-foot foe. Potential danger past, I made my way down to the lower park and crossed in the process an old, broken dyke I presumed in bygone days to have demarcated the original grazings. Thereafter I passed a sheep pen more recently established—again built out of massive boulders and of strips of turf—and before long found myself facing the back door of the house and being loudly hailed (appropriately, I thought) by a fulsome rendering of *Vesti la giubba*.

A hirsute and slightly tipsy Mac greeted me with astonishment.

"Ma Goad, laddie, what's happen' tae ye? Ye look as if ye took a tumbledoon the clough. And who had a go at ye wi' yon gun? Aye! Dinna look sae doped and dozen'd. Is that no a nasty beit o' blood at the back of yer heid?"

I put my fingers to the crown of my head. Sure enough, upon lowering my arm I saw a daub of crimson in the peaty palm of my hand. A crack against rock—endured at the burn's lip—had not been a blow against stone after all: the accidental sighting I had given my enemy had almost made of a shameful deed a thing of success.

CHAPTER 12

The Game Afoot

Good as his word Mac had prepared as handsome a table as any man could wish. Already the Lapsang was infusing in the pot and the fat in the pan sizzled merrily as I vied for his attention.

"Look, Mac, if you're ready to listen I'd like to put you in the picture. I doubt this game can be played by any man alone, though I confess I've been playing it solitaire for the past seven days. I believe I've the measure of you when I say you're honest, reliable, and can take care of yourself should the going get tough. Added to which this cut on my head has come as a timely reminder, that if anything should happen to me there would be no-one to halt the devil in his tracks or hinder the transmission of his damnable Red Pepper."

"Steady there, laddie, steady. I'm flattered fine by your proposal, only it would assist us greatly if yud get that heid o' yours stuck in yon burn. It'll cool ye doon a bit. We dinna want ye gaspin' away afore ye've told me what's what…now do we?"

He flung me a partly-decent hand towel and a fresh slab of carbolic. The stench of the phenol and the icy touch of water soon had their effect. I returned to the table a new man and began quickly to devour the heap of victuals there set out before me. A couple of mugs of Mac's Souchong—brewed till it was as tarry in consistency as it was in scent—and I was all set for the first pipe of the day. I had earned it, I reflected, and stepped out in the cool of the evening to tap it clean and fill it afresh. When I returned Mac had an announcement to make.

"We haf, laddie, a visit-orr. He's the excise man and I've taken him through to the back room. He's been here before and seems on the whole a decent enough squaddie—if, naturally, a little too inquisitive. Come on through when you're ready."

I wasted no time in joining my companion and stepped into a room that was as homely and inviting as one could wish to discover. The walls and ceiling were throughout panelled in pine and were stained dark after the colour of burnt sienna. The furniture was both simple and eccentric, comprising a typical collection of easy chairs, leather sofa, and stout table, but also boasting a magnificent wardrobe—the outer mirror of which caught the light of a single window and thereby helped to alleviate what otherwise might have been a gloomy place to sit. As it was the room had about it a secretive, most enchanting character. Another mirror was fastened above the mantelpiece while next to that stood a mahogany bookcase. There was also a fine-looking sideboard stationed against the opposite wall. In the former was housed both an indifferent set of Dickens and two shelves of the *National Geographic* magazine.

After I'd been introduced to Sandy Galbraith, the local Customs Officer, I sat down to face the window and contemplate the view, which—it must be said—was quite exquisite. The sleeve of water in the frame had become a smooth, milky blue, while the low hills beyond had turned to a light brown and were mottled with bright patches of yellow where the evening sun continued to shine. It was an entrancing picture, constantly changing with the slow fall of dusk and made the more arresting by the distant flight of gulls, a sudden circle of kittiwakes and an occasionally careering gannet.

To begin with I was occupied simply supping my dram contentedly and absorbing the ambience both within and without. After a while, though, I began to observe the stranger, Sandy Galbraith.

He was a lofty upright man, rather on the lean side with a crop of curling black hair and a small moustache. His forehead, moreover, was unusually high while his nose had about it a slight kink. He wore trousers made of black-twilled worsted and had a white shirt with an official tie and over that a grey v-neck sweater. Oddly, perhaps, he also wore a pair of black Wellington boots almost entirely concealed by his turn-ups. His voice was curiously thin and seemed a trifle anomalous. My ears pricked up, however, when he mentioned the drug heroine. Almost immediately he turned to me.

"Major Delman, I wonder if I might ask you if you've observed anything you'd consider at all unusual or untoward."

"Not I, old man, not a thing. Not unless you can count a couple of unshorn gimmers or an Englishman falling into a bog."

He laughed pleasantly—seeing the state of my clothes—and then added:

"No curious yachts on the loch? No queer customers on the hill?"

"As I say, none I saw. Only myself."

The reader may marvel at my reply, but I did not wish to muddy my own operation by involving this chap in the intricacies of M.Q.1 or in the pursuit of either Ishbaal or his infamous Red Pepper. Galbraith's work was clearly straightforward and his call just then entirely routine. He was based, he said, somewhere in Fort William and for a while we discussed there the siting of the present railway station and the plans recently projected for a new skiing-complex.

Later on the conversation spanned the globe somewhat further—as far, indeed, as the Persian Gulf. Mac was bemoaning his size and gathering years and said it was high time the Iraqi president paid the price of his iniquity. Galbraith, for his part, commented on the religious and cultural antecedents of Mesopotamia and went on to argue for a greater degree of British involvement.

"All right, so it was only a mandate intended for twelve years. Thereafter, as we know, the state opted first for independence and then for the status of a republic. Nevertheless, were we not partly responsible for drawing up the territorial boundaries? Again, was it not perverse to deny the Iraqis effective access to the Gulf? It is, is it not, a pity to have to contemplate war—and there of all places? Think of it: the greed and capitalism of western democracies about to ravage and lay waste the Garden of Eden. The fall of man has extended its influence far and wide but not tardily like the fabled ramifications of that other tree of Paradise: life and death, perhaps; but as to the knowledge of good and evil, of that I have my doubts—for truly it has been a slow and tortuous growth. And the forbidden fruit? Today it is oil. The children of Adam in Britain, the children of Eve in America—they must have it and at whatever cost. Yet fancy turning the first paradise into a bomb-pitted battlefield! It is shameful, downright shameful. We should be in at the forefront of every diplomatic initiative, not lagging behind like Lot's wife. Why do Western governments find the prospect and calamity of war so fascinating? It petrifies their thinking, makes postlapsarian, pithecoid brutes of the denizens of our so-called civilised world. It is shameful, truly shameful."

"Eh, Sandy, lad," spoke up Mac, "not so harsh on the apes noo. At least the peasties haf none of our consciousness. Trupple wi' the folk o' this generation is that they ken well and they ken fine what it iss that they are doin': what they dinna ken is how they might make the petter use of their wits—any more than they dae to protect or distrypute their oil."

I confess I found Galbraith's talk a touch depressing. Accepting he was no mere whiffler but had a genuine commitment to peace, his admonition against the hurdy-gurdy of war and the picture it conjured—with the dreadful crump-crump of shells over the cradle of civilisation—depicted a disastrous and appalling prospect. It seemed predicated on the worst kind of craziness. I wondered, given the possibility that diplomacy might fail, how the process would conclude: it was far easier to start a war than to finish one. Mac seemed to be thinking along similar lines for he started before the other could reply.

"Ye see, suppose we go chargin' in there, tae give back yon scrunty kingdom tae the Kuwaitis—which maybe we haf tae dae : 'specially if we wanna knock oot the missils—how, and when, do we stop? We canna presumably gan' aal the way tae Baghdad—the Harraps, they would neffer swalla that at aal—then how can we help the Iraqis get quit o' Hussein? The Yanks'll haf tae advance a wee bittie—say as far as Basra—then hang on till the Resistance can regroup and give time enough for a popular uprising tae develop. That is it as I see it, anyhow. Basra as the intermediate capital, that's the best ploy tae adopt. What say yersel, Maechur?"

"I think what you say makes a lot of sense. Still, let's hope it doesn't come to that."

Again I thought of Ruairidh; then I thought of the rampant and ensuing destruction—of oil terminals set ablaze and lighting up the dark and polluted skies.

"Is it not though a lovely evening? The Gulf seems far removed from all this peace and tranquillity. Yet, here we are talking of war."

"Aye, it iss a bonny night, right enough. Well now, if I light us a lamp or two—and some candles an' aal—will you, Maechur, play Sandy at the Chess? It'll taak yer minds off-of aal this gloomy stuff and the days ye both haf had."

"Good Lord, Mac, how ever did you know I played Chess?"

"I didna. Now I dae, though. I'll bring through some beer. It's canned, but you'll no be mindin'."

My friend's linguistic performance, which I allow had persuaded me hitherto without need to demur, now began to amuse me and I began to find it difficult to take him with the degree of seriousness our situation warranted. Galbraith called me to attention, however, with the charge, “I take it you abide, Major, by the principle of touch-a-piece, move-a-piece.”

“Whatever you say, old chap.”

“And shall we toss to see who commences play?”

“No need, no need. You take white. I dare say it’ll not make much difference.”

The excise man then emptied from a small wooden box its varied contents and the jumbled armies of pieces fell with a clatter on the chequered board. For a moment I hesitated. Galbraith was waiting for me to position the battlefield. Then I remembered the dictum, “White square on the right” and turned the board accordingly. Very soon the game had begun and by the third move I’d already suffered my first loss in playing the Queen’s Gambit.

Mac himself returned at this point carrying a tray of cans and some hefty looking glasses. I was pausing to contemplate my next move when he slammed the thing down on the table causing thereby several of the pieces to tremble in their squares. He added to this irreverence by chucking in an outspoken reproof.

“Ach, I wonna ye can be pothered with such a game. It’s no the same as Pridge. At least wi’ that ye dinna haf tae descend to the level of a compute-tah! There’s no psychology in Chess. Anyway, Mae-chur, it’s yer ain go. Cummon noo, if ye’ve the smeddum tae start yud better have the wits tae finish.”

Mercifully our host turned aside then and began to busy himself with a pair of wicks, carefully trimming them. It was not long before he had set the room aglow in a flickering chiaroscuro, conjuring an atmosphere of paraffin-reek to blend in with the already resinous smell of pine. The sticks he had lain took quickly and a ferocious heat began to permeate the room. Now and then the fire would spit forth some remnant of charred or burning timber, and at such times Mac would scramble to his feet to retrieve the scorching ember from its illicit occupation in rug or chair. He went off after a while to hunt for a fireguard, coming back with a makeshift one of wire netting coupled to some old coat hangers. Leaning this over the open hearth he made it possible for Galbraith and I to resume our concentration. Mac seemed to take such a delight in the wearing of eccentricity that I began to wonder how much of it was put on and how much was endogenous.

The verdict he'd given, moreover, concerning the game of Chess did not seem entirely apt. Even allowing that the element of luck, inherent in the dealing of thirteen random cards, might seem to have no obvious counterpart in the equal division of thirty-two pieces, nevertheless I could not agree with Mac upon the matter of "psychology." There might not be those ingredients of bluff and counter-bluff—with which the common player is apt to imbue his game of Bridge—yet there was in Chess a weighing-up of the adversary's personality and the taking of that into account when deploying tactics and devising stratagems. Leastwise that was how it had always seemed to me.

Not—I hasten to add—that I possessed anything which could be said to resemble a strategy. What usually happened was if I owned a Black King I would play in response to the plan of my opponent—that is, defensively—but as I went along would keep an eye open in case serendipity might present the possibility of Mate; or, if I was to land a White King, I would practise the technique of approximating to the so-called "perfect position"—getting as many of my pieces as possible towards the centre-ground. As a matter of fact I opted for this last alternative even though I had started second.

We were about half way into the game, some thirty-five minutes having passed, when I began to thank God in earnest for Dougie Robertson's tutorials. This was what happened. While Galbraith and I had been pursuing each other along the same flank, inadvertently I had pushed forward my Queen to a highly exposed position allowing her to become hedged about by a number of pieces. Suddenly Galbraith seized the initiative. With his last remaining pawn of the second line he moved forward two squares and revealed thereby a discovered-check (to use the jargon) on the King's better half. If I was to retaliate directly, through the use of that Queen, what would almost certainly follow would be the loss of that piece in an exchange for a Bishop. Yet I could not free her from this diagonal attack. It was a serious oversight on my part not to have anticipated such an occurrence. I was unable moreover to see a way forward.

Then it came to me: if I was to use the manoeuvre of *en passant*—so felicitously recalled by Dougie on my second game—then I might seize my foe's troublesome pawn and put Galbraith's Queen in instant jeopardy. I carried out this move while my adversary (not surprisingly) took my pawn. This in turn allowed the Black Queen to take Galbraith's Bishop, which was no longer protected. I should add, incidentally, that the White Queen could not be removed from the vertical—which at that stage she occupied—because to have done so would have illegitimately exposed the King (from one of my Castles) to a spontaneous Check.

Unfortunately—as I fear the astute reader will appreciate—I'd already missed the opportunity of using the aforementioned Rook to capture my adversary's Queen! Galbraith lost no time in reversing that advantage, and, though I'd kept my Queen secure, I'd lost a point thereby and had let the zugzwang established receive a royal rebuff. I gave out a loud sigh.

"Not goin' yer way, Maechur?" Mac inquired, mischievously.

I ignored the interjection, though, as I'd suddenly become enthralled by my opponent's countenance. His face and neck (as I'd already noticed) were of a brown complexion, and when I looked now into his eyes I expected them to be of like colour complementing his pitch-black hair. What I observed in fact was a pair of eyes more green than turquoise and with a curious tendency to water—so that every now and then Galbraith would pull out a small silk handkerchief and surreptitiously wipe them. His hairline, moreover, was rather in recession and that tended to accentuate an already high forehead.

Yet it wasn't any individual feature which aroused my interest so much as my competitor's overall and animated expression. The lamp behind me—which incidentally had the effect of casting my own visage in shadow—illumined Galbraith's mien and uncovered thereby a thousand moods. Initially he'd appeared thoroughly relaxed, confident—even perhaps a trifle smug. That expression had given way, however, to a look of the most extraordinary concentration, with his left eyebrow arched above his right and with a fierce indentation of lines scouring his forehead. In addition, shortly before his attack on my Queen, I'd detected a most disturbing aspect that I can only depict as one approaching horror. In the flickering half-light my imagination was apt to cast him in the role of victim before torturer, of prisoner before executioner. With hindsight I see it must have been the expeditious positioning of a Rook that had prompted amazingly such horrified features. Almost immediately, however, they were displaced by a look of the most incredible glee—as if any hint of simple relief had been superseded by a wild and exultant sense of certain victory. Moreover, incredible though it sounds in the same exchange of play, my rival seemed to lose in age some fifteen to twenty years. Yet I'd only to push my pawn—from one square to another—and the expression of triumph was completely lost to one of pitiable tragedy. The effect was heightened, withal, by the natural tendency of Galbraith's chrysoprase-eyes to water involuntarily. To tell the truth—and for sanity's sake—when the Black Rook fell to the Queen I found myself glancing through the window to look out on a passing trawler: its bright beacon of light gliding in the darkness imparted a welcome contrast—a reminder (if you will) of the real world. Then, when I next turned to Galbraith, he had my own face fixed in a hard, steely stare impatient for my next move.

The effect of my rival's mien was to translate my own mood of calmness to one of increasing misery. I knew of course we were only playing a game, yet Galbraith's intensity was not so much ludicrous as forbidding, so much so I rapidly began to feel he would not be able to countenance defeat. The game to him mattered too much, and consciousness of that fact produced in me a feeling akin to nausea. I wanted nothing more than to knock over the Black King with the tip of my finger, signifying both an insouciant disregard for the game and a frivolous contempt for my childish opponent. Indeed I might well have done so had I not at that moment heard the taunt of a chilling and sinister laugh.

I glanced briefly at my vis-à-vis but there saw only a grave and portentous face, solemn in the extreme. Had I been wrong then? Had I only imagined Galbraith to have been mocking? For the first time that evening I noticed the mobile portrait before me fasten to an expression of inscrutable calm: I believe I feared that even more than the man's agitation. At any event, I determined then and there to make his victory as costly as I could: I should be like some Roman soldier on that fateful day at Asculum.

The immediate problem, though, was to discern his strategy. I filled our glasses and studied the board carefully. I know it sounds daft but I'd recently done the same thing with the King as earlier I'd done with the Queen: I'd pushed the poor-but-regal fellow forward into a similarly vulnerable position. Now, by reflecting with some keenness on Galbraith's likely attack, I saw that in three moves' time he must have the option of giving Checkmate. The situation was not hopeless, however, for I might retrieve it by sacrificing my remaining Rook in an intervening pin. Nonetheless it was a most gloomy prospect.

Then I noticed how—if I was to advance my Knight-Dexter to a particular position—I should not only cover a square Galbraith might wish to occupy but threaten also the two vacant stances flanking his King. In addition to which, I should be leaving my Queen standing entirely at his mercy, for she stood proud but defenceless rooted on the diagonal pathway of a hostile Bishop.

I decided to employ a little psychology. I allowed my left hand to hover over the Knight, but then retrieved it and began to pore intently over the other side of the battlefield. I put my right hand meanwhile over my head and made as if the quandary now suffered was causing me to extract a veritable tonsure, so desperate my predicament. Next, I allowed my left hand once more to linger over the advanced Knight. Then swooping all of a sudden I had the mare wrested from her stance—the armoured rider forwarded to a place near the King—and my own hapless Queen seducing my adversary's regard.

It was a bold move, but would it work? I took from my pocket a handkerchief which Madge had given me and wiped my forehead. Then I gulped down my beer like a man in need of solace. Galbraith all the while looked by turns puzzled, worried, depressed, and finally triumphant. With a click of wood against wood he swapped at last his Bishop for a Queen. An ultramontane church had reproved a cisalpine state for the impudence of its importunate king. So, perhaps, my rival might have thought. But just as one should not confuse chauvinism with misogyny, so should one not disparage the historic importance of sacrifice. It was the turn now of my own prelate to make a decisive move and to illustrate thereby that a national church may sometimes show forgiveness to a discomforted king. Standing the piece on the same diagonal as my opposing monarch, I declared with as much firmness as courtesy might allow, "Mate!" The White King had at last been toppled.

Galbraith's reaction to his defeat surprised me. His manner was relaxed and his face composed. He extended his hand to me and congratulated me most cordially. Then turning to Mac he bade his host farewell.

"I must thank you again for your hospitality. It's been a most pleasant evening."

"I am chusst sorry that we couldna help ye. Ach well, Sandy lad, call again if ye passin' this way. Good night tae ye noo."

"And to you, Mac. The major as well. Give him a dram if you've got one, he's earned it. Good night, good night."

So saying, the excise man stepped into the darkness, letting the beam of his torch illumine the path ahead. How he was going to get to Fort William at that hour, I had no idea—for he must surely have missed the last train. Then it occurred to me he must have a vehicle parked at Mallaig Bheag.

"What did you think, laddie?" queried Mac sensibly. "He's a fair enough sort, wouldn't you say?"

"I'd give him the benefit of the doubt," I replied.

"Oh, it is like that, is it now? There is doubt, then?"

"I could be wrong, of course, but to me he seemed a mite too preoccupied with the game of Chess. And his face, did you notice the way he looked?"

"No, laddie. I canna say I did."

"I'm probably just tired, Mac. When I've put you in the picture I'll take myself off to bed."

I flopped into a chair, lit up a pipe and began to describe the course of events that had brought me thus far. I told Mac everything—my meeting with Monty at the club, my encounter with the old Etonian, the episode at the Grand Hotel, the fortunate escape that had followed as well as the skirmishes subsequently with the twins in both Kerrera and Mallaig; I informed him, too, of Ishbaal, the deadly powder he dealt in and the exchange of that for a haul of narcotics. Finally I told Mac about Henrik Meyer and his own possible involvement in the crisis we faced.

"A rough-sounding Johnny, if ever there was," let out my companion, sounding genuinely concerned. "And from what you say, laddie, he's no half so bad as the other. Ishbaal, eh? Can't say I've heard of either of them, though the description you give of Meyer could fit two or three I've been warned of in the past. I presume you feel unable, therefore, to trust even Galbraith?"

"That's about the size of it," I conceded. "Maybe we'll be glad enough of his assistance later. What about yourself, though, are you ready to lend a hand?"

"Did I no say, laddie? No? Well, take it as said then, just as surely as I accept who you are and what you're about. It'll no be a favour, either. Right now I'm as bored as a coot in a pond. It'll be a rare treat to get back into the mainstream. Oh yes, laddie, you can count me in. One more thing—what on earth happened tae ye upbye?"

I finished off my narrative and was about to retire when suddenly Mac queried, "The boy, then, he's still on the hill?"

"'Fraid so, Mac. It was no time to be detained by a corpse. I'll see you in the morning."

A few minutes later I found myself lying in an ancient and none-too-generous double-bed awkwardly stretched out under the winceyette and contemplating the ceiling. For a little while it was a relief merely to listen to the wind—soughing evocatively amidst the rustling of firs: that, and the relentless trenching of tide upon shore. Soon, however, the exertions of the day caught up with me and I passed off into a deep sleep.

I awoke abruptly at 4.00 a.m. I'd been having the most appalling nightmare. It was about the blond-haired boy, the one I'd seen sitting with Meyer. He'd been under the latter's dominion, it seemed, for about five years. Prior to that he'd been through a succession of foster homes and had had a nasty episode in London in which he'd been forced into compliance during the making of a film. It was after that, badly damaged and psychologically scarred, that he'd come across Henrik Meyer. The Norwegian, whilst taking pity on the lad, had also permitted himself to feel towards him a growing attachment. In due course, however, the boy had become something of a dropout, got into drugs and for a while seemed totally lost. But Meyer—wandering like Jean Valjean through the sewers of the city—had somehow found him. His prospects began to look brighter. Then there he was, all of a sudden, limp and bloodied upon a moorland heath, the very same in fact whence I myself had hastened but hours beforehand. With his pitiable eyes staring at me from the heather, his mouth then opened and his whole face contorted into a silent scream.

I awoke dripping with perspiration even though the air in the room was sharp and cold. My unconscious had made the connection. The young man I'd witnessed slaughtered in front of me was none other than that boy, concerned but fearful, whom I'd observed earlier in the Belhaven Ward. And as Mac had so properly elicited, I had abandoned the dead body of that youth to whatever molestation man or beast might there devise. Instantly I was on my feet and making ready for the return. I knew I must make my way back to that same spot and convey the poor unfortunate to whomsoever would give him an appropriate burial. I'd put my own safety before common decency. It was a wonder I'd slept at all.

I crept out of the house finding to my satisfaction a full moon lighting up the entire landscape, suffusing it thereby with an eerie but magical glow. Whole swathes of hill and glen and a wide sleeve of water were bathed in a wonderful brilliance, a silver-blue aura that lent to the scene all about a superb and luminous sheen.

I wasted no time in retracing the pathway beside the burn and very soon was standing once more on the raised level of the mire. It may sound foolish but I'd put behind me all thoughts of Ishbaal and took only the minimal precaution of attending to sights and sounds occasioning surprise: a dog crossing the park, for instance, but with such feline grace that in reality it must have been a fox searching for prey or else a way back to its den; whilst a raised hand above the lip of a burn turned out to be but the disjointed bough of a fallen tree. I suppose I felt happier now, seeing the burden of my quest was shared by another; and, were it to prove necessary, Mac could always bring in Galbraith to lend support. After a while I left behind me the purling stream of light and took again to the higher ground. During all this time the way ahead remained clear, while I could see in the sky above huge clouds tinged with white or glimpse the great heavens between pierced by a multitude of stars.

At last I reached the small reservoir and began to scout around for the body I'd come to retrieve. A slight breeze had got up which made the silver water ripple in the chill of the air. I got as far as the rock and paused there beside the tree. Slowly the truth started to dawn. There was no sign of the youth's body, and, though I searched again and again, I could discover not a trace.

I was casting about thus in vain, at the point at which the pool of water fell into the burn, when I saw that lodged tightly there was the decaying carcass of a sheep. Exactly how it had got stranded was hard to say: perhaps it had fallen and drowned, thence got carried to the edge whence it had become stuck; or, failing that, perhaps it had simply been thrown in in some vandal-like act of recklessness. But whatever the explanation, and for some reason I couldn't fathom, it became terribly important to shift the poor brute, and I began frantically to wrench away at the single horn now remaining. Unfortunately the latter broke off and I then could no longer avoid grappling with its shaggy and bloodied remnants. The water I remember was ice-cold and when at length I disengaged the wretched creature I stood wet, trembling, and close to tears. Perhaps it was the combined effect of my exertion the previous day, my abortive attempt to carry out a burial, and now this grim tussle with a grave and sodden beast. Anyhow the strangely romantic setting of moorland and moonlight seemed peculiarly at odds with my present task. Once more the sheer absurdity of my position was being most miserably conveyed to me. I had thought of decency, of what was right; I had thought of Freya—how lovely if she were to behold this majestic land, this beautiful place; and I had thought of poor Monty, gone for ever. Now I stood staring into the indifferent night and wondering what to do with a corrupting animal. I felt cheated and mocked. I felt angry.

Blow the wretched creature—I should hasten back to Aridhghlinne and catch up on what sleep was due. I broke into a run and made good progress as far as the main burn. At that point I needed to take a slower, more cautious descent. All at once I became aware that two white dogs (terriers, I took them to be) were in the heather clumps surrounding me, racing round my feet and impeding my advance. Apart from the fact that they were harrying me at every footfall, they yelped and yattered incessantly: this again put me in a most ferocious temper. When I saw Mac standing by the pen, calling to the animals, I was not best pleased.

"Sae, laddie, ye've met Pibroch and Pishak, mi two canine accomplices. But why choose to meet them in the moonshine?"

"What on earth are you talking about? For heaven's sake, Mac, call them off!"

"There they go, laddie, there they go. I fear we have acted unilaterally. It's sometimes not a good idea that. In this case I think I got to your destination before you."

"What?" I gasped.

"The boy. I found him, just as ye said. I saw yon Ishbaal, too. Leastwise, reckon I did. I carried the poor youth as far as Bracora and left him there to be given a proper burial—they're Christians, so they'll no object. Then, as I was coming back, I noticed up by on the knoll the profile of a man. He was limping and appeared to be in haste. He was making some fine hirple of it, too—forging off in the direction of Loch Eireagoraidh and intent, presumably, on just the same business as ourselves."

"Did he see you?" I snapped.

"Not a chance, laddie, not a chance. I took every precaution a reasonable man might take, plus one or two others besides. No, no, I'm sure he didna. I was just coming alongside the pen when here mi two beauties began to summon up a racket to stonker the deid. I was thinkin' maybe Ishbaal has a sidekick, when who should I see drivin' mi dogs daft but yer very ain self."

By now we were coming down to the house and the first lights of dawn were showing the horizon in layers of agate: grey and yellow and delicate white. Though one or two stars still winked above the oystercatchers at the shoreline were sounding off the familiar pip-and-cry of daybreak.

Once inside we lit a roaring fire and breakfasted early. Then we dozed off a while in easy chairs and let the morning come upon us gradually. It must have been around eleven—and Mac was, I recall, expounding upon the problems of dichlorovus in salmon fishing—when I noticed that the surround of the window was beginning to rattle and that the wind must have shifted its direction. I therefore interrupted the diatribe my companion had so eloquently launched in order to signal the fact.

"Aye, so it hass, laddie, so it hass. It's swung a wee bittie to the north—though it's no fro' the west aal the same. By now—were a westerly brewing—the door in the far room would have banged tight. And that infernal wheepling at the shore, it has ceased. No, yon's moved from sou' sou' west to east nor' east, and it's freshening. What conclusion do you draw?"

"That shortly the *Queen of Sheba* will be heading our way. Look, suppose she's to land a largish cargo of drugs, Galbraith is surely correct to imagine the location here—or hereabouts—to be the ideal venue. Consider the bay, consider the road nearby, consider the railway line. If they are indeed going to exchange any Red Pepper for a haul of narcotics they may well do so this very night. What's more—if we did but know where!—the villain has probably stowed his cache somewhere in the vicinity. For all we know it could be up at the old house or down at the boatshed."

"Not, I think, the latter. That's where I keep Pibroch and Pishak. They'd never let anyone in without my being there and they'd ferret out a package as does a whippet a rat. No, but you've a point or two there, laddie. Maybe it's time to make a plan."

"I already have," I retorted. "I'm going to take a brisk march up to the first summit—"

"The Hill of the Goats, you mean, Carn a Ghobair, as the old map would have it…"

"It was steep enough, certainly. And high enough, too. All I need though is to see where the *Sheba's* anchored. My hunch is she'll soon be moored nearby. I'll come down at that point and we can prepare ourselves for nightfall."

"What then, laddie? What then?"

The question was, I confess, all too pertinent and deserving of reply—though of the latter I had little to make. I had no gun and to rely on wits alone would be foolish indeed. We were not dealing with maiden aunts and elderly gentlemen.

"Have you a shotgun, Mac?"

"No, laddie, I have not. I've no truck wi that sort of thing, not anymore. I have a bow and a set of arrows, if that's of any use."

"Your aim—is it true?"

"I normally hit the mark."

"Okay, well let's have you down by the boatshed while I'll keep low in the lee of the burn—I mean over by the old house where I can keep an eye on the proceedings. It'll be touch and go of course. We must not concern ourselves with the drugs, vicious though they are. Our sole aim must be to capture Ishbaal and to retrieve the Red Pepper."

"Capture, you say?"

"Capture or kill. But we must get the Red Pepper, and one or other of us must make good his escape. As I hope to be that one myself, I guess that leaves you in a pretty tight corner."

"Sae what's new, laddie, sae what's new? But dinna worry aboot me aal the same. I can take guy care o' missel'!"

"Stout fellow, Mac. Now I'd best be off. If you can get us something cooked—by say a couple of hours' time—I reckon I'll be more than ready for it."

"A couple of hours, eh? You're the fit one. It takes me nearer the three. See you later then."

CHAPTER 13

The Devil and the Ghost

I took to the west face of the Hill of the Goats with a vengeance. I knew the way well enough to proceed with some confidence and was avid to put into action the intent which all that morning had been simmering steadily. The air I recollect was wondrously fresh and on rounding a bluff exposing me to the rising breeze I caught the tang of the sea blowing in my face. In truth it was good to be alive and finer still to have my nerves pitched high and my muscles braced hard to purposeful effect.

I made such progress in pursuit of the top that barely three quarters of an hour had passed before the summit eluded me by a mere fifteen feet. It was then that I almost lost my balance—for I had suddenly to duck as would a warrior before the sweep of a claymore: only this was no cutting edge of an ancient clansman but the deafening passage of a low-flying jet roaring overhead. It shot into the distance like the fabled bat-out-of-hell.

I recovered my balance and paused to watch the aircraft disappear into a distant clot of cloud. Doing so a handful of frightened sheep brought to a halt their scurrying through the heather. I could imagine what a miserable reputation the pilots of such aircraft must suffer. The many peaceable folk going about their daily business, to say nothing of idyll-seeking visitors to the west, all alike would be resentful at such noisy and violent intrusions. For my part, momentarily stunned as I was, I could not do other than admire the nerve of the crew. I reckoned that that flight had missed my head by a mere thirty-so feet. Given it was a rehearsal for action in time of trouble, some risks surely had to be taken: but standing there staring at the face of the Sgurr beyond, and contemplating the awfulness of a miscalculation—even by a hair's breadth—I couldn't be anything other than astounded at the hardiness of those having the nerve to fly so fast yet so close to the ground. Were we not lucky to have such courageous souls? Set alongside their rare uplifting bravery, complaints about temporary inconvenience or protestations about sound seemed but unwarranted unworthy murmurings. Who could doubt that if called upon to act in the Gulf it would be pilots and navigators such as these who would thwart the enemy's radar, and do so time and time again? It was precisely their type who would defend democracy and stave from our peaceful kingdom the lunatic madness of war. Then and there did I thank God for their presence.

Lowering my gaze towards Loch Nevis at first I could see no sign of any boat bar an occasional fishing vessel. I took from my pocket the telescope and began to study the southern fringes of the water below me. I shifted position several times and finally caught sight of a port side which I fancied looked familiar. I again moved ground and was certain this time I had the *Queen of Sheba* in sight. Her sails were down and she appeared to be riding at anchor. Secure in the knowledge that the yacht was now waiting for nightfall, I began my descent. I had thirty-five minutes to get down if I were to arrive at the house within the stated two hours. Though in reality there was no rush, having given Mac an estimated time, my preference was not to be late. Then in hurrying not to be late I ended up typically by being early. In fact, drawing close to the original habitation of the croft, I had several minutes to spare.

That building by the way was in a sorry state of disrepair and constituted a cheerless spectacle of sanctioned decline. Seeing a date of 1810 scored into a large cornerstone, I couldn't help but reflect on the perceived struggles and doughty persistence of those first inhabitants. Even now the main structure of walls remained intact, although the internal fittings and woodwork had deteriorated badly in the wake of inevitable and encroaching damp. Whole pieces of panelling had been prised from the walls, windows stove in, and once-good timbers allowed to rot.

I ambled over to the byre to see if the dwelling place of creatures had fared any better. I stepped cautiously through the low doorway and peered about me. Suddenly I heard and felt simultaneously the crack of wood upon my bowed head. Then of sight and sound I lost all consciousness.

When I came to I was lying ingloriously on what appeared to be a mat made up of turf, nettles and stone. Slowly I focused and began to squint at the rotting-timber frames before me, imagining them to be all that was left of the original cattle-stalls. Once more attaining to the full possession of my senses, I gradually became aware of a presence immediately to my right; the presence of a figure it was, bent-over—the figure of a man. His face looked familiar.

"G-Galbraith," I stuttered. "Good Lord, man, whatever are you doing here? Give me a hand up, will you, there's a good chap. I must have knocked my head on the lintel there. It's good to see you."

"Perhaps, Major Delman. Perhaps not. I regret to say you've been doing a mite too much snooping for the good of my schedule."

"What? You're not saying I'm…"

I broke off. For the first time I noticed I was unable to loosen the torso of my body or to raise myself properly up from the ground. Two belts of leather had been firmly secured about my middle and were tied to the wall behind me.

"Now look here, Galbraith…," I continued but was soon interrupted.

"No, *you* look here. This is a risky and finely-tuned business. We're hoping to make contact this evening with known purveyors of narcotics. Yes, that's right—drug-runners. And we've calculated it's going to involve a pretty large haul too. There's just no way I can afford to have you interfering. As a matter of fact I've sent one of my colleagues to inform the police. You could be mixed up in this for all I know."

He spoke forcibly and his face was clearly agitated. An open sweat lay about his brow and on his breath I could detect something unpleasant—as if recently he had not been taking care of himself. This had been less noticeable in the smoke-filled room of the previous night. Now I wondered if there was something wrong with the man. I put it to him.

"Don't be an ass, old fellow. You must be sick. You can't actually think I'd have anything to do with smuggling heroine. I'm just as much against that sort of thing as you. In any case, Mac will vouch for me."

"'Fraid not, Major. It was Mac who told me. He said you'd been prying about asking folk too many questions."

"What!" I exclaimed.

"You heard. No, I'd not trust you as far as I could throw you. And I don't intend you to make a noise, either."

So saying and despite my protestations, Galbraith produced a large linen cloth with which patently he meant to gag me. Restrained though I was I might still have prevented him were it not for a sudden whiff of chloroform which assailed me and overcame me at once. For the second time I lost consciousness.

When I next came round it was already dusk. From my confined position I could see a mass of cloud had accumulated in the sky and could feel cold draughts of air coming in through gaps in the drystone walls. It may have been the latter which revived me, for the stench and taste of the rag in my mouth were truly appalling. Neither could I remove the cloth since my hands were both tied.

Nonetheless Galbraith had made one mistake at least. He'd pinioned me to the wall using a large, rusted wedge, and this protruded through two stones the cavity of which had been filled with plaster. The latter was clearly cracked, however, for by yanking myself from one side to the other I could feel the iron pin wearing loose. At length, with a slight jingle, it fell to the floor.

From then on it was relatively easy. First I found a sharp edge—a broken piece of corrugated roof—and cut the rope binding my wrists. Next I removed the gag. Lastly I managed to disengage the two belts from around my middle. However, standing over by the window, I got the fright of my life.

A mere ten yards or so to my right stood the deceptive figure of Galbraith. Somehow I'd remained out of earshot. I presumed the breeze and his sense of preoccupation had combined to distract him. It was fortunate too I'd not stepped into the open, for just at that moment a sheep scurried from a hollow and in just the same instant Galbraith swung round.

It was at this juncture—shifting my position—I discovered stationed a little to the left my adversary from a London-cab. Although at first I couldn't be sure when I had my telescope trained on his features, the last of the light revealed a broad forehead puckered with creases. So, my foe from Kerrera had picked up the trail.

For a while I could make no sense of such a coincidence. What was the remaining twin doing at Aridhghlinne and in cahoots with Galbraith? Then I noticed about Galbraith something that fairly drove the blood from the temples. As he stood there, his gaze fastened to the promontory opposite—a place known locally as Mary Anne's Point—I perceived his left shoulder to be lower by inches than his right. Not only that, but the man was quite erect and held his stance akimbo.

Suddenly the truth dawned. I was looking not at an excise-man from Fort William but at the master of shame, not at Galbraith but at Ishbaal himself. The man whom Mac had addressed as Sandy in reality he was none other than Ishbosheth, the very devil we were chasing. I'd been a fool not to realise it before. I'd thought it strange my opponent at chess should have worn beneath turn-ups a pair of black gum boots. Now I had the explanation. He would not as Galbraith have employed the same unwieldly shoe with which he'd been equipped during that day upon the moor. Instead, he'd managed in visiting Aridhghlinne to fabricate an alternative support in the foot of his Wellington. It must have hurt like hell, too. Either that or he'd somehow been able to contrive his form in a manner as to appear normal. Perhaps he'd acquired an ability to contort his shoulder or twist his frame to evidence a more regular profile. Whatever—he'd proved himself to be a consummate chameleon and had kept Monty's men guessing for many a long day. It was then the earlier description bore in on me and I recalled the uncertainty over Ishbaal's height. One thing was definite: there was no possibility this fellow had inspanned Mac either to his company or his purpose. Of that I could be certain. With Galbraith and for the sake of expediency it might have been different, although I thought even that to have made little sense. But with the devil incarnate there could have been no truck whatever.

Unfortunately I'd no sooner consoled myself on the matter of Mac's innocence than I began to torment myself with the notion that my friend might have been beguiled. Supposing Ishbaal had drawn him in under the guise of Galbraith, was there just then the iota of a chance that Mac might have been persuaded to assist the enemy? The very idea seemed absurd, yet the thought alas continued to vex me. I had to get free. I couldn't risk quitting the byre, however, as my adversaries were stationed too close to the exit. I should have to be patient and wait for the shadows to deepen.

To while away my time I made a closer inspection of the cattle-shed in which I was closeted. This turned out to be a surprisingly compact affair and of a design that was rudimentary yet well considered. The stalls themselves had clearly had their day and it was mostly wool which their remnants now housed. Above them an iron roof was nailed to stout beams of wood joined at the top. But it was the floor that chiefly interested me, for it had been built on two levels and with a wide channel separating one from the other, acting presumably as some sort of drain. The one to which I'd been prisoner was the higher of these and was made of concrete. The other, though, consisted simply of boulders with large stones driven into the ground and yet lain sufficiently close to convey the semblance of a floor. The latter incidentally was quite easy to discern while the former was a lot less evident to the eye. Nonetheless (as I have had cause to mention) there existed there a mat of turf and stone and nettle, and it just so happened that a corner of this had got tugged apart from the rest. Now, as I idly put my shoe to the tear, I found that it was not at all difficult to raise. It sounds stupid, perhaps, but before long I was down on my haunches and pulling back this turf like a roll of carpet. Sure enough, a concrete floor lay tidily beneath.

Something else, however, caught my attention to elicit further wonder and which was to have a direct bearing on the tale I tell. For immediately below the open window there appeared a perfectly-shaped square hole with a massive stone lodged in its aperture. The sight intrigued me and soon I found myself trying to dislodge this enormous plug. Try as I might, however, I was unable to shift the thing. All I could do was to rock it—a useless inch or two—from side to side. It was, moreover, so close-fitting and so awkwardly-shaped I couldn't get my hands far enough down its sides to get a decent hold. It was tantalising, and before long I'd got my knuckles and fingers thoroughly scraped.

Still, there was no sign outside of either Ishbaal or his accomplice making a move. Then I spotted a piece of discarded wire and attempted to loop that down under the stone but could only manage to wrap it about a single corner, thus once more a proper grasp eluded me. All the jolting and knocking, however, seemed to have angled the thing into a slightly different, perhaps easier position.

Suddenly I found my fingers had got far enough down to discover a grip. Bending them taut—underneath the thin ribbing of stone and along its narrow grooving—I succeeded thereby in lifting the weight an inch or two from the ground. Nervously, my fingers edged down.

Grimacing with concentration I now essayed to haul the stone upward. Half way up, though, it again lodged awkwardly and it looked as if my fingers were going to get in a mess, for I could neither withdraw the blessed rock nor lower it straightforwardly. I did not panic though but drew in my breath, leant forward, and jostled it just a fraction to one side. Then, all at once, I pulled it clear and was able to roll it away to reveal the hole.

By now I was kneeling down and trying my best not to pant out loud in the wake of my endeavours. Again I glanced through the window. The prospect was the same as before—though I noticed in addition a few spots of rain had begun to fall. Towards the bottom of the hole a well-contrived circular drain ran out from the far side. I put my hand and forearm into it and grubbed about for any objects lying there. All I retrieved was a little siltstone and a bit of twig. The drain was remarkably clean and almost entirely dry.

The reader may well marvel at my curious and distracted progress. Just the same I am bound to confess I was thoroughly intrigued. The rough boulder itself was much as you'd expect, though some of its multifaceted aspects seemed smoother and less opaque than others and here and there I seemed to glimpse the colour pink: but it was the fact it fitted so perfectly as a plug which fascinated me most. Why, indeed, had not a flat stone been used and one intended to cover the aperture instead of blocking the entire hole? And why insert something so cumbersome and so difficult to manoeuvre? Come to think of it, why prevent the passage in the first place from functioning as a drain? I couldn't help but conclude that somebody had deliberately wished to obstruct access whilst keeping the channel itself clear. If so, what was down there?

The question was vexing me to a funk when I noticed an abandoned roll of fencing. Woven through this was a single strand of detached, crumpled wire. Furthermore it was both thicker and stronger than the rusted measure I'd earlier employed. I managed to unravel a good length of the stuff and then let it probe and prod the extent of the drain. I even bent it slightly to negotiate a corner. But labours notwithstanding I brought from that hole nothing at all. I sat back against the wall weary and perplexed. Thank heavens for the breeze. If only the two outside would make a move. I put my head to the edge of the window and to my surprise discovered they'd gone!

Look about me as I did I was unable to see them. I ought to have been pleased, as now I was free to take up my position as planned in the burn beneath the cottage. Oddly, however, something had gotten into me. I felt frightfully alone and in a ferocious temper. I lifted up that infernal rock, and, raising it then to the level of my head, flung it down hard on the concrete floor. Somewhat to my amazement it fell apart!

I checked at the window again, lest anyone heard the blow and be eager to discern the cause. I paused for several minutes. No-one came. All the while I kept glancing at the broken stone. At length I focused my gaze and seemed then to see a lump of something more or less at its centre. Intrigued, I picked this object up and felt it in my hands. It appeared to be some kind of leather pouch.

By this stage my heart was beating frantically—and my blood had adopted a runaway pulse. Could *this* be it? I folded back the velvet skin and held in my hand a small container shaped like a jar. At the top of it I could detect no lid of any kind but instead my fingers ran over it smoothly from one side of the neck down to the other. The entire receptacle had somehow been fashioned as a single piece of glass. What, to be sure, had been so strangely and so carefully secured?

I struck a match in the cowl of my hand and proceeded to examine the bulb of glass, elongated and whole as it was. Though the light was poor I nonetheless discovered that which I fully anticipated to find. The queer-looking jar was filled with a powder of which the colour was that of a certain cactus-eating insect of Mexico, the homopterous cochinilla. There could be no doubt whatever—it was the Devil's Redpepper!

Had I been less excited by my fortuitous discovery I should surely have been rooted to the spot, being petrified with terror at what lay within my grasp. I should have been like the fellow depicted who guards the infamous red button—he has only to press a finger and the whole caboodle goes up; or again, like the febrile Prince of Denmark shivering before the ghost of his father and being tempted to step forward either to the flood or "to the dreadful summit of the cliff"—and so to madness. As it was, I felt so thrilled and relieved to have got back for Monty his charge that I tossed the thing twice or thrice in my palm. Then I rewrapped it and thrust it deep in my pocket.

I might have departed there and then to make straightaway for Porton Down, only just as I was about to decamp I noticed the clot of a man's presence on the lower park. Like it or not, even though the ball be in my care, I had to admit I might at any moment be brought to the ground knowing as I did neither the extent of the pitch nor the full complement of its players. What if Ishbaal had other aids, beside the remaining twin, posted on the hill? Where was Henrik Meyer? On the Burma Road perhaps. Then there was the strategy I'd negotiated with Mac. I could hardly leave him in the lurch, for all that I'd said; besides, it might be important to enlist his help if I were to make good my escape. I was pondering these questions when suddenly I heard voices. They sounded as if they were coming from the bay and on glancing in that direction I noticed a small searchlight scanning the cove. I decided after all to head for the burn.

I slipped back to the rear of the byre and proceeded to use the cover of the buildings to secure the vantage area of the earthen gully. Once established in the slope of the burn's ravine I was able to worm my way downwards to a position affording views of the road, park, bay and sward. Not only was the moon itself partly visible, but the beam below also gave considerable light. Clearly the crew of the *Sheba* considered that they were safe.

Then the moon shortly divested herself of her garment of cloud and shone magnificently in all her brilliance. At once the beacon of light vanished. A strange sight greeted all who watched. About the eastern horn of the bay there now emerged a wooden dinghy—already presaged by the steady *plish-plash* of oars slicing the waters. No majestic yacht this, but a humble affair and astonishingly laden. What I now gazed on was a small craft piled high with dozens of woollen fleeces. One man rowed single-handedly the weighed-down vessel while opposite sat another idle in the stern. At the prow of the boat I could catch the straining outline of a collie.

As the vessel came into the shallows it didn't make for the pier by the boatshed but found alternative anchorage nearer to hand, forcing me to conclude that a slipway of some sort must lie between the rocks. All sight of the dinghy had now been eclipsed. I dropped down as far as I dared and there, to my astonishment, saw the eerie, fey spectres of huge white animals (looking for all the world like gigantic sheep) stumbling towards me. I remained well hid and was able to observe this extraordinary sight as it gradually grew nearer.

Suspicions as to what these monstrous creatures might actually be were soon confirmed, the more so when a sheepdog barked at the first of them and a voice bellowed back at it to be still. What in truth I was watching was the progress of two shepherds. They were carrying great mounds of fleeces about their shoulders and were so burdened by them that each man was bent almost double. Somehow it seemed an ancient, curious scene borne of the timeless and in the silvery-blue cast of moon wonderful to behold. Totally enthralled I watched them making their way wearily to the boatshed opposite.

It occurred to me then I should perhaps detain these shepherds. Going in the direction they were, might they not scupper the entire operation? Indeed I got as far as standing out in the open when an almighty row erupted, for racing from the shed were a certain two terriers whom I recognised—only too well—as Pibroch and Pishak. They made straight for the single dog and began to worry and fret the poor creature, making it twist and turn in maddening circles. The dog then put up its own clamour of barking to which one of the men responded in a foreign-sounding tongue that at that juncture I was inclined to equate with the Gaelic.

The two herds, it must be said, appeared surprised by this, and though they called out to the animals, the canine mayhem continued as before. I next heard more shouting and along with it the abrupt sound of machine-gun fire. The gable-end of the shed was being peppered by a dire and frenzied attack. Amazingly the perpetrator of this assault was one of the shepherds!

All at once I saw the deception. These men were not rustics but members of *Sheba's* crew aptly disguised to avoid suspicion. Indeed, had they not been able to talk out loud using torches to illumine their way? I reckoned underneath the uppermost fleeces there probably lay secreted sacks of heroin. And this illicit connection was being expedited before my very eyes! Of Ishbaal himself, regrettably, I could see not a sign. I myself, moreover, still had the Red Pepper hidden in my pocket. I was obliged to conclude that Ishbaal never had had any intention of making an exchange and would dispose of these men as he had done others besides.

But when I heard a cry go up—and saw an arrow protruding from the first man's chest—I knew then that Mac himself was busy arresting their progress. The very next moment I had him in view. He stood up among the boulders at the leeward side of the shed and had a second shaft already trained on the victim's accomplice. Alas! I could make out a third fellow too coming up from the rear and about to knock him for six. Reckoning I should have a fair start on the opposition in front, I opted to follow my instincts: which is to say I put my hands to my face and roared out to Mac the vital warning.

In an instant he'd ducked and had slued round to the enemy. A further commotion then ensued while the wolf-in-sheep's-dress dashed forward to lessen Mac's chances by a hundred per cent

The worst of it all was I could do nothing to avail him. I'd broken my cover and must face the consequence. I scrambled back to the cottage and thence to the cowhouse. I was too late however to prevent that wily fox Ishbosheth from making his escape. As I now discovered, he'd made his way directly to the byre. He must all the while have been in close proximity, for I'd wasted no time myself and yet saw him depart the entrance while still a fair way off. He took to the hill—game leg and all—like a spirited goat.

Of all the nights of my life there then began one of the most awful if also (let it be said) awe-inspiring. As the way to the rear appeared barred to fortune I was forced to go forward. My chances of not being hit by a bullet seemed perilously slim. I suppose I was fully minded to catch up with Ishbaal: after all, if I could put out the main foe and then bury the concoction he'd devised it would not much matter what happened thereafter. Thank God I'd not married.

The problem now confronting me was the awkward nature of the terrain—that, and the agonising pace which my disabled enemy paradoxically was able to set. I can only describe his ability as superhuman; for sheer strength of will, sheer stubbornness of purpose I should say I have yet to meet his equal. How he managed with that handicap of his to climb, limp, trot—just to keep going—I shall never know. But keep going he did. Any thoughts I'd earlier entertained of "Galbraith" being unwell now seemed utterly without base. At one point—having overtaken Sgurr Eireagoraidh itself—I saw Ishbaal fall several feet down a particularly steep gradient: yet he regained his ground before I was able to close the distance separating us by as much as a half. Furthermore, the territory through which we now passed was unknown to me so that I was forced to rely ever more on Ishbaal's superior knowledge. I hesitate to say it, but increasingly—in that weird, moonlit and fantastical setting—I came to bear towards that lone creature an attitude I can only describe as akin to admiration: admiration that a being so disadvantaged could encompass within his frame such formidable mettle, such sureness of intent. At another juncture—when we were gaining the heights over Earnsaig—I saw him actually stop, turn round, and for several seconds watch dispassionately my attempt to pursue him. I believe in that lunatic-but-beautiful atmosphere a kind of bond, albeit subliminal, was being forged between us. Perhaps it's only fancy, yet I would have said that neither lacked a certain respect for the other. Evil he may once have been, but as a creature made impotent he exhibited a tenacity second to none.

The descent to the ruined habitation of Earnsaig seemed formidable, what with the steepness of the decline and the rough nature of the ground that jolted and jarred underfoot. The endeavour would have been unthinkable were it not for the fortuitous presence of the moon. As it was, it was probably a model of foolhardiness. In addition, I myself was ravenously hungry, having been unable to enjoy the anticipated lunch scheduled with Mac. Happily I'd kept about my person some of the chocolate and cake provided by Madge. Had it been daylight I dare say I should have made a pretty queer sight clambering down that precipitous mountainside whilst at the same time attempting to feed myself on sweetmeats.

The last part of it was, as may be imagined, a thoroughly bruising and uncomfortable experience. However at last the end came in sight and I caught a glimpse of the *Sheba* anchored in the shimmering waters below. Evidently Ishbaal was intending to swim to her moorings. Already he was flashing a torch and gesticulating to the remaining crew. He spoke the same strange tongue as that adopted by the men at Aridhghlinne.

Seeing my prey about to elude me I put on a sprint over those last hundred yards and entered the shallows before Ishbaal had reached the deeper section. However, even that short distance—for I am no use whatever in water—seemed a deal more than the fifty or so yards it must actually have been. The miserable apophthegm, "So near yet so far," came inescapably to mind. What I needed now was a miracle.

I found one in the shape of a large discarded door come in with the tide. I pushed it out some way and flung myself onto it. I then propelled the rudimentary raft by the use of my arms, much as might a surf-rider do on the crest of a wave. My progress unfortunately was rather less spectacular and altogether less rapid. Even so, the distance between door and boat started to diminish while I closed in steadily on the now faltering Ishbaal.

What surprised me all the while—as no doubt it did my enemy—was the apparent absence of any member of crew: none stood alert on deck and none was ready to lend a supportive hand. For me of course it was just as well, as it was hard to imagine they would do anything other than shoot me. I should drown, for sure.

It was in a moment of desperation—as I saw Ishbosheth pull hard on the ladder and heave himself free of the water—that I badly misjudged my actions and almost came a cropper. The door and I parted company as it was for it rolled over onto my shoulder, temporarily pulling me down. I came up in a state of panic, flailing my limbs and yelling like mad. I'd just about swallowed my fill of the ocean when astride the yacht's ladder a fresh figure emerged. As he reached down towards me, however, I was convinced it was too late—for it seemed I was staring at a being no longer of our world. It was the form of a ghost that seemed to come over me and the unreal hand of a spectre that drew me from the depths: for at the point I lost consciousness I caught sight of a face familiar and dear, the face of a friend, but of a friend taken from me plucked from life. You see, it belonged to none other than to Montagu Fiennes.

Yet several moments later, awaking to find myself below deck, the familiar countenance was the same. The only difference was that it was creased by a wide and mischievous smile.

"But you're..."

"Dead? I know. Don't worry, Fred, it's me all right. Now sit up, will you, there's a good chap, and see if you can down a bit of this tea. I thought you were a gonna back there. It's a good job you hollered or I'd have been too late. Your loss of memory is a deceptive thing."

I failed to pick up my friend on this last remark, being at the time too much in need of an explanation as to how he'd survived. After all, the last occasion I'd seen him he was engaged in a mortal free-fall from the Glenfinnan viaduct. I was pleased, of course, but bewildered as well—and, to my surprise, irritated and angry.

"But Monty," I stammered, "I saw you plummet to your death, saw you with my own eyes. No man could have survived a fall like that!"

"No, and no-one did. The body you saw did indeed depart this life and I hope for his sake he never regained consciousness. It is unlikely that he did."

"But damn it, I *saw* the cyclist—the one with the cape—I saw him hurl you over the edge."

"No, Fred, that's what you *thought* you saw. You believed you saw a cyclist. Well, in reality, it was one of the Lopez twins from Peru and dressed not in a cyclist's cape but in some new-fangled aquascutum. It was, to be precise, the senseless body of a certain Alberto Lopez, one of Lima's up-and-coming mafiosi and the very same thug who'd driven you to Euston. His brother, you will recall, you'd observed on the train—his own name, by the way, was Sancho. Time was when it would have been hard to have found a more intelligent bandit. It's a shame he fell in with Ishbaal, for once he did some useful work for the C.I.A. Anyhow he's dead now, and I gather it was you who put him down—so Malahide informs me. It's no great loss to humanity that he's out of the picture."

"Malahide?" I queried. "Up here?"

"Certainly. Has been for days. He's undercover, of course, so I doubt you'd have spotted him."

"Hang on though, Monty," I added—my mind going back again—"I believe I saw that chap—Alberto you called him—only a few hours ago up at Aridhghlinne."

"Fooled again, I'm afraid. That was Jose, a cousin of the Lopez twins and no mean chameleon himself."

I sat there in that smartly polished cabin staring disbelievingly at the person in front of me, scarcely able to take in a word of what he said. Somehow Monty was alive; somewhere around Mallaig Malahide was acting for MQ1; and somebody called Jose was impersonating the man whom I'd seen careering to his death. Still, the picture looked incomplete and I pursued my questioning.

"But why on earth did you disappear at Fort William? What in heaven's name were you up to?"

"Listen, Fred, I don't blame you at all for being angry. You've had to endure more than friendship allows. No, let me continue. The problem, you see, well, it arose on 'The West Highlander'—when that wretched youth with the earphones announced news of a possible attempt on the life of the P.M. I realised I'd need then to detach myself from you as soon as I could. If the police had connected me with your doings in Brighton the delicate and secret nature of my mission would have been blown apart. That's why, as soon as the train reached Fort William, I grabbed the only taxi available and backtracked to Spean Bridge. From the hotel there I was able to make a series of telephone calls, but none to the Alexandra. That would have been too risky—I couldn't consider it. Besides, I'd already slipped you a covert warning and alerted you to the possible presence—in the Belhaven Ward—of Henrik Meyer. I hoped you might follow that up, although I should have realised your loyalty to a friend was sure to make you come looking for me. Anyhow, I was able at last to get through to Malahide and I arranged for him to come up here the following day. He travelled on the morning train, second class only, and was—he told me—cursing all the way. It's largely through him, though, that we learnt of the *Sheba's* passage along this infernal loch."

Seeing I was still shivering, Monty broke off and lit up a couple of cigarettes, pushing one of them into my mouth.

"Draw on that, Fred, it'll bring you round. Now, what was I saying? Oh yes…Malahide, he's been invaluable. Same goes for that chap from Customs. Told us the most probable venue and said he'd do everything to assist us. The problem, however"—and here Montagu Fiennes became grim in the extreme—"is that we are no further forward in relation to Ishbaal or to his cache of Red Pepper. Our hope is he'll make his transaction with the beached drug-runners. If so, one of our chaps—and there are four altogether—will apprehend him or else it's my guess he'll make his way to the *Sheba*. What he doesn't know is that when two of his crew took off in a dinghy—disguised, I might add, as shepherds, nice touch that—we ourselves came up in the *Little Hebrides*, sent ahead a couple of our men to take out the opposition, before coming over here to board the *Sheba*. It's possible any moment now Ishbaal will attempt to gatecrash the party. In fact, I must have a word with Galbraith. Poor fellow, he looked about in."

"Where's he, then?"

"Up on deck. Look here, 'fraid I'll have to continue with this in a minute."

"Wait!" I snapped. "That's not the excise man you've got. It's the devil himself—it's Ishbaal!"

"What!"

"You heard! If you'll observe, Monty my old friend, I've not exactly been idle myself. Yet—as you point out—now is not the time. Suffice it to say you'll find Galbraith's shorter in one leg than the other, while not long ago he believed a certain major to be stowed away in a ruined cowhouse. He's every bit the tricky customer you made him out."

With the delivery of that broadcast I saw my companion's face shift from a preliminary look of disbelief, to one of surprise, to one of astonishment. Then he was in control again.

"Quick, Fred, he may try to escape!"

We dashed to the wheelhouse only to find both pilot and Galbraith gone. Each of us searched about in the darkness, the wind freshening our senses and putting into our faces occasional spits of rain. I could easily imagine my friend's desperation, for he still did not know I had the Red Pepper. Then I tried a ruse.

"Supposing he's gone! Supposing we never see him again, I've already got the Red Pepper—here in my pocket!"

With the cry of that admission there followed a lull even in the noise of the wind and the slapping of the waves. It was as if I had put into that elemental confusion a moment of command—of poise or stillness.

Monty stood there, flabbergasted, staring at me. He was confounded still more when I produced from my pocket a small jar of ruddled powder.

"We've won, Monty!" I shouted into the dark. "We've won! Ishbaal is powerless. The devil's no more!"

Speaking thus I held aloft the jar. There then happened that which I calculated must come to pass. Ishbaal, who all the while had been clinging to the starboard-exterior, swung over the railings like a trapeze artist and leapt to my side. I tossed the object of his attention into the air and for several dread-filled seconds we watched the lid tremble on Pandora's box as the devil's work rose upwards. Then it fell.

Not for nothing is Montagu Fiennes the mastermind and overseer of MQ1. He caught the offending object with the alacrity of a cricketer. As for myself, I thanked God that the *Queen of Sheba* had not at that moment been jolted by some lump of wave.

After that came a fiendish, bloodcurdling cry as Ishbaal threw himself into the now boisterous sea-loch and struck out with a vengeance through the drawing tide. Monty and I watched helplessly as our worst enemy inched steadily shoreward. It came as a surprise, moreover, to observe that whilst below *Sheba's* decks the good lady had but turned the corner at Earnsaig and was still within sight of Aridhghlinne. Even now, therefore, Ishbaal might call upon the assistance of some remaining accomplice.

Then Monty, grave-faced, turned towards me to speak above the racket of the wind. But it was not, alas, to offer praise to Allah for the return of Red Pepper. Instead, it was to recall a sentiment expressed earlier about my failed recollection.

"What do you mean?" I cried, more than vexed by what seemed a mindless non sequitur. "What is it that makes my memory-loss so deceptive?"

"No need to worry!" he yelled. "It's just I remember how well you swam at Oxford and more recently on our jaunt in the Atlantic."

Both of us at this time were standing abaft the main mast, our hands firm upon the stays and adjacent shrouds, relief-crew battling at the helm. It wasn't exactly terra firma but it seemed a whole lot better than the motioning surface into which Ishbaal had plunged. In addition, the moon was nowhere in sight and only an infrequent star could still be seen. A single sail flapped and walloped in the breeze. Then I got angry.

"For heaven's sake, man, I've returned you your precious Red Pepper, isn't that enough? God knows I'd like to apprehend the fellow—of course—if I could only swim!"

By now Ishbaal was halfway to the shore.

"But one time you *could*. They say once you've learnt you always remember. I'm no swimmer myself and can't corroborate that. As I said, don't worry. It's a pity. That's all."

I stood on that wretched vessel peering into the gloom and bluster of the loch and feeling nauseous at the sheer sight of all that turbid water. I thought of the evil Ishbaal intended, the evil he might do. I thought of our troops stationed in the Gulf and ready to wage war. I thought of Freya, of the boy on the moor. Finally I thought of Ruairidh and of my promise to the Robertsons. Then I swung myself over the railings and entrusted myself to the Almighty and to the word of my friend.

In two seconds flat I felt the shock of the impact and the terror of drowning that had earlier befallen me. My head went down. Was I about to see the whole of my life now pictured before me? Then this word, the one word, iterated and reiterated in my mind—Freya, Freya, Freya!

All at once I began to move my arms more purposefully and the flailing about became a steady stroke, powerful and vigorous. My head once more broke the surface and I gasped and swallowed less of water, more of air. I could see Ishbaal pulling towards the bay and I began then to pursue him more relentlessly I think than I had upon the hill.

But then disaster! My foe had reached the shore and I myself the area of the bay, when a bullet whizzed out across my head. Then another, and another. I ducked beneath the surface and tried to impel myself forward, keeping in the same direction. However there came to me at that point a remark Mac had once made in discussing the nets—about vast underwater quantities of bootlace and of fronds, of great swathes, leathery and slippery, of bladderwrack and ropes and tangles of weed. It was in the midst of such an underwater mess that I now began to struggle and swim. I could feel my head and lungs ready to explode, panic tempting me at every turn.

Yet it was also then that I encountered a series of stones, regular and slab-like and appearing to slope. At once I recognised my location: I was situated at the foot of the pier. The knowledge calmed me. I began to breathe out—slowly, slowly—and to haul myself gradually from stone to stone. I surfaced. Nothing happened. I descended once more. Then I stood dripping before the front of the shed. Thankfully it appeared I must be out of view of anyone either on the road or watching from the park.

A little way off were two bodies. I could tell at a glance neither belonged to the redoubtable Mac. With that fillip to my senses I straightaway headed for the track at the shore—the original path of Ecky Donaldson and the same exit to safety which Ishbaal must follow.

To start with, progress was relatively straightforward: the rocks and slabs of that first path were large ones and they had been lain with great care, even if every now and then one of them would tilt or wobble alarmingly. Once the corner of the bay had been turned, however, the way was periodically overcome by a profusion of vegetation, being in at least two places broken by the incessant erosion of shore-rubble and sea: on these occasions it was necessary either to forge an exit through the undergrowth or to tackle the slanting piles of rock in the rapidly incoming tide. Even in the midst of my labours I regretted an insufficiency of time to take proper note of the craftsmanship—the darkness of the night demanding concentration be focused strictly on orienteering. All the same I found the temptation irresistible at one point to note how a curtain of rock had been adroitly cornered by this carefully elevated path: at its extremity the latter was supported by a single column of slabs some twenty feet high; the water beneath splashed unnervingly, yet that contrived tower stood firm as Peter before the fires of Gehenna.

It must have been shortly after this I heard—sounding above the wind—a familiar drumming of blades. The noise to my ear was unmistakable; it was the rotatory *thump-thump-thump* of a helicopter and was fast approaching. When it came into view I thought I recognised it as a Lynx—certainly it was smaller than either a Wessex or a Sea King—and it was coming dangerously close to the side of the cliff. Then I noticed a line being let down and observed Ishbaal leaving the path, scrambling towards a small outcrop of rock jutting from the line of the shore. I would have hastened to detain him were it not that the surrounding boulders were suddenly alive with ricochet and I was forced to take cover.

I watched helplessly as the deafening rhythm of the machine proclaimed Ishbaal's escape and the futility of my efforts. There was nothing I could do! At least the young King David had been granted a sling.

Just as the enemy had recovered its leader I spotted—high above my own position—the shadowy figure of a man. He was wearing on his head what looked like a Balaclava, whilst in his hands he wielded a substantial firearm. The next thing I knew was that a terrific explosion had occurred and the helicopter was spinning uncontrollably down into the sea. A crash soon followed and there seemed little hope of anyone's survival. All the same I had not actually seen Ishbaal enter the machine. Granted he had got as far as the extended hand of some henchman, but had he or had he not got the full force of the crash? Or had he instead fallen with his ghost intact?

I was about to investigate when a fresh hazard of bullets began to rebound about the rocks. Whoever had brought down the Lynx now seemed intent on felling me! After a while, though, the attacker fell silent and I tentatively moved forward. I soon discovered I was at the foot of a gorge, and finding the initial gradient fair and the ground not difficult, I decided to make a climb of it to see what else the Norns had in store.

I had not even got beyond the first rim of the ascent when I realised my mistake. The deep gloom of the early night had lifted somewhat and the sky gave off enough light now to reveal a precipitous wall of scree terminating above a bridge. So, I had come half way now, being directly below the Burma Road—at the very point where the main chasm had been breached. In for a penny, in for a pound, I reckoned I'd have a go at it despite the risk of falling or of starting an avalanche.

It was awkward going and I took my time. A little over half way I paused to take breath and to take account of my position. It was just then that my attention became distracted by a patch of white. It was, on inspection, a small piece of paper folded in four. Next to it I struck a more impressive find, for there lying in the fretwork of stones was the widely used “Gimpy” of our elite forces. Three feet higher up there lay an additional, more formidable weapon—a “Stinger” 70 mm anti-aircraft missile. That explained the hasty demise of Ishbosheth’s helicopter. Of the owner of these weapons there was no sign. I could only speculate as to what had happened. I considered it most likely he’d departed in some haste. Why else would he abandon his combat-equipment? Intrigued by my discovery I pocketed the folded paper for good measure and then temporarily forgot about it.

After one or two nasty slips and a thorough scraping by wet and jostling stones I eventually came out beneath the bridge itself. I heaved myself up and sat on the edge. I was facing Mallaig Bheag and admiring the silhouette of Skye—almost in touch it seemed with the road—when who should come into my view but Henrik Meyer! I had just enough time to disconnect a freshly lain plank before the fellow was upon me.

I struck Meyer a manful blow in the flank and saw him totter to one side. The piece of timber, however, proved to be less resistant than my opponent’s ribs, for I was left standing with but half a beam. My adversary flung back his head and roared with pleasure. Seeing his middle thus distended I bent my head and rammed myself into his solar plexus with as much force as I could muster. This made more impact, and the Norwegian emitted a guffaw of pain.

I attempted at this point to sidestep Meyer and to make thereby an undignified but rapid exit. My intention was foiled, though, by the sheer size of the man, for as I moved towards him he simply fell across my path making me trip over his torso. For a moment stunned, I allowed my foe to regain his feet. As he did so, however, I registered a degree of surprise: the thing I dreaded most was to be pinned beneath his weight—yet Meyer had held back from doing that.

Taking my astonishment for fear the giant in front of me gave out a deep bellow. Oddly, however, he did more than just that. Like some character from a fable he stamped his foot onto the bridge in a gesture of defiance. And this was his undoing. The rotten wood gave way and immediately his boot wedged into the crumbling splinters. This time I moved more quickly. In two seconds flat I was on my feet and in no more had thrown the whole of my weight at his distorted figure. Both of us went down—he with his back over the side and I on top. But it was I who'd won the initiative. I pulled his foot from the hole and yanked his leg—and he plunged, head first, down into the chasm. A careering of rocks signalled his descent as I left him there to sort out his fate as best he could.

The first proper light of dawn lifted from Mallaig Bheag the earlier impress of night, allowing me thereby to make my way back to the glen and thence to the Circular Walk. It was there that I benefited from a stroke of good luck. Tied to some railings surrounding the garden of a house was an old bicycle. I freed the thing from its anchor and thereby set up some wretched animal howling in protest. But—as Mac might have said—I was 'no caring.' Unsteady though I be, I hoped to put in several good miles before Mallaig had awoken.

CHAPTER 14

Towards God's House

I left Mallaig early that morning in a state of some ignorance and devoid of any plan. All I knew for certain was that the infamous Red Pepper was safe in Monty's hands and that in all probability Ishbaal was dead. Other than that, it was still possible the latter's henchmen were posted on the high ground where they might be intending to dispose of either me or the unfortunate Mac. My companion from MQ1 would hopefully tie up any loose ends and ensure that my ally at Aridhghlinne be duly rewarded. Looking about me as I went though, seeing the fresh and windswept sea with Rum and Eigg beyond, I determined that before very long I should revisit my former host and that on doing so I should be accompanied by Freya. Finally, my mind had yet to take cognisance of the local constabulary.

The problem in that regard was I might still be taken in for questioning as a wanted man. Not only that, but it was possible Ishbaal under the guise of custom's inspector might have alerted the interest of otherwise apathetic police officers. For all I knew—speeding past the cemetery at Morar—I could be summoned once more to a chase: only this time the exchange of four wheels for two must surely see me apprehended.

In the meantime one broad bay succeeded another: links, shore, and sea. And with them the wild birds—sandpipers, oystercatchers, "hoodies" and gulls—they rose, they fell—while always to my left was a bastion of hill or a levelling lower down to a bleak piece of moorland or wooded glen. The sleepy little town of Arisaig came and went. I left behind the coast and headed eastward into that deep and mountainous terrain between Lochailort and Glenfinnan.

When I came at last in sight of the celebrated viaduct I stopped and stood again in awe. I think I felt giddier this time looking up to that great edifice—seeing it put into perspective by still greater heights—than I'd earlier been from my vantage point on the railway line. I thanked God that my worst fears had been but fancy and my friend was alive and succeeding still.

It was when I stopped too that I realised the extent of my fatigue. Remember, I had slept little in the last couple of days and not at all for the past twenty-four hours. I was in addition thoroughly famished, dishevelled in appearance, and in obvious need of a shave. Notwithstanding the dirt on my dungarees—and in spite of a tear or two in my homespun—I ambled on down, bicycle at my side, to a nearby and grand-looking hotel above the shoreline of Loch Shiel. It was on inspection a place of baronial splendour, wreathed in rust-red creeper and surrounded by resplendent scenery.

Leaving the cycle outside the front door I proceeded to the area of the lounge bar to discover I was almost alone. The exception was a small figure of a man who had just collected his change and was lifting up nervously what looked like the first dram of the day. He emptied the glass in two gulps and then ordered another with a half a pint of beer. Next he lit up a cigarette. Suddenly his face grew more expansive and he began to chide the bargirl for not serving me more promptly!

Not being in any mood for bar-room badinage I carried my own measure-and-a-half to a seat by the window. I took out my pipe to smoke and began thereafter to feel not only a certain distance from the previous evening but also the pleasantness of my present location. However, it was not long before a handful of locals entered who themselves preceded a party of visitors. The place was getting busy and I wondered if a quieter spot might not be found.

I ordered a second drink and made my way to the foyer. There, and to my pleasure, was a great hearth surrounded by comfortable chairs. At its centre a marvellous wood-and-peat fire blazed beneath the mantelpiece. A mellow sweetish smell permeated the atmosphere, peatsmoke filling the interior. Though modern lights here and there burned discreetly behind shades, the place had about it for the greater part an air that was almost antique: dark too perhaps, but altogether too welcoming to be described as "dingy." Best of all though the entire space was devoid of occupants. I collapsed into a chair and allowed my thoughts to unravel in the reverie of long-awaited sleep.

It must have been about four-thirty when I came to, for I heard a waitress whispering to a young couple, "Any more orders for tea? Last call."

"Please," I replied, and then added to her amusement, "Know anywhere I can get a shave?"

Again I was in luck. A passing attendant pointed me to a washroom where I should find an ivory-covered blade and an old leather strop. After a wash and a shave the next priority, naturally, was to get something to eat. In the event I dined rather handsomely—off trout, venison, and a plate of plum pudding—and drank with it a bottle of claret commended by the house.

It was not until I was in the main lounge, and there seated with a pot of tea and some petits fours, that I remembered the piece of paper I'd put in my pocket. I unfolded it and at once discovered the following cryptogram.

N
O
N
SED SARUM
A
L
S
U
M

It looked and sounded patently nonsensical: still, I'd seen this sort of thing before and confess to being thoroughly intrigued by it. The *non...sed* formula was easy enough to decipher. I knew sufficient Latin to translate the construction "not...but." Furthermore, I knew the Roman *salsum* denoted the English word "salt". So, straightaway I'd got three quarters of the message: "not salt, but..." Presumably it must end, I reflected, in the word "pepper." Now that made every bit of sense, for while Red Pepper had been the object of my quest it might also have been the concern of one of Ishbaal's hirelings. Moreover, the predicate "red" was itself contained in the "crosspiece" *sed sarum*.

As soon as my mind had registered the evidence of a "transverse beam" I caught, naturally, the allusion to a cross but wondered what significance that might have for Ishbaal whom I'd taken to be both irreligious and without scruple. It was possible, of course, that the cryptogram was of an accomplice's devising: yet as an explanation that didn't entirely convince—it just didn't seem likely. Conversely, and on reflection, an artifice of this kind was precisely what I could conceive Ishbaal to be capable of—a man of shame might well resort to the pivotal symbol of Christian faith to intimate his devilish intent; in his case, it would merely be par for the course. All the same, what particular meaning might the sign carry in the context of

Red Pepper? That was the question vexing me now. X marks the spot, they say; but I'd found the Red Pepper and the marking was either a plus or a cross—not an X.

I must admit, however, sitting there smoking my pipe and enjoying the feelings of a man who has exercised hard and eaten well, I began to feel rather pleased with myself, congratulatory even. Had I not (albeit with luck) beaten my foe and thwarted his purpose? Had I not virtually deciphered his code—a foolish bagatelle, no more than some iced overlay adorning a wedding cake? Then an intrusive piece of knowledge robbed the celebratory confection of its decorative top. The Latin for the noun "pepper" I recalled was piper, piperis. I had got the cipher wrong and with the realisation soon started to tire of the thing. What did it matter, anyhow?

I returned to the bar to contemplate my next move. Perhaps I needed to make directly for Westminster and there make enquiries regarding Monty and the whereabouts of MQ1. The difficulty though was I still didn't know whether man or organisation was officially recognised. Until Monty himself prepared the way, till, that is, he'd declared the precise nature of my dealings in the affair—as precise as facts would allow—then it seemed best I bide my time and avoid the police. On the other hand he might well expect me to make contact either with Freya or my aunt in Winchester. Yet I myself was determined to keep them both as far removed from the entire business as possible. After all, was it not conceivable that Ishbaal's network—in seeking to ensnare myself—might trepan in the process those in my association? So it was, then, I found myself returning to my first notion—though now with the firm resolve of remaining incognito throughout. Perhaps, too, I might make inquiries at the Livery Club and gain word of my friend there. In any event, the time seemed ripe to be quit of Scotland and to proceed henceforward in the direction of London. For the moment, however, I had no wish to spend the night in an hotel any more than did I to travel by train the following morning. Then, curiously, an alternative possibility presented itself.

Standing a little distance from the bar was the same fellow I'd observed earlier, the one to be absolutely truthful I'd sought to avoid. Now I overheard him talking, making some private boast to the barman who'd taken over from the girl. It appeared he'd made a great deal of money in the previous ten days, his earnings amounting even after deductions to a considerable sum. His drift assumed the following course.

"I know what it is that is my weakness," he averred, striking up a match for a further cigarette. "It is what is in this glass here. I like the drink, it is true. I know I do. For another man it might be something different. But on the other hand I work for it, I work very hard for it. As a matter of fact I'd say I work harder than most of the people up here. That ways I pays for my dram and nobody loses out."

The barman served me and slyly winked before raising his gaze upward to the ceiling. He spoke softly.

"That's wee Murdo, a whippet and a wisecrack if ever there was. He's in from the fish farm, the one by Lochailort, you'll have seen it I dare say. Tonight, he's taking an old truck of his down to Dover. He'll be up again—day after tomorrow—for last call at lunch time. Then he's going to do a spot of shearing—which should have been done already—then after that he'll take a real skinful. If he can sleep at all he will, but in either event he'll be the first up in the morning at Lochailort."

Raising his voice the barman then turned to the till, keeping his back to his customers.

"I was just telling our guest here what an awful man you are, Murdo Murchison…Eh? One for the road, is it? What time are you off then, and have you told the missus?"

"Oh she knows fine my comings and goings. And if she did not she would no be caring. As a matter of fact she might prefer it. Aye, I would say that…I would."

I could not at this point be sure whether I was in the company of an alcoholic, a workaholic, or a candidate for marriage guidance. In any event, I decided to take a chance.

"Would you have room for a passenger?" I asked.

"I might," replied the other. "Then again, I might not. Where is it you're heading for?"

"London. Will you have another? To clear the head."

"Oh there's nothing wrong with my head. But I'll take another if you're offering."

"Only I've to get there as soon as I can. There's a hundred in it if you'll do it."

"Oh, I'll do it all right. As a matter of fact I'll get you there in less time than you think. Hand over the money to Donald Alastair here. He can do the sums tomorrow and I can drink in peace."

I did as I was bid. Afterwards Murdo Murchison led the way to his lorry. He seemed none too steady on his feet and lit another cigarette at the side of the vehicle. Then he coughed, spat, and hoisted himself up behind the wheel. In five minutes we had put Glenfinnan behind us and were heading for the "Fort."

Fearing my chauffeur be in loquacious mood I pleaded tiredness and made as if to sleep. I did so speculating on the likely outcome of our shared passage: indeed a room in London; a cell, perhaps, in a police station; maybe a casualty ward in a hospital. I needn't have worried, though, for even if "wee Murdo" did put on a frightful pace he gave every impression of being wholly in control.

I woke up at one juncture to discover the lorry had stopped and that the driver's seat had been abandoned. Before I'd time to be alarmed, however, the fellow Murchison returned. I asked him where we were.

"Coming up York," he proclaimed.

Five minutes later, just again on the verge of sleep, I caught the following pronouncement.

"Eh—borr—achum, eh—borr—achum."

"What?" I asked, ungrateful at being summoned from slumber.

"It's Latin. Did you not know that? Well, well, I'm surprised. And you an educated fella, an' all. Or so I took you for, anyhow."

"Oh, *Eboracum*, you mean. Quite, quite."

"That is what I said, is it not? Eh—borr—achum." Then he added. "Are you all right, there? Do you want a cigarette?"

I stayed silent and allowed the word to sink in. As I did so another word shot into consciousness.

Sarum—Old Sarum. Suddenly I was awake. Wide awake. I sat up and took out my pipe.

"Oh, it is the pipe you smoke, is it?"

Over the next two hours I found myself half attending to the "whippet" and half turning over the implications of this subliminal revelation. I might indeed have been grateful to Murchison had he not kept asking questions and jolting thereby the flow of my meditation. All the same, a picture began slowly to emerge.

Old Sarum was as commonly known the name given to an ancient Hill Fort situated beyond the city of Salisbury. It was there that the present town had had its Iron Age antecedents and whence derived its designation of New Sarum. So, New Sarum stood for Salisbury. Now Salisbury itself was chiefly famous for its spired cathedral—for far and wide the dominating landmark and an inspiration to paint for both Constable and Turner. In addition to which, a church or chapel not infrequently was signified by the symbol of a cross cast in the form of a plus-sign. Accordingly the cryptogram in my pocket ought to have read, "Not salt, but Salisbury Cathedral." Moreover, any connection with Ishbaal would make the inclusion of Red Pepper entirely plausible. The actual message was simply this: Red Pepper / Salisbury Cathedral.

While I was smoking another bowl of tobacco a further realisation occurred. Salisbury was the nearest major conurbation to a certain venue whence a dubious American had fled complete with devilish charge. Porton Down, in other words, lay only a few miles north by east from the city itself. Given Ishbaal hadn't wished to be deprived of his invention, might he not have intended to use the stolen narcotics in a further trade-off? Perhaps he still needed access to the facilities at Porton Down. Maybe he would make an offer to an employee there of the Sicilian type—handsome, and to be turned down only at one's peril. For some transaction—be it in drugs or Red Pepper—was certainly about to take place and it seemed Salisbury Cathedral was the likely location. But bearing in mind what had happened, could the operation still proceed? That was the question, and there was only one way to find out. First I should have to get there.

Then sometime during the "wee small hours" my diminutive companion stopped his truck at a scruffy roadside establishment denominated 'Alfredo's Caff.' I went in with him and sat down to a pot of tea and some hot-buttered toast. He, however, spotting someone he knew, walked over to a table on the far side of the room. I noticed then that a quarter bottle of amber was being poured into two plastic cups and regretted at once I'd not had my own flask filled as a fillip to loyalty.

I wandered over to the window and peered out toward the asphalt park. There were three lorries stationed close to the entrance and emblazoned across the nearest of these were the words 'Arkinshaws of Reading, Removals.' The driver of this vehicle was just about to get into his cab. Without a moment's delay I slipped out of the 'caff' and ran straight towards him—he was already pulling away at the steering wheel intending to reverse. He was on the point of saying something discourteous when I held up in my hand a familiar piece of plastic. He got the message and ordered me to climb up inside. Very soon had I left behind me the truck destined for London and was heading instead, post-haste, for the town of Reading. Once there I could abandon the lorry and attempt to hitchhike my way to Basingstoke and thence to Salisbury.

Getting away from the centre of Reading, however, was expedited more easily in the imagination than executed in the event. I seemed to do a great deal of walking and only obtained lifts irregularly and over short distances. At length though I succeeded and sometime around dawn found myself standing in the pouring rain at the heart of Basingstoke.

It was an unpleasant experience, I'm bound to say, for I very soon found myself soaked to the skin. However, this inauspicious start proved to be only temporary, for I'd barely got on to the A303 road to Exeter when a Morris Minor saloon screeched—more or less and after its fashion—to an abrupt halt, while out of the front seat there jumped a figure whom I instantly recognised and who straightaway hailed me to go over to him. It was none other than the schoolmaster, Stalbridge.

"Major Delman!" he cried. "Is it really you? I thought so—only you are turned out a little differently from when last we met."

He eyed me up and down, miserable hitchhiker that I was.

"May I offer you a lift?"

"Why, Stalbridge, I'd be most grateful if you would. I trust you'll excuse the attire. It's been a long story and I'm sworn to secrecy."

We got into the car and were soon on our way. Stalbridge it seemed had acquired leave from his headmaster to attend a symposium in London entitled, 'Patterns of Meaning: The Interface of Physics and Theology.' It had been hosted at the Queen Elizabeth II Conference Hall and led by an international team of experts. Actually the poor chap was rather full of it, so I didn't feel the need to vindicate either my intentions or my appearance. Of course he himself was bound for his school—near Sherborne as it turned out—and so had no objection whatever to dropping me in Salisbury.

It wasn't till we were well out of Andover—and had passed a place called Amesbury—that he suddenly became curious.

"Pardon my asking, Major, but should I take it you are currently engaged in some sort of espionage? I mean you were acting rather strangely, were you not, as we passed through Glenfinnan? What have you been up to exactly, between then and now? It'll be more exciting than teaching I dare say."

No sooner had Stalbridge finished his questioning than happily for me a celebrated henge of stones loomed large in front—like solidifying spectres, they were, convening in the mist. It provided me with something of a diversion, so that by the time we had turned south to Salisbury I was vigorously expounding upon—would you believe it?—the aesthetic and spiritual entitlements of gypsies: in particular, I urged that they be left free to attend solstices without harassment from the police. More than that, by the time we approached the city centre I was in full flow about a group of hippies expelled from Skye. Dougie Robertson had told me about them and had claimed it was only local bigotry which had forced them to decamp. Mere prejudice, then, was all it had taken to uproot them from their site beyond Broadford.

I felt sure when we drew up that Stalbridge was going to add to this his own threepennyworth. What he actually said was quite different.

"If I'd time, Major, I'd take you to the railway exhibition housed at the station. As it is I'm afraid I must hurry along. I'm due for dinner-duty, you see, in about half an hour."

So saying, the conscientious Stalbridge drove off in the direction of Yeovil, leaving me once more to feel both solitary and in debt to another. It was a grand thing just the same to be left in view of Salisbury Cathedral—he had dropped me off on the very edge of the Green—and to be able to gaze up at its tall and tapering spire. I was standing to be precise between the area of the old belfry—removed by the architect, James Wyatt—and an unusual representation of the Madonna cast with her back to God's house—all the better perhaps to confront God's world. As it happened this sculpture in bronze was not unknown to me. I'd observed it on previous visits to the cathedral and had long pondered on the curious design the sculptress,

Elizabeth Frink, had adopted. Patently there was nothing pietistic or docile about the figure in question; caught in a perambulatory stance, she seemed to stride out purposefully, a woman of the eighties destined to challenge the chauvinistic assumptions of both layman and cleric.

There was, as I say, a pleasing familiarity about all this and the day would have seemed jolly enough had I not all at once taken note of my disreputable appearance. I was still attired for the high places and scrambling about the glens. A busy workman—I might be that; but on what tasks could cathedral precincts detain me on what was now a clear October day?

Then I noticed the scaffolding that lay clustered about the spire. Throughout my previous visits a small amount of metal framework had grown here and there about the steeple, while an interlocking ladder had connected then the two levels. Now a more elaborate system of platforms—with sloping rungs and interfacing supports—straddled the erection. This suggested to me that there would in all likelihood be some cradle or ascending cage to facilitate the job of the repairers. If there be something approaching a building site then even now I might be able to excuse my unhallowed appearance on God's grounds.

Being careful to avoid the main concourse of people I paced down the north transept, past the Morning Chapel, till I had come to the cathedral's east front. I realised then that I had reached the exterior of Trinity Chapel and paused to contemplate what lay within. Just on the other side of that window stood the haunting portrayal of a thousand faces, each one ennobled through suffering, each tested through the fires of injustice: such was the famous depiction of the Prisoners of Conscience—that most uplifting of testimonies to human courage, fine instance of creative genius and the work of one Gabriel Loire of Chatres. I stood awhile, rapt in meditation, awed by that mirrored spectacle of man's inhumanity to man, yet awed no less by man's contempt for his own brutality and bold attempt to transcend it—to find in its correlate of bravery something beautiful, something precious: even, perhaps, something divine.

The thirteenth-century chapterhouse had come into view when I noticed a work-site abutting onto the southern transept. However I did not make an approach to it but continued my perambulation. Almost immediately I spotted an alternative entrance to the cathedral at the southern corner of the cloisters. Looking down the easterly enclave I observed a dozen or so individuals gathered about an exhibition of brass rubbings, at least two of whom were engaged in tracing designs with coloured crayons. This gave me an idea. I took out my cap from my pocket, placed it on my head at a slight angle and ambled over to the group there assembled. I might, I considered, hope to abandon for the time being the work-site and assume the semblance of a bohemian artist.

I need not detain the reader with an account of my doings by the garth that Tuesday afternoon. Suffice it to say I'd again adopted a forthright approach—believing that a strong and persuasive character, by no means devoid of eccentricity, was less likely to arouse suspicion than a person appearing nondescript or overtly shadowy: in my eyes the wisest front to adopt was that of a man who has nothing to hide but something to declare. And, say it who shouldn't, the three brass rubbings I produced were not bad representations of the originals. Truth to tell I rather enjoyed the diversion provided and fancy I made a friend or two as I went along. In particular a female student—a slim young thing in her twenties—seemed especially impressed. Exactly what the motifs were I am now no longer certain, though I rather think one was of a medieval rendering of the Trinity—cleverly executed by an artist from the locality—while the last was of greater size and (if memory serves me correctly) bore in its central design upon some noble courtesan. This piece proved particularly handy because I was able to roll it up, thrust it under my arm and swagger forth thus into the coffee shop. My queer get-up no longer bothered me.

Believing it to be the main meal of the day there seemed little point in stinting myself as I pronounced my order. It was of course the usual fare, being a choice of jacket potatoes with mixed salads, and even if I am not a great one for fresh fruit I took that too, as well as a slice of chocolate cake and several cups of tea. Fearing lest my appetite prove a sensation—even if my clothes did not—I eventually got to my feet, retraced my steps to the corner of the southern transept and went to take another look at the cathedral work-site. As three or four men were occupied at the gate it was not a good time to proceed. Instead I made my way back to the place where earlier on I'd seen several worksheds. Putting myself well to the side of one of these, and in the lee of a bulky tree, I sat down to light up my pipe and allow myself a good dose of nicotine to steady my nerves.

Admittedly the reader may think me a fool for having got thus far. After all I'd no idea whether or not the operation would still go ahead and even if it did I'd no precise notion as to its timing, the identity of its protagonists or where they would convene. If ever there was a long shot, this was it.

Conversely, I still had the piece of paper inadvertently discarded by the rifleman, while it must surely be worth trying to tie up any loose ends beyond the purlieus of Aridhghlinne. Then there was Monty. In a day-or-two's time it would be easier to make contact, while I did not doubt my friend would permit his inquiries to be pretty far-reaching. The police, in particular, would be amongst the first informed and would be given strict instructions as to my proper treatment. In the meantime all I could do was to wait. I had succeeded in coming to the cathedral at Salisbury where it seemed unlikely that infidels from Porton Down would strike before dusk: any meeting must surely take place at night or at first break of day.

CHAPTER 15

Further Dealings With An Old Etonian

I decided to pass that night in Salisbury hidden amongst the rubble and tarpaulin lying about the cathedral. So when the last of the day's visitors had dispersed I clambered over the wire gates and there settled down to sleep. I could not retire for long, however, because I needed to be alert during most of that night and ensuing dawn.

To begin with my plan succeeded. I must have slept for about four hours before—on waking to no great bed of comfort—I got up to make a reconnaissance of the cathedral precincts. However, I had barely shifted my position when a beam of light fell across my path. In all my deliberations I'd given no thought whatever to the presence of any watchman. Now here precisely was such a one and waging in on me with all the indignation attendant on making a rightful arrest. What was I doing loitering about the work-site? Didn't I know it was private property? It was necessary, it was vital—I ought to have appreciated this—to safeguard the proper functioning of the cathedral lifts and other appurtenances from any outside interference. Et cetera, et cetera.

However, in examining the day quarters of the accredited workforce the workman had been obliged to push wide one of the previously locked gates. I decided to make a run for it, believing I should in all likelihood be taken for a lone but importunate tramp, one to be pitied perhaps rather than feared. On that account though I was sorely mistaken. The guard if elderly was also a sprightly and wiry individual on whose side the initiative had clearly fallen. He was in fact every bit braced for a chase, and—give the fellow his due—he hounded me round the precincts like an aggrieved canine. I ducked and darted, hither and thither, but that blessed chap would not give up—not, that is, until I had quit the grounds entirely. Fearing lest I create an even greater disturbance, I slipped away into town and accepted defeat.

I decided next to make a more circuitous tour of the cathedral and to close in by degrees. This I duly did and once more found my way to the cathedral workshops. I could see the night watchman patrolling the area and keeping an especial eye on the entrance to the site. There then followed what seemed an interminable period of waiting which—in my own case at least—lacked the pleasant distraction of either flask or sandwich box. For a second time was I impressed by the canniness of the watchman. Patently the fellow had done himself proud as he was for some while engaged on his meal and at the end of it lit up a sizeable cigar. When I caught a whiff of Havana I realised I must be sufficiently downwind to make the lighting of a pipe devoid of risk. I had just done so when I noticed the surrounding streetlamps had been switched off. Morning had officially arrived. I could hear, moreover, the irregular rush of traffic sounding in the distance.

If Ishbaal's cronies were to make a move they would have to do so soon. Even if theoretically they might wait till later that week, my own judgement was that the happenings by Mallaig would brook no delay but prompt an imminent resolution. And in this verdict I was proved presently to be correct.

What happened was I decided to wander around the cathedral's west front. I'd barely done so before I spied two figures walking away from the north porch towards the corner of the transept. To my amazement the taller of these—a clergyman no less—was noticeably disadvantaged by a debilitating limp. His progress was distressingly slow while he himself seemed to be in considerable pain. Now and then, moreover, he would allow his left hand to rest upon the other's shoulder. The conclusion was inescapable. Once again had I come into the company of Ishbaal—former master of shame and now of most miserable disguise. I made a light run to the side of the Frink Madonna and waited, with bated breath, to see what would happen.

It seemed remarkable all this while that there had occurred no intrusion from the conscientious watchman. Perhaps the wounded rogue hirpling in front of me had succeeded in passing himself off as visiting dean or enfeebled cleric. In reality though it was all too likely the night guard had fallen prey to mischief or misadventure. I could well imagine the brave front he would have put up: he would not have gone down without a struggle. As to the identity of Ishbaal's accomplice, I had no idea: only perhaps that he might be some associate or other from Porton Down—though the relationship between the two of them was clearly not a viable one, for they were arguing, with Ishbaal himself now having let go of his grip and stepping back a pace.

All at once the smaller of the pair produced a firearm and pointed it towards his opposite number. His intention was clear. Yet a man who has scaled so high in the world of infamy as Ishbaal was not now so easily to be put down. Quick as a flash there sprang from his sleeve the arrow of a dagger, and it caught the other straight in the hand. A cry went up and the revolver dropped to the ground. There then began an almighty tussle with each deploying whatever he could muster in the way of pummelling fist, striking foot or banging head. It was as well I hadn't put money on the more capable, as it was he who was finally knocked down leaving Ishbaal very brokenly to lope across the green. He did so in the direction of that path to which I myself was adjacent.

Torturously the fellow grew closer, the fallen pistol now in his hand, the extent of his difficulty increasingly apparent. No more was there any point in disguising his malady. It was as a bent and staggering cripple that the disciple of shame now tottered towards me. His face, moreover, had been extensively cut as well as bandaged awkwardly above his left eye. From the scrap he'd just suffered his other eye too appeared muddied, while blood was beginning to issue from the corner of his mouth. Furthermore he would intermittently lay his hand to his stomach as if creased by some grave if hidden wound. Had at this point the Dean or Precentor emerged on the green it is doubtful whether the white collar worn would have assisted him one jot. As he came towards me, beaten and humiliated yet still clinging to some vestige of pride, I confess I felt for him again a degree of wonder. Yet stronger than admiration in me were the feelings he provoked of pity and contempt: bleak contempt for what he had done, profound pity for what he'd become.

Then all at once I noticed the chap who'd been slugged to the ground had somehow got to his feet. More than that, he had in his hand the same injurious knife to which minutes beforehand he had himself fallen victim. Now hopping along the grass he had the weapon drawn back to deliver a mortal blow to his erstwhile master. It was just that then I stepped aside from the ambulant Madonna.

"Watch out, man!" I yelled. "Behind you!"

Quick as a hawk Ishbaal dropped to the ground. He rolled over to one side and fired the automatic. The assassin *manque* fell obliquely across the lawn, the dagger falling uselessly from his limp hand. He was dead. Dead as surely as Ishbaal himself now required urgent attention. Precariously, the latter struggled to his feet.

It was I who spoke first. "Galbraith, old chap, you seem to have got yourself in the devil of a mess. You're all in. It's help you need. Give me the gun."

He put again his hand to his stomach. For the first time I noticed an increasing discoloration showing about his waistcoat. He tried to hold himself erect, lifting his sunken shoulder. But it was no good, the effort had become too great. He looked towards me feebly and made as if to speak.

"Delman," he groaned. "You may forget me. I can take care of myself. I suggest it's your own soul for which you should have regard. You see, I am going to kill you."

He raised his hand with deliberate slowness, then pointed the weapon towards me, standing as I was some twelve feet before him.

"Don't be an ass," I insisted. "You're in no position to do anything."

Slowly, very slowly, I moved towards him.

"Now be a good fellow there and give me that gun"

The gap narrowed. Eleven feet. Ten. Nine. Eight.

"You're a dead man, Delman."

Seven, six…

Suddenly a shot rang out. It detonated the silence: a thousand shards, a thousand splintered fragments.

A look of agony passed over Ishbaal's countenance. Then the victim of shame fell to the ground. Beneath the weight of his head about the back of his neck a wide seam opened; from it a steady flow of blood streamed. The prince of degradation had departed this world.

It may be imagined my response was one of relief, if not satisfaction. The villain after all had merely received his just deserts. Yet that was not at all my reaction. Seeing the person I'd formally defeated at Chess and eluded at Aridhghlinne, subsequently chased across the Sgurr and tricked as passenger on board the *Sheba* before pursuing to a broken escape and near drowning, seeing that same person now shot down—like some miserable dog—before my very eyes: that filled me only with horror; horror that such brutality could be meted out by one of our kind even to another. Granted Ishbaal should've been made to pay, but had he not escaped justice—its process, its verdict, its punishment—by having his life quenched in the instant of a bullet?

Not only that, but I'd wished him to surrender and to find thereby in what ruth I could muster some earnest of compassion, some signal that humankind was not founded solely on revenge and covetousness: that there was another way. Now that chance had been snatched, irrevocably. The principles of might and cunning had triumphed as usual. The bottom line, as they say, had been reached and acted on. It had not been transcended.

So I felt angry—and cheated—and crazed by the sheer madness of it. I wanted to know who'd seen fit to execute—without a trial. I wanted to know why the method of shame had been demonstrated even to its master, as if that indeed were the only course to assume. I wanted to beat a different kind of drum, instil a different kind of sense into the executioner. Quite what I thought I'd say or do—should I succeed in finding him—seemed less important than that I essay the attempt. Yet when it came down to it I was perhaps not so different from the next man, for I chiefly desired to give to the fellow a hiding and only subsequently a homily.

With all this in mind I reached at once for the telescope in my pocket only to discover it had a large dent in it and that water had got in beneath one of the lenses. I pointed it upward towards the spire—the very place whence the shot was fired—but alas! could make out nothing. Then I remembered a public telescope stood but yards away. Putting a coin in this I swirled it up and around for a prospect of the cathedral-top.

At first I could descry very little, the view afforded being hardly less poor than that obtained earlier. Yet just when I though it futile I caught a glimpse of a helmeted man crouching above the northern transept. He appeared to carry a rifle by his side, hanging loose from his shoulder.

Without delay I raced to the southern side of the cathedral. The gate to the work-site being already ajar I was able to enter and make directly for the cage. To my relief the latter was stationed on the ground and had its doors open. However, I had underestimated the hardiness of the night watchman who'd survived his blows, kept to one side and now came towards me with a raised crowbar. I fielded his attack with a relative ease and, not wishing to put him out properly, bound and gagged him with his belt and shirt. Reluctantly leaving the poor fellow in a nearby shed I made at once for the inside of the lift. I pulled down the doors, pressed a button, and the cradle started to rise.

There are those doubtless who would have found the prospect then rendered as uplifting as the ascent. Indeed, had the occasion been different from what it was, it is just possible—but only just—that I too should have marvelled with the rest. But at the time of which I write I felt only a sense of nausea and a dizziness in the head. After two hundred feet the cradle stopped.

I attempted to open the doors only to discover in so doing that they'd jammed. In that moment—with the cage swaying and my exit barred—I felt completely at the mercy of my importunate assassin. In my haste, moreover, I had not even collected a helmet—though I'd the ironic recollection of a dozen or so hanging upon hooks precisely for that purpose. And without one I felt even more disadvantaged—as if the absence of headgear, however paltry or ineffective, in some way highlighted my exposure and increased my vulnerability. Just when panic was getting the better of me I paused, tried more slowly, more calmly, and the doors lifted. I stepped out onto a walkway of double planks.

It must be obvious by now that whilst a lover of mountains I am quite useless when it comes to those artificial heights created by man. I became instantly aware of the smallest movement in the boards below me, of the not inconsiderable breeze blowing from the south, and of a panorama becoming—in a sense all too disturbingly literal—breathtaking. It was in this frame of mind and set of nerves that I hazarded now to seek out a killer. It could hardly have been more foolish.

I was so inept in making the attempt; moreover, I could hardly credit my endeavours with the necessary degree of thoroughness. True, I did at one point climb over a protective barrier and there stood for a whole moment trembling on the brink. And in addition I managed to crawl on all fours for several minutes before making my return (successfully) to rejoin the doubtful terra firma of the established walkway. I wondered thereafter what to do next.

The answer all too regrettably stared me in the face: waiting calmly for me to continue the ascent stood the unwanted cage. (Not inconveniently, note, did I despise the network of ladders proffering the only alternate route.) Quite how I coped with it all surprises me yet: somehow all the same I managed to reach the next level in that same infernal cradle, coming to a halt at a similarly increased gradation. This time I escaped without difficulty—but, had no sooner done so than a figure emerged from the corner of the spire sporting a torn combat jacket and a yellow helmet. He called above the wind, a voice of command.

"Major Delman! Stop where you are!"

I might have froze then and there, only I'd not come through the baptism I had not to notice that the man's rifle even yet swung free. I had perhaps a handful of seconds. I ran to the opposite corner of the spire, all fear of heights eclipsed by the virtual certainty of being killed by a bullet.

As I turned the corner, however, I straightaway noticed a small doorway to my left. It looked as if it gave access to the interior of the spire. I hadn't time naturally to secure an immediate entry—I should have been shot in the process—but instead fell flat on my side, finding concealment in the adjacent scaffolding. I first heard the speedy fall of my pursuer's footsteps, then watched him almost at once pass from view.

Here was my chance! I grabbed the handle of the small door, gave it a substantial pull and dived inside. I slammed the door shut, pressed down the light-switch and gazed all around.

At the centre of the spire was situated what looked like an original construction of woodwork, but upon which fresh wiring had recently been fixed and a variety of ladders installed. A reconnoitre of that dim and dusky apex revealed a cluster of joints with leaning timbers and a narrowing space, but it wasn't easy to gauge from such a restricted prospect the true elevation of the edifice as a whole. Behind me stood a large circular frame which rotated and which appeared to act as a hoist still operable by hand. At the same time there was sufficient in the way of modern equipment to hint at more sophisticated, mechanical means. I'd no time to ponder such refinements, however, and made immediately for the ladders.

To my satisfaction I found I was quite soon hid in the interlocking beams. I then lifted the first ladder, containing it partly with one hand and partly with the aid of a joist. I knew my pursuer must shortly gain entry, but I might at least now deter his upward progress. Suddenly the door banged wide.

Thereupon a tall, lean figure lowering his head somersaulted into the interior, rolled over to one side and bore his rifle at the ready. He had hardly done so before he was stationed anew under the protection of the hoist.

"Don't be an idiot, Major!" he called out. "I only want to talk!"

I uttered not a word of reply but remained as still as an attendant snake. At last what I anticipated came to pass: the fellow stepped into the centre—his face creased with anxiety—to look right up into the depth of the spire. In just the same instant I released the first ladder from the joist and with the hand which partly held it jammed it downward onto the victim beneath.

The gunman took the blow fully in his upper chest and shoulders. He fell backwards saving his head by courtesy of the helmet he wore. I leapt to his side and fell upon him in earnest. Not wishing him to recover in such confined quarters, I put him out for as long as it would take to bind and gag him with the strap of his gun. When the fellow came to he was already tightly secured to a wooden upright. He looked in a deuce of a temper and was obviously anxious to speak.

But I was in no mood for conversation. All I wanted was to be free of the spire, telephone the police, and have word passed on to MQ1 (if that were possible) and thereafter to make as soon as I could for the centre of the capital. Once there I should find shops aplenty, a comfortable hotel, and by no means least the City Livery Club. From there I might even obtain word of Montagu Fiennes.

In the meantime I was standing again on solid ground. It was as well I'd not delayed for there then took place an incident that enabled me to escape more readily than otherwise would have been possible—though it seems even less credible now in the recounting than it did at the time it happened.

Having exited once more the gates, and making my departure from the cathedral precincts, a burly-looking official suddenly called out to me: "Hey you there, Johnny, what ye doin'?"

Although not sure of my movements at this stage, it seemed I was engaged in a detour set to bring me to the side of an imposing residence looking over the River Avon. Though unknown to me at the time, this place—being in the ownership of a former prime minister—had been afforded a larger than usual degree of security. It looked as if my wish—I now hoped to be taken for the gardener—was not to be granted.

The official steadily began to pace towards me. Then a ludicrous gambit suddenly occurred. Once more I must seize the initiative.

"Look here, old son," I remonstrated. "It's you that's stolen my car keys. See over there—that grey Ford Cortina. There's no other explanation. I haven't got them any more. Here's my pockets—empty, nothing at all. I must have dropped them. You were there. Yes, I'm sure you were. You've taken my keys. Now, let me have them back at once."

The stout chap stood back a minute. Then he whistled.

"Well, you're a one aren't you! How can you talk such—?"

"Look here," I interrupted, "I'm not going to mess about. Either you give me those keys or your breakfast's going for the high jump. Come on, let's be seeing them. You can tell they're mine—they've a miraculous medal attached to them."

That did the trick.

"Then we can soon settle this nonsense. My keys, Johnny, as you can see have no such medal."

The man, of course, told the truth. There was no evidence whatever of any sacramental object. The only thing secured in the palm of his hand was a bunch of keys belonging to his vehicle. I was nearly there.

"I still say those keys are for the grey Ford Cortina."

"And I say, Johnny, they belong to my red Sierra."

Bingo! With that I seized the items under discussion, threw the official to the ground, and raced as hard as I could across the encompassing green.

Just the same I believed my ploy at first not to have succeeded, for I could get no sign at all of any red Sierra. Then all of a sudden it came into view. The hour still being quite early, no other car of that design was observable. I put the main key in the driver's door and turned it. Then having no difficulty in starting up the engine I straightaway headed for the nearest exit to Basingstoke.

I had not got far though before I realised I had not telephoned the police. In the process of looking for a kiosk, however, I found myself troubled by an uneasiness that began to bother and irritate me—much perhaps as did the celebrated thorn in the flesh of the Apostle. It was occasioned by the recollection of my encounter in the apex of the cathedral. There seemed something odd about Ishbaal's assassin which, try as I might, I simply couldn't place. The confusion gradually cleared as my mind focused upon two memories: to start with, the first glimpse of the fellow after I'd come from the cage—he hadn't had his weapon raised ready to fire; then there was his voice—I could not rid myself of a notion that I'd heard it before.

It wasn't till I was drawn up at the kiosk and hunting for a coin that the realisation bore in on me as to whom Ishbaal's killer really was. It was as I went through my pockets in search of loose silver—and came thereby on my tobacco pouch—that there then entered my imagination the image of a railway carriage, one in which there sat a man whom I'd earlier judged to be an old Etonian. It was indeed the very same fellow whom I'd thought to have designs on the life of the P.M., the same indeed who'd detained me and who had sought thereafter to have me falsely arrested. However, the element of unease remained. After all, was there not a difference between attempting to wipe out the Head of Cabinet and shooting instead an arch villain and perpetrator of crime? And still with a nagging insistence came back the question: why had the man merely hailed me and done me no harm?

I was consoling myself with the thought that harm would have followed on the heels of interrogation when my call was received. I'd taken the liberty of going straight to the top where, due to my predicament, I needed to be pretty brisk with the official who answered.

"I am in a telephone kiosk. I have only a couple of minutes. This is to go to the Head of Scotland Yard. Write it down quickly. There are two dead bodies beside Salisbury Cathedral, while the body of a third is tied-up alive in the interior of the spire. The dead clergyman is Ishbaal. Tell that to MQ1. Thereafter you will be told what to do. It may be you will need an ambulance for the one who is bound, who also incidentally shot down Ishbaal. The night watchman in a nearby shed also requires attention. He is to be commended for his endeavours and deserves to be rewarded. Inform Harold Hardanger that he may contact me at the usual rendezvous."

I don't think the message cut much ice for a stony silence followed, while it looked as if the primary effect of my dictation had been to nonplus the unfortunate inspector. I got the feeling he was about to protest when the pips went. I put down the receiver and returned to the car. There was no time to lose.

Then it came to me. Something was puzzling me still about the old Etonian. Seeing him with a protective helmet on his head, and noticing the face thus framed both rivelled and strong as well as deeply tanned, another if similar countenance came starkly to mind. This time the visage was topped by a balaclava. The man was sitting alone in the corner of a bar. Then the same man was stationed beneath the Burma Road, not exactly firing at me but more directly and more surely at the helicopter and at the fugitive Ishbaal.

Suddenly the truth dawned. I slammed on the brakes, swung the car round, and put my foot down as hard as I could. I'd been a fool, a complete idiot! Could I get to the cathedral before the police? Could I safeguard the assassin's identity? I threw caution to the wind and gave to the attempt my best endeavour.

I drove like a madman in that early morn. It was just as well the main rush of the day had not yet begun—though it could not be far off. Then I began to feel the effects of my troubled night and the preceding days. My eyes wanted desperately to close, while my stomach groaned in mutual protest.

I allowed the Sierra to screech to a halt right beside the cathedral workshop. I jumped out and raced towards the work-site. Still no sign of the workmen. The cage itself, still in place. I pressed the button and kept the thing going to the uppermost level. The view, I opined, was starting to improve.

A moment later I burst into the tapering space and halted once more before the struggling Etonian. "Rupert Malahide," I declared. "I owe you an apology." And as if to prove my astuteness I removed the chin-strap, lifted up the helmet and beheld, as I knew I should, the shining pate of MQ1's finest agent.

Then I laughed and quickly set about untying my captive's bonds. When I'd finished the prisoner leapt to his feet and extended me his hand. Tough nut and sport that he was, he took it like a gentleman showing not a flicker of indignation.

"Major Delman," he grinned. "It would be good to have you in at the beginning next time. I fear we've been working widdershins for too long. Next time let's go sunwise together."

Then he added more gravely, "Thank God you came to your senses. You see, it's important I keep clear of the establishment."

There being no time for explanations, we both made at once for the cage. By now I was almost sad to watch the steadily disappearing panorama, whilst the coming into view of the stable and familiar seemed almost like an encroachment. A workman by the gate restored me to the moment.

I told Malahide to follow me closely while I myself went up to greet the foreman—for such I took him to be—with as much authority as I could decently muster.

"Good morning!" I cried. "You've arrived, then? You'd better get up to the top—p.d.q. There's been some sort of set-to in the spire and there's a redundant firearm to show for it. I'm going for the police directly, but you might like to send up a couple of your own chaps just in case. There's bound to be an inquiry, you know."

My comments produced the intended degree of astonishment while for the time it took Malahide and I to negotiate the green it was clear the initiative was all our own. We marched past the tardy Madonna as if we had not a care in the world.

I'd decided to abandon the red Sierra and to trust my fate once more to British Rail. We broke off our progress to the station however to visit a Betjeman's teashop. There, over a speciality-infusion, we held our first, ad hoc debriefing.

Malahide it seemed had been no better advised of political timetables than I, which was why of course he'd made up his yarn about playing the flute at the Tory-party conference. He had shown little diffidence in so doing because he was indeed heading for the Grand Hotel. However, the target in sight was no minister of democratic government but the arch anarchist himself. Ishbaal, as it turned out, had been scheduled to fly across the Channel in a light aircraft coming down at the nearby training school of Shoreham-by-Sea. From there it was expected he would visit the Grand Hotel so as to rendezvous with a young man in the employ of one Henrik Meyer. Malahide's contacts had been keeping tabs on the youth since his name cropped up in a climbing accident—in the infamous Pass of Glencoe—in which Meyer too had been personally involved. At that stage the hunch was the youth would take the place of the Norwegian who'd been temporarily hospitalised. When he'd booked in as a salesperson, from a famous sporting company and at Brighton's most prestigious hotel, the assumption had naturally been that Ishbaal would follow. According to Monty, who had himself been in touch with Malahide, such a meeting had indeed been finalised—though only as part of an elaborate plan to keep hid Ishbaal's whereabouts from the officials of MQ1. In the event a small aircraft had landed on the cockle strand lying to the northern end of the Isle of Barra. It was from there (and as a tourist) that the master of shame had set forth to Skye from which place he would decamp in turn and disappear in the hills behind Mallaig. When Malahide got word of these developments he'd travelled to the western seaboard and there taken the cover of a fisherman ousted from St. Ives. It was a part he knew well, having formerly adopted it whilst working in Gibraltar and having first devised it during a visit to Cyprus. He could not (he considered) use it again. He'd been lucky as it was.

To me all this sounded quite preposterous. I am certain I should never have believed it had I not myself been caught up in the same web of intrigue. Of the writer's own part in the matter the reader already knows. I had now to give a brief account of it to my newfound friend. He it was who imparted to me the news that Mac himself, thank God, had sustained only bruises and minor cuts, while the chap who'd been killed by Ishbaal was believed to have been a former research worker at Porton Down.

"And the Red Pepper?" I asked. "Can we be certain its formula is dead?"

"More or less, Major, more or less. You don't get certainty in this game though and the nightmares of yesteryear give way to the visions of tomorrow. What they in their turn will be—whether for good or ill—we cannot tell. But remember this, that those who devise such wickedness must be put away resolutely and for good. A man like Ishbaal, he is capable of perpetrating a thousand such horrors. It is the human process with all its ingenuity and cleverness—its conative resourcefulness—that proffers the key to such doyens of shame. When the process becomes poisoned the impulse to do evil intensifies, and then the devil gets a purchase to wreak havoc where he may. That's why Ishbaal had to be killed. We were not dealing merely with some fellow-human being—some tragic soul capable of healing—no, but we were facing in Ishbaal evil incarnate. That's why I shot him, and I am glad for your sake that I did."

There was nothing more to be said. I didn't like it, of course. I should have preferred myself to have distinguished between what a man does and who he really is. But I also appreciated that men change, they become other than what they were—and it must be admitted it is not always easy to separate a person from his works; indeed, there are times when the former is lost to some process—fiendish, deadly—and becomes himself a kind of evil deed. That such a one should have worn the mask of Galbraith simply made more hideous the fact. It did not redeem the man.

As I prepared to take my leave of Malahide I was effusive therefore in my thanks. I remember at the time we were waiting on platform four.

"Look, Malahide, I know I expressed reservations earlier about your putting down Ishbaal, but I want you to know how much I respect your part in all this and for firing when you did. I hope you can accept my apologies for giving you a bit of a trouncing back there."

"Think nothing of it. I dare say I should have acted similarly had our roles have been reversed. Though, as I said before, let's have you in at the start next time."

Next time! Again that expression. I queried it out loud, wondering if there was fresh mischief afoot.

"Oh, of that I'm certain. As long as the good globe turns."

I had no time to demur as I was about to change platforms for the service to Waterloo. However an announcement was made which caught my attention. The next train to Exeter was shortly to arrive and it seemed among the stations included was a place called Gillingham. I couldn't actually recall that particular halt so I questioned Malahide about it.

"That's funny," I said. "I was thinking Gillingham was in Kent. Only a young lady I know has just purchased a house there."

Pronouncing the word with the first consonant soft, the Etonian replied, "Oh, but you mean Gillingham. The hard guttural belongs down the line."

"Why of course, I was forgetting, and that's the one where my friend lives! Look, I've changed my mind about London. Do me a favour, will you? Telephone Fiennes and tell him Harold Hardanger won't be needed a while. I'll get in touch."

The din of the train bore our conversation away. When the engine had stopped I got into a compartment and through the window held out my hand.

"All the best then!"

"Same to you! Incidentally, where is it that you live?"

I'd no chance to reply, however, for the train was already gathering speed and putting a widening gap between myself and my acquaintance. All I could do was to grin and give a shrug of the shoulders. Nonetheless I'd decided I rather liked this Etonian and that my first impression had been a correct one. Bald-headed he might be, but he was a good sport and brave with it. I laughed at the thought and reached for my pipe. To my amazement I found next to it a tin of tobacco: it was the same brand my father had smoked!

It wasn't long however before I began to nod off. Being wary of missing my stop I pressed the old lady opposite—she being the only other traveller in the compartment—to awaken me on our departure from Tisbury. This she duly did—somewhere beneath the hilltop town of Shaftesbury—and then questioned me whether or not normally I travelled first class. Seeing the state of my clothes and unshaven face it seemed a fair enough question, though I forget now what I said in reply.

I couldn't have awoken properly, however, for when I disembarked at Gillingham—trying desperately to recollect the address—I tripped over someone's suitcase and fell flat on my face.

The hand of a young woman came immediately to my assistance. I looked up and found to my surprise I need search no more.

"Freya!" I cried. "How in heaven's name did you get here? I was just coming to see you."

"Yes, apparently. But don't sound so shocked, Fred. There's such a thing as a phone, you know. Someone by the name of Montagu Fiennes rang and said he'd heard from an agent of his you would shortly be arriving. He said he was very pleased. Also, that somebody called Mac had informed him that what the Major needed was a good woman. So, there you are! And here am I!"

I steadied myself and took her hand.

"I think," said she, "we'd better get you a proper set of clothes and a good square meal. There's a performance of some madrigals tonight at Stourhead House, and I'd rather like us to be there."

THE END